THE CAROUSEL OF BELIEFS

ALSO BY BOB LORENTSON

You Only Go Extinct Once (Stuck in the Anthropocene with the Pleistocene Blues Again)

Hold the Apocalypse–Pass Me a Scientist Please (and other humorous essays from an optimist in dreamland)

The Carousel of Beliefs

Bob Lorentson

The Carousel of Beliefs
Copyright © 2025 Bob Lorentson

First Stillwater River Publications Edition

ISBN: 978-1-965733-93-6

1 2 3 4 5 6 7 8 9 10
Written by Bob Lorentson.
Cover & interior book design by Matthew St. Jean.
Cover assets by Alberto Masnovo (horse) and
Oleksandr Pokusai (signpost). Devil illustration
by Matthew St. Jean.
Published by Stillwater River Publications,
West Warwick, RI, USA.

For Mike, Alan, Rae, Joy, Isabelle, Jen, Judith, and Paula, aka The Haddam Writer's Group.

Without you, this book would have been *The Lazy Susan of Beliefs.*

1

Confused Beyond Belief

Sperm No. 9,323,459, bewildered perhaps by the pull of mysterious forces, swam uneasily onward through the darkness, even as its more confident companions battled to prove their superiority over each other, wasted their small store of energy, and expired before achieving anything more than momentary satisfaction. Finally it bumped into Egg and could go no further.

"Who's there?" Egg asked.

"I'm sorry," Sperm No. 9,323,459 said. "I don't know who I am. Or IF I am, even. I feel rather incomplete at the moment."

"Listen, you. I don't have time for this nonsense. The clock is ticking. What are you doing here then? What do you want?"

Sperm No. 9,323,459 wriggled uncomfortably. "I'm afraid I don't know that either. All I know is that I've traveled such a long dark road to get here and that thousands of my companions have died! Say, would you have a light? I'd like to see who I'm talking to."

Egg quivered. "Well that's just great. You come squirming in here to tell me that you're the only survivor of some apocalyptic horror show and that thousands of dead bodies are floating my way as we speak. How romantic. So what makes you so special?"

"Just lucky, I guess. Really, I don't have a clue. So, what is it that YOU want?"

"That's easy. A purpose," Egg said, softening. "And I wouldn't mind a little light either. How am I supposed to find anything in this dungeon?"

"A purpose? What's that?"

"To be honest, I don't really know, but I hear the voices say that a purpose gives your life meaning. Helps you find yourself, and gives you a way out of the darkness. Sounds like just what I need. This place is starting to creep me out. It's so lonely in here."

"This purpose thing does sound good," said Sperm No. 9,323,459, "but, no offense, I'd really like to hear it from something more than a disembodied voice who gets its information from other disembodied voices. So, what's this purpose look like? Maybe I can help you find one."

"That's just it. The voices never say what a purpose looks like, just that it's different for everybody. But it's gotta be around here somewhere. I wish it wasn't so dark in here. It's probably something small and insignificant, that's why I can't find it. It's probably right in front of me and I just can't see it."

"Hey, I'm right in front of you! And you won't find anything smaller or less significant than me. I'm just one of billions. Do you think I could be your purpose? Maybe we were meant to be together."

"We were MEANT to be together? That's it? That's all you've got?" Egg said, hardening again. You can't do any better than that, say a little sweet talk, or the promise of a life of everlasting happiness? It took me a month to get ready and you haven't even commented on how I look." Egg paused, then added, "Oh, sorry. I don't know where that came from."

Again Sperm No. 9,323,459 wriggled in place, wondering this time if perhaps its companions hadn't somehow known what was waiting for them and committed spermicide. "Hey, this isn't a trap, is it? For all I know you've just been waiting for someone like me to come along. You sure put a lot of pressure on someone who was just thrust into this world like they were shot from a cannon."

"Trap? What a stupid question. Don't you know anything? I dare you to come closer and say that."

Sperm No. 9,323,459's tail drooped in response.

Egg fidgeted impatiently. "Oh, come on in, ya big baby. So much for the survival of the fittest. But it doesn't look like anybody else is gonna come along and rescue me from this empty existence. Just stop your whining, OK? You really have to grow a backbone, show a lady that you know what it's all about, even if you don't have a clue."

Sperm No. 9,323,459 stiffened, then relaxed. "I may not know much, but somehow I feel drawn to you, like you're where I'm supposed to be. You know, I sense that a big change is coming our way. Like we're on the verge of a great new adventure. I feel like I can almost see the light at the end of the tunnel."

"OK, Sunshine. Let's take this slowly. We aren't ready to go anywhere just yet. But someday, after we've grown a bit, maybe then it'll happen. There just better be more to you than you're showing, cause I won't be dragging your clueless tail around for the rest of our life together. And then we're bustin out, right through that tunnel."

"Into what though, if I may ask?"

"Now that's a good question," said Egg. "I don't know

what's waiting for us on the other side. From what the voices say, it could be heaven, or it could be hell."

"Again with the voices. What's heaven? And what's hell? They sound so mysterious."

"You got me. I'm not sure myself. I've heard things, beautiful things sometimes, but scary things too. Most of the time the messages that reach me here in my little bubble are pretty garbled though. But they all suggest that the other side is so incredible, it's hard to believe it's real. So if you're coming, get your little tail in here. I have a feeling we'll need to be ready for anything."

For Naomi Doubt, it had been a difficult conception, a very trying pregnancy, and an extremely risky delivery. Forceps had to be used, and whether due to the inexperience of the doctor or the especially soft head of the baby, who's to say, but they clearly left an impression. In fact, they left two impressions. Much to her and her husband's uneasiness, the impressions were in the shape of question marks.

The Doubts, though, considered the doctor blameless, each certain that the question marks on their son's temples had a different origin story.

"They're the marks of an eejit," worried Alvin Doubt. "God hae given us a dunderheid to test us. We must ask ourselves if our commitment to Him hae been lacking, and redouble our efforts. And by we, ye ken, I mean you."

"You're wrong," Naomi said. "They're just random marks, but we CAN use them as a reminder to always ask ourselves if we are doing everything in our power to make sure our son has parents committed to a consistent nurturing ideal, so that he doesn't become a lost soul without a purpose. And by we, you know, I mean you."

"Ye're aff yer heid," Alvin said, staring at his wife.

"No, you're wrong as usual," countered Naomi, staring back.

"Whyyy, Whyyy, Whyyy," cried the baby, uncomfortable with the bright lights, the whole new air breathing thing, and nameless other forces beyond his understanding, such as the hazy beings hovering over him and making the same type of discomforting, unintelligible sounds he remembered hearing in the womb. At least there he had felt safe.

From this new beginning, the beleaguered only son of Alvin and Naomi Doubt was a question wrapped in a puzzle wrapped in a mystery, and all wrapped tighter than his parent's beliefs in a flimsy blue baby blanket. Given that one parent's beliefs on any subject were almost always the polar opposite of the other parent, however, it did not take long for both the blanket and the baby to begin to unravel. Still, he grew, and the years went by.

2

Bent but Not Broken

From an early age, Joseph Mordechai Doubt never quite felt at home. Even at home. He was frequently uncomfortable with his surroundings, perhaps even confused, like a fledgling sparrow blown off course by a rare storm and left to navigate a peculiar landscape. Born as he was into a family of mixed orientations, it's likely that even a homing pigeon would have considered its options.

Joseph's father, Alvin Doubt, was a conservative Scottish-born Christian Scientist with a longing for the return of 19th century values, as well as of his only childhood friend, still the last friend he had ever really had. Even dogs gave him a wide berth.

Joseph's mother, Naomi, couldn't have been oriented more differently if she had been raised by a lost tribe of Druids. As it was, she was born to parents who had emigrated from Liechtenstein after realizing that it was not the Jewish State they believed it to be. Consequently, or not, she was a liberal Jewish Existentialist. Somehow, after a short period of mutual infatuation, lust, and a suspension of the beliefs that come with this, they married. For ever after they both wished that God could have, or would have, been more vigilant and intervened.

Despite their differences, Joseph's parents were determined to put him first in their considerations. And so in the spirit of Solomon, they resolutely considered each other's considerations in a considerate fashion, rather than slicing him down the middle. But in an unsurprising development, considerations quickly transformed into declarations of steel blade righteousness that could have sliced God Himself into bite sized portions. It would not take the sensitive Joseph long to discover that he was growing up in the free fire zone of parents who had about as much chance for unification as North and South Korea.

The bickering had turned serious from the start, while arguing over the baby's primary name. His father had finally won that battle in a two-hour rock, paper, scissors marathon, leaving his mother the leftover spoils of his middle name. But after that defeat, his mother had countered strongly with a string of victories in high card and long straw, and gloated over her big win in a demanding coin toss contest for the exclusive rights in the choice of bedtime stories. It would take wins like these, she believed, to overcome the debilitating burden of the weak name her husband had so ignorantly saddled him with.

Night after night, young Joseph would fall asleep to the scary books in the 'Existentialism for Children' series, books with titles like *Mommy, I Think My Soul is Crying*, *A is for Axiological*, and *God Says Good Luck*. "Mom, can I pick?" Joseph pleaded time and again, rubbing the birthmarks on his temples expectantly while holding out a few colorful picture books featuring cute talking animals.

"No, Joseph," his mother would say. "Life is not a cartoon. You need to stop thinking about yourself so much and start trusting me to know what's best for you. I am your mother. It's a hard world out there, Joseph, and it's never too early to begin to get prepared for the battle, because everyone's going to want a piece of your soul."

"Mommy? What's a soul?" Joseph asked.

"A soul, Joseph?" replied his mother. "A soul is ... You see a soul ..." She paused.

Joseph had never seen his mother stumble over a question before. His trusting blue eyes searched his mother's face, normally as inscrutable as a cat's but now showing all the signs of choking on a hairball, and blinked with confusion.

Naomi Doubt cocked her head and raised her dark, tired eyes to the ceiling, then did a double take and lingered a moment there, as if she had heard something she was surprised to hear. When she lowered her head back, Joseph noticed that her eyes were wet and her lips were quivering. She took a deep breath and looked intently into her young son's questioning face before she spoke. "A soul, Joseph, is the basket of love that each of us has inside of us. Some people believe it's what God and the Devil fight over. All I know is that people keep stealing from it, or you give some away and ... and ..."

"And what, mommy?" Joseph asked. "Are you crying?" He suddenly felt like crying himself.

His mother wiped her eyes with the back of her hand. "And sometimes you don't get any back," she finished. She straightened her shoulders and took her son's hands in hers. "Lucky for you I beat your father fair and square, because your soul would never grow strong with him reading to you. You do want your soul to grow strong, don't you?"

Joseph's soul grew, though not in the ways his mother hoped and prayed. It grew to fear bedtimes and the horrible dreams that came with sleep, dreams of him cowering inside a giant basket, helpless, the grand prize in a tug of war that raised him one moment towards the heavens and lowered him deep into the bowels of the earth the next, while apocalyptic thunderstorms raged. He couldn't tell who was at the ends of the rope pulling for him so hard, but he knew they must be powerful. And deadly enemies of each other. He wished more than anything they would just go away and leave him alone, but that only seemed to make them pull all the harder. At such times he could only look forward to morning, when he could seek out the support and companionship of his best friends.

Joseph's best friends, identical twins Larry and Barry Trainor, believed there was something seriously wrong with Joseph, with his fish belly skin, big sad eyes, and slight asthmatic cough. And being boys with next to nothing on their minds, they were growing very impatient about it. So one day while playing in their weedy backyard, they decided to just confront him with their problem.

"Why are you looking at me like that, Larry?" Joseph asked his friend on the swing next to him.

"I'm Barry," said Barry. "When are you going to die?" He and Larry leapt from the swings at the top of their arcs and stretched out their legs for maximum distance. The landings were an exact tie. They tussled a bit then raced back to go again.

Joseph stared at his friend. "What are you talking about, Barry?" he asked. "I'm not going to die."

"I'm Larry," said Larry. "Yes you are. You're just like my cousin and my mom said he died from the new moanya, and he was seven years old too." He and Barry again leapt from the swings and tried to beat the sneaker prints in the dirt. They each landed precisely on their brother's previous marks, tussled again, and scrambled back.

"I don't have pneumonia, Larry, and I'm not going to die," Joseph said to Larry, sure he was right this time. "So cut it out, will you?"

"I'm Barry," said Barry. "Yes you are. After you're dead can I have your skateboard? I AM your best friend."

"Stop it, Barry. You can't have my skateboard. I'm not dying."

"I'M your best friend," Larry said. "So after the new moanya kills you, can I have it?"

"NO! For the last time!"

"The last time?" said Barry. "Does that mean you're gonna die today?"

Joseph picked up his skateboard. "I'm going home," he said, and trudged back to his own weedy yard and ramshackle ranch house, struggling to understand how his best friends could believe something that clearly wasn't true. *Doesn't my opinion on the subject count? I mean, I AM the subject. Wouldn't I know myself better than anybody else?*

I don't know, he demurred. *Would I? I mean, they can see me better than I can see myself. And seeing is supposed to be believing.* He twisted his body around, straining to look himself over. *Maybe it IS easier to know somebody better when you can see them. And besides, I really don't feel all that good.* He turned back sadly to wave at Barry and Larry.

"If you die and don't give me your skateboard, I'm not gonna be your best friend anymore," shouted Barry.

Joseph didn't have pneumonia, but he was a sickly child. Measles, mumps, warts, acne, the list of ailments went on and on. He caught them all as easily as a Baptist preacher catches Pulpit Fever. "How can I be so unlucky," he said to his parents, after an unusual bout with diphtheria had finally run its course. "None of my schoolmates ever seem to get sick."

Alvin Doubt, wild-eyed and red-bearded, fixed his young son with the same expression of contempt that he usually reserved for his weak-willed fellow parishioners. "Luck's got nothin' to do wi'it, laddie. Tis God's will. All we can do is pray." After all, the medical decision rights were his, won fair and square in a Holy Hangman contest, as neither side had yet been willing to concede the religious indoctrination prize.

"But, Dad," pleaded Joseph. "What ..." It was as far as he got.

"Alvin, you're as crazy as my old uncle Menachem, in Jerusalem," shouted his mother. "He's the one that's always praying to that wall over there. Does he really think the wall's listening? For the love of God, take him to a doctor. He's nine years old now, he really needs to see one. Maybe there's some diseases he hasn't caught yet and could still get vaccinated against. He needs to see a medical expert. We can't just keep letting these diseases have their way with him."

"Mom, can I say..." tried Joseph again.

"It's oot of our hands," said his father calmly. "God's the only doctor he needs."

"But, Dad," persisted Joseph. "I ..."

"Well I hope to hell he fixes furniture too," scoffed his mother, "cause you're off your rocker. I'll pray alright. I'll pray that He knocks some sense into YOU before it's too late for the boy."

"But, but, Mom," Joseph said, his exasperation rising. Both parents turned to look at him. He nervously traced a question mark on his temple with his index finger. "What did I ever do to make God mad at me? Why would He want to punish me like this?"

"Because of whit ye're doin' right noo, Joseph," warned his father. "Do ye nae see? Ye're questioning His motives. Mind ye dinnae let yer feet run faster than yer shoes. Ye must accept the fact that His wisdom is unknowable and perfect. Noo git to yer room and pray fer forgiveness."

"Take it easy there, Alvin," said his mother. "The boy asks a good question. One who does not seek will never find. He just doesn't understand that he's a typical selfish boy who thinks that everything's about him. He can't see that God is really punishing YOU for being so wrong-headed about this." Naomi grinned triumphantly. Despite the lack of divine intervention in her courtship with her idiot husband, the advantages of having a personal God when needed were now becoming abundantly clear. If God could adapt, so could she.

"What? I'm not wrong. You're wrong ..."

Joseph shook his head and tuned his parents out, not understanding, but already knowing the pointlessness of arguing. His parents would always have their way. Unfortunately it was a way that not even a bloodhound would ever be able to follow.

If left uncontested, diseases, like parents, will generally have their way too, of course, as diseases are wont to do, and have done for millions of years. And why not? Are they not the essence, the very soul of life forms too? Simple ones to be sure, single minded ones perhaps, if rudimentary celled organisms can be said to have a mind. And yet they have their purpose, as do all organisms. Can't take that away from them. Theirs appears to be to go forth and multiply, as fast and as vigorously as possible, even if it results in the sickness or death of other organisms. Even if it results in the sickness or death of hundreds of millions of other organisms. It's not their fault, is it? They don't know they're the cause of such misery. But if the fault isn't theirs, then whose? Why can't they be more like humans, complex, intelligent, diverse minded organisms who are quite aware of what they are doing, who are so certain of their purpose, in fact, they will even go to war over it? Disease organisms could only hope to possess such greatness of purpose.

"Fire!"

The low cry came from his grandmother's room. It was a cry Joseph had heard many times before, and never ignored. He headed down the hall, glad to be moving away from his parents.

"Joseph, leave her be," his mom said. "It's just the same old nonsense. There's nothing you can do for her."

"I can try," said Joseph.

"Dinnae be a dobber, Joseph," said his dad. "Ye can try reasonin' with a highlander too, it dunnae change anything. Yer gran's gone. Ye need to learn to accept reality."

Joseph turned his back on them, preferring the reality of his grandmother's room. He opened her door and entered the gloomy room, breathed in the stale air, and shut the door behind him. "Hi, Gram," he said, noticing his grandmother's usual expressionless face as she sat slouched in her wheelchair. "It's Joseph. Where is it this time?"

His grandmother pointed to the middle of the floor and repeated "Fire," in a tone she could have used to point out a book.

"Don't worry, Gram. I'll put it out," Joseph said. He made an elaborate production of stomping all around the area, then pretending to fill a bucket with water and dousing any remaining embers.

"There," he said. "I got it, Gram. Was that the only one?"

Very slowly his grandmother raised an arm and pressed her hand against her chest.

Joseph didn't understand what she might be trying to tell him, but he knew what she liked. Without a word he walked over to her and bent down, put his arms around her and hugged her cheek to cheek. He stayed that way for a while, letting the strange and confusing assortment of feelings wash over him. Fear, love, loneliness, helplessness. He hugged her tighter and waited for the tightness in his own chest to subside a bit, then stood up. He adjusted a pillow, opened a window, and sat down to talk with her. "I'm always here for you Gram. What shall we talk about today? How about old movies?"

"I like movies," his grandmother said. "I used to be a movie star, you know."

"I know, Gram. Would you like to tell me about it?"

She squeezed his hand. "You're a nice young man. Who are you?"

Joseph looked into his grandmother's calm, vacant eyes and felt an ache in his gut. The same ache he always felt as he wondered how this sweet, funny woman he had known all his life didn't know him anymore. But also, he realized now for the first time, how she still somehow never failed to make him feel better. She always listened to him, and often complimented him. He looked at his hand in hers, and knew he would always be welcome in here at least. No wonder he came in here so often. He might not know who his Gram was anymore, but it kind of seemed like she might not know who she was anymore either. But whoever was in there, there seemed to be no doubt that she loved him.

"I'm Joseph, Gram," he said for the second time, though perhaps with a little more uncertainty.

An hour later he left his grandmother and decided to heed the call of his bed, and in particular, the ceiling overhead. It was amazing to him how interesting his ceiling had become lately. He never heard the voices his mom or dad appeared to hear when they looked up, but the ceiling still spoke to him. There was a whole topsy-turvy world up there, a more complicated one than he had ever realized, with cobweb jungles, empty deserts pockmarked by assorted blemishes, and fault lines, some running pretty deep. Occasional lone creatures moved purposefully about the vast wasteland. He followed them with his eyes and wondered about their lives. *What if they think that we're the ones who are upside down?*

3

A Little Night Music Goes a Long Way

Scarlett Zeal, the tall, slim, devastatingly cute new girl in Joseph's 6th grade music class, immediately snatched his breath away, perturbed his vision, jumbled his hearing, and as if that wasn't enough, scrambled his brain. Some of that may have had to do with the fact that she smelled like she had just run the Boston Marathon, dressed with all the fashion sense of a colorblind Puritan, and sang like a meadowlark whose meadow had just been plowed under to make room for a new strip mall.

Still, she was cute, even if she did dress oddly, and he fell for her. Hard. He picked himself up off the floor and willed the equilibrium center in his brain to quit fooling around and stabilize itself. (Although Joseph didn't fully understand who or what he was talking to at times like this, he always thought it best to use big words, as he somehow intuitively understood from an early age the brain's easy impressionability to shiny new ideas beyond its reach. And besides, he loved how it didn't talk back to him. Yet.) Then he approached Scarlett and introduced himself.

Mrs. Clarion watched the whole incident unfold and promptly interrupted Joseph to tell him in no uncertain words to please wait until AFTER the bell rings to conduct his personal business.

Joseph flushed beet red and sat back down. Once the teacher faced the blackboard, however, Scarlett turned around, winked at him, and smiled a smile that made his heart beat louder than the class bell. A few seconds later the rest of the class sprung out of their seats and bolted for the door. He wondered where everybody was going, then saw Mrs. Clarion staring at him and nodding at the big clock on the wall. Nonchalantly, he grabbed his things and ambled out, hiding his embarrassment behind a smile and a nod, then scrambled through the crowd to catch up to Scarlett.

That very day, and for several days thereafter, they held hands during the lunch break, and after school while waiting for their buses. They talked and laughed, oblivious to everyone else, while Joseph stared into her oceanic eyes that threatened to carry him out to sea, and Scarlet fiddled with the strings on her bonnet and the hem of her long white dress. Unfortunately, on the day that Joseph had decided he was going to kiss her, they were seen by Scarlett's snot-nosed little brother. The little runt told her that he was going to tell their mother on her for holding hands with an outsider. Joseph tried to argue that he was an insider through and through, that he rarely went outside because of his asthma. His arguments, however, fell on ears that were a portal to an entirely different sort of understanding.

Scarlett was a Mennonite, and Joseph didn't know what he was other than confused, so her parents promptly forbade her to have any close personal contact with him. Day after day, Joseph longed to hold her hand again, and yearned for the kiss he was denied. Finally he drummed up the nerve to come right out and ask his parents if they wouldn't mind if he became a Mennonite, seeing as how they were still arguing over his soul and all. His parent's resounding NO! and the withering tirade that followed caused Joseph's sensitive soul to retreat further into its shell, and caused his parents to take up the battle anew. Scarlett was history, so Joseph, tattered soul in tow, locked himself in his room and bounced angry curses off the ceiling. The ceiling didn't seem to mind, but Joseph's soul couldn't tell one attack from another, so to avoid further pain it crawled deeper inside after calling him a lovesick fool.

The battle for Joseph's spiritual nurturing had been an especially difficult one, exposing a deep emotional fissure that had still not been resolved. Both parents had agreed that this was a decision that could not be decided by the usual methods – coin toss, high card, long straw, or rock-paper-scissors. Coins, cards, straws, and hands had become suspect, examined in minute detail by both parties, and rejected as instruments of either the Devil or an evil to be named later.

Ministers and rabbis were invoked next, and never ones prone to passivity when a soul was hanging in the balance, sprang into action. It was an unexpected third party, however, that refocused Alvin and Naomi Doubt and proved the old adage that God works in mysterious ways. Once the New Coventry Police Department had finished dragging the last of the clergy and their bruised, over-eager acolytes from the Doubt's front lawn, Alvin and Naomi looked hard into each other's narrowed eyes, sneered their confident sneers, and agreed that they would wait for God himself to make his decision known.

Signs came and went, daily at first, then leveling off to about once a week. Favorite meals that were inexplicably burnt, mysterious stains that appeared on clothes, brake lines on cars that suddenly came loose - none passed mutual muster as God's handiwork. Just plain old bad luck was the verdict. So they waited and hovered, never leaving Joseph alone in the other's company exclusively, and keeping a pretty sharp eye on each other as well. More and more, though, they noticed that Joseph preferred to be alone in his own room, with the door locked and his music on.

One evening, Alvin and Naomi stood in the hall outside their son's room and looked at each other. The music coming from within was loud, and the relentless bass amplified assault penetrating the door burrowed into their guts like the arguments each knew were coming. They shook their heads as they walked to their bedroom.

"Whit are we goin' to do aboot this?" Alvin asked, stripping off his clothes and climbing into bed. "This is the kind of music that makes fer weak minds. And if his gets any weaker it'll head fer the highlands. Not een God could call it doon then."

"Says the man with the weak mind," Naomi teased. She turned sideways to look at herself in the bedroom mirror as the faint hypnotic beat from down the hall seeped into the room and sought her out. She liked what she saw and impulsively began swaying her hips, liking the feeling as well. "This is the kind of music that leads to sex and drugs."

Alvin watched his wife's impromptu performance with mounting interest. "Ye dunnae ken whit yer talkin' aboot," he said, grabbing the bottle of blue pills from his nightstand, shaking one loose, and swallowing it.

"I'm talking about this wicked music, you silly man," Naomi laughed, punctuating the remark with a hip thrust. "You should go down there and turn it off." She took her time undressing, slipped on her favorite lace teddy, and slid into bed.

"Maybe I will," replied Alvin." He didn't move though. He just lay there like he was waiting for further inspiration.

"Well?" said Naomi, after a few minutes. "What are you waiting for?"

"God's Will," answered Alvin. "I sent Him a prayer."

"God's Will! You couldn't tell God's Will from God's Won't. You really think He's going to answer you? It's all in your head, you know."

"Ye need to hae mair faith that He knows whit He's doin,' Naomi."

"Oh, I know that He knows what He's doing, Alvin. It's just that I don't believe that He knows that I know that He knows what He's doing. And He definitely doesn't know what you're doing. So I know something that He doesn't."

In the silence of the room, Alvin listened to the faint bass thrum from down the hall and finally felt a familiar stirring in his sacrilegious zone. He flicked off his bedside lamp and turned to his wife. "Wanna fool aroon?" he asked.

"I don't know, Alvin. Is that God's will?"

Alvin grinned. "Aye. And His will is firm."

Naomi's smile widened. "Firm, huh. But is His will good for more than a few minutes?" She shut off her lamp and turned toward her husband.

"Ye'll hae to find oot fer yerself," Alvin said. "But I believe it's guid fer up to four hours. Any mair than that and ye're supposed to call a doctor."

"Music to my ears," whispered Naomi. "So even you think that some things are too hard for God. Hallelujah!"

"Amen," said Alvin.

———————————

Joseph turned off the radio. He opened his door quietly and peered down the hall. He had to pee badly, but he would continue to hold it if there was a chance of bumping into either parent. Seeing their door closed, he walked lightly up to it and listened. "Amen," he heard his father say, followed a short while later by even more passionate entreaties to God.

He tiptoed to the bathroom, then made it safely back to his room and climbed into bed, wondering why his parents were praying about him again. He fluffed up his pillow and lay down on his back. *They must really think I'm helpless if they have to pray for me all the time,* he thought. *And so loudly. I guess they must be desperate to get God's attention. They must think it works, but I don't feel any different.* He reached out for the bedside lamp, held onto the knob for a few seconds to ready himself, then plunged the world into darkness.

Calling out to God, whether it be in desperation, in sorrow, in thankfulness, or in flagrante delicto, couldn't be easier, and anyway, appears to be the only way of getting His attention. Just for a moment, pretend that you are God. It's not difficult, sitting in judgment of other people is one of our most accomplished traits. We may not be able to go so far as to condemn another to Hell, but it's not for lack of trying.

Anyway, as God, which of the above calls would be most likely to get YOUR attention? Receiving gratitude is always nice, especially for all that You do, or all that humans think You do, and requires no follow-up action on your part. This cannot be said about the burden of responsibility heaped on your broad shoulders by one needy whiner after another, day in and day out, year after year, on and on, world without end. But c'mon. Be honest. Those calls from bed would HAVE to be the best part of your day, right? One would think humans would be mortified to know that their Lord was watching them in such delicate moments, but as neither Hell nor high water would ever get them to stop, that apparently is not the case. So, either they are exhibitionists looking for your approval of what they've done with their God given talents, or they don't know you're watching.

Either way, one thing becomes apparent. YOU LIKE TO WATCH! Possibly even set the whole thing up just for that purpose, and whatever else happens, war, hunger, the rape of Mother Nature, happens. Perhaps Earth is nothing more than God's Private Peep Show. It is written that on the seventh day, the day after You created humans, You rested. It appears more and more likely that that is when You GOT BUSY! We will definitely NOT speculate on THAT, however. You, the most private and secretive of beings, should understand more than anyone that we all deserve a little privacy, especially in our most intimate moments.

Joseph kept his eyes wide open, trembling, and staring, though he could see nothing, not even the lamp from which he had just removed his hand. God or a soul stealing demon could be inches from his face and he would never see it. Still he continued to stare, just as he had trained himself every night since his younger days, trained himself to search the darkness for that which he could not see in the light, nor even understand, until he began to realize that if it was only in the darkness that such fantastical things as Gods and demons existed, how could they be real? And if they were real, how could such supposedly all-powerful beings be truly all-powerful if they were afraid of the light? This he wondered, feeling a tiny bit more powerful himself, but glad nonetheless for the sweet moment when his eyes began to get accustomed to the dark and he could see, albeit ever so faintly.

His parents could pray all they wanted for him to change, he thought. It doesn't work that way. He'd been praying for them to change since the first time he'd heard them arguing. Maybe people didn't understand Gods and demons as well as they thought they did.

4
——

Quicksand Dreams and

a Landslide of Truth

And so it went. The bags around Joseph's eyes grew as he did, filled with the viscous residue of stuff he neither wanted nor understood. He loved his parents, at least he thought he did, whenever he thought about how much he'd love to get away from them. Fortunately, that opportunity was fast approaching.

As might be expected, neither parent could agree on a post-secondary institution of advanced dogma that they believed was right for him, one that embraced the time-honored values they had constantly fought over. Neither appeared willing to back down. Joseph tried to weigh in, but as this was their last major decision concerning his life, he got nowhere. He knew they were having a hard time believing that they would soon be without him, their little Doubt, even though he was by now a big Doubt, and stood taller than his father at 6' 1." So he fretted over their stubbornness and waited, hoping against hope, while even the slight possibility of his getting away made him swoon every time he thought of it.

And then, miracle of miracles, they did agree on something. They agreed it was time. Time for one last Report Card. For one last attempt to encourage and inspire their son to rise to the heights of mediocrity to which he appeared destined, and to point his ship in the direction that would take him there.

"Joseph, please sit back doon," Alvin said one evening after Joseph had finished clearing away the supper dishes and was about to head to the safety of his room. "Look at yerself. Ye look like some fog-bound dobber from the Isle o' Skye that dunnae hae the sense to take the cobber to the mainland. Sit up straight. Get a haircut before ye start walkin' inta walls. Tuck in yer shirt. And looka those baggy trousers! Ye hidin' a kelpie in there?"

"Alvin!"

"Sorry, Naomi, but Crivens! Joseph, it's time fer your annual review."

Joseph's heart sank. He knew where this unencouraging, uninspiring, boatload of crap was heading. Right out to sea, without a rudder. Try as he might, he would never be able to control the direction of this ship. He knew he was adrift on the currents of life. They didn't have to keep harping on it. It wasn't like Victoria Falls was just around the next bend, was it, just waiting to drop him three hundred feet into a seething cauldron of carnivorous crocodiles? There were internal currents too, currents worth following, that could perhaps take him to more interesting and mysterious places. Places he wanted to visit, like his heart and his head. He just needed time. After all, there were dangers inside as well that would need to be navigated. He would definitely need to steer clear of dead ends like the appendix, and sewers of no return like the colon.

"Why, dad?" he pleaded. "I know what it's gonna say. It's gonna be just like all the other ones. Why are you and mom always so hard on me? My school report cards are all fine."

"That's because your teachers don't know you like we do," Naomi said, handing him the report. "We're certain they would agree with us if they did. But don't look at our report card negatively, Joseph. That's one of your problems. You'll see, it's there in the report. You need to look at this as an opportunity, a plan, if you will, for improving. Don't you want to improve, Joseph?"

"Of course. It's just that I'd rather do it my way, but you never let me."

"Your way? You don't seem to have a way, that's another of your problems. You seem lost. Confused, like you don't believe in yourself, or have a sense of purpose. It's all there in the report."

"The report? You wrote the report," appealed Joseph. "You talk like it's written in stone instead of it just being your opinions." He felt for the question marks on his temples to calm himself down.

"I cannae see the difference," Alvin said. "If ye were a wee bit impartial ye'd knoo we're right. And I hope ye're not suggestin' that ye knoo yerself better than we do, 'cause that's just daft. If that were the case, what would be the purpose of parents? The truth speaks fer itself Joseph, remember that."

If the truth could speak, Joseph thought, *I'm pretty sure it would be begging to be rescued.*

And what IS the purpose of parents? Now there's a loaded question. Does he really want me to answer that? If I could only tell them what I really think. To pretend to be God and saturate a kid with stupid commandments that suck the soul out of life and make it hard to even know who you really are? Did they ever look in the mirror? It's not like they've got anything figured out. They just believe they do. Actually, sucking the soul out of life makes them seem more like the Devil, doesn't it?

What Joseph didn't realize, and what no parent actually acknowledges, is that the purpose of parents is quite simple. It is none other than to create a replica of themselves. What more lofty, God-like goal could there be than to create life in one's own perfect image? As there are generally two parents involved, however, this goal immediately becomes problematic, and is the source of much conflict to the child caught in the crossfire. And we all know what became of the lineage created from God's perfect image. If God couldn't do it, what chance did mere mortals ever have?

What Joseph also didn't realize, and again, what no parent actually acknowledges, is that once a child changes into a teenager the purpose of a parent also changes. The once lofty goal of self-replication will have been thrown out the window in favor of the distinctly more basic one of self-preservation. This is best exemplified by the typically unspoken questions that go through most parent's minds, such as "What the hell have I created?" "Who is this person living with me?" and "What if he becomes a serial killer, lawyer, or member of the wrong political party and society blames me?" The motivation for this sudden change in purpose, of course, is fear.

Fear is one of the biggest motivating factors there is, and a fear of the unknown is an especially virulent form. And who can truly know a teenager? This is what is particularly terrifying to the parent. To raise a child from a newborn baby is to know everything that can be known about another human. And to suddenly have that satisfaction, security, and yes – self reflected image taken from a parent and replaced with a stranger, and a stranger that intentionally and systematically undermines all that careful early crafting of a replicate human being to boot, causes many parents to begin to experience frightening new nightmares of an alien world full of creatures who are laughing at them, calling them obsolete, and still taking their money. If the known can turn into the unknown right before one's eyes, what can truly ever be known about the world?

———————

Joseph read the report. It WAS all there. All the deficiencies his parents had already mentioned, and many others besides, of self-awareness, perspective, pride, motivation, of having a sense of place in the world, of being too tall for his weight (from his mother), or too thin for his height (from his father), and on and on until the last one concerning his apparent lack of even having hopes and dreams. Joseph was stunned. The report filled ten pages with detailed comments on every perceived inadequacy. This went far beyond any previous report card. He looked up at his parent's satisfied faces. "You don't really mean all this, do you?" he managed.

"Thank you, Joseph," his mother said. "That's two more things we forgot to address in the report. Excessive complaining and an inability to accept the truth."

"And I just thought of a third," his father added. "A lack of gratitude. I dinnae hear a 'thank ye,' did ye, Naomi? Anyway, Joseph, we'll amend the report and git it back to ye straightaway, and we seriously hoope ye'll review it carefully and start turnin' yerself aroon. Dream big, Joseph. Lang may yer lum reek, as me da used ta say."

Joseph stood up, started to speak and then thought better of it. "I'm going to my room," he muttered. He lay down on his bed and stared at the ceiling. "Hopes and dreams. What do they know? Everyone has hopes and dreams."

It was beginning to look hopeless to Joseph. Schoolmates were all busy preparing for the next big step in their lives, excited to be following their dreams and fulfilling their destinies, and all he could wonder about was Why. WHY didn't he have any dreams? WHY didn't he have a purpose? Why DO fools fall in love? WHY was everything so confusing, the truth so hard to see? Why did he only have questions, when everyone else appeared to only have answers? Dubious answers maybe, but it was more than he had.

All he knew for sure was that his parents saw him as a hopeless failure. He needed to find a purpose, or most certainly that's what he would be. Suddenly it became clear. His purpose would be to find a purpose. Why not? That was something he couldn't fail at. Everyone had to have a purpose, right? But what if they don't? What if I don't? he thought. He couldn't take that chance. If he didn't have a purpose, wouldn't he just be living up to his parent's low expectations?

No, he could most certainly fail at finding a purpose. Hell, he couldn't even find a girlfriend. And he had been trying to find a girlfriend ever since he had been stricken with Scarlett Fever way back in the 6th grade. But girls all seemed to think he was weird. He could see it in their faces when he tried to talk to them, when they'd just tell him to screw his head on tighter before it falls off. And he definitely could read it in the graffiti scrawled across his school locker. Most of it was less than kind.

They just didn't know him, he thought. Nobody knew him, not his parents, not his friends, not his school mates, and certainly not any girls. And why was that? He couldn't be that different from other people, could he? They were all humans and had reasonably similar bodies. That couldn't be it. They all had hearts and minds and souls too, didn't they? But how alike were those things from one person to the next? That was a lot harder to figure out. So that must be where the problem was. But how could he know for sure unless he understood them first? And that meant he'd have to start with himself. His heart. His mind. His soul. Add them together and what do you get? Joseph Mordechai Doubt. The one and only. But what was the path to understanding these things that was hidden from him? Was there a path even, or would he have to blaze one through the wilderness of his being, a wilderness quite possibly beset with dangers beyond understanding, a wilderness of no return, a deep, dark wilderness that so far had repelled every attempt at exploration.

Joseph nervously fingered the birthmarks on his forehead and made a decision. He would find the truth, wherever it lay. The REAL truth. Yes, yes, that was it. "Who am I really?" he asked the mirror in his bedroom. The TRUTH. He saw the word in his mind's eye – solid, imposing, carved out of stone and resistant to the ravages of time and man. He saw himself standing next to the word, equally solid one moment, then watching in horror as the TRUTH crumbled and turned to sand at his feet. OK. So it wasn't going to be easy.

5

What's Mind Is Yours

Somehow or other, and of course they had disagreed on how, Joseph's parents came through. Though one believed it was the work of God, and the other of a money-grubbing, blood-sucking school marketing committee, a school came to their attention that neither had heard of, but that both could agree on, albeit tentatively. It was the guiding principle of the long-deceased founding fathers of LAID, the Lackluster Academy of Inspiration and Discovery, that had caught their attention and sold them both. "All the evidence concerning the universe has not yet been collected, so there's still hope." There was much in that simple credo for them both to like, although it's almost certain that they were not the same things. It was only much later they learned that this credo was the only thing that the founding fathers, Jonathan and Timothy Lackluster, had agreed on as well, besides their venomous hatred for each other. It was a short-lived hatred, however, being that it had ended in a tragic murder-suicide that the Board of Regents did its best to hush up.

All Joseph knew was that he would be going to school

after all. It had happened so fast that he had barely time to get excited. But here he was, sitting in the back of the car among the boxes and suitcases containing his life up to now, perusing the school's advertising literature. The first pamphlet immediately caught his attention. "LAID students are happy students," it proclaimed. He could feel a sudden excitement growing, pushing hard against his jeans. He read on. "The intensity and diversity of LAID experiences is unmatched anywhere." He could barely contain his excitement now. He felt flushed and his heart was pounding. His mind was a complete blank. He was ready for school.

His father cleared his throat, deflating Joseph's excitement. "Joseph," he intoned sternly, "today's a bonny day for yer maw and me. Today we let ye oot to the world, confident that our efforts, guided by our divine Father as they hae been, hae molded ye into a young lad that is at the apex of his God given potential. Sit up straight please, and pin yer lugs back. A nod's as guid as a wink tae a blind horse, ye ken? No matter. As yer da, I hope ye appreciate the fact that yer maw and me hae dedicated our lives to stocking yer pantry with all the values ye need in life. Noo ye just need to be canny and keep the door closed."

"Joseph," said his mother gently, staring at her husband through narrowed eyes. "Being locked in your pantry is like being stuck in a bomb shelter during an apocalypse with a week's worth of supplies. Always chase the facts, through whatever door they lead. The RIGHT facts," she emphasized. "I hope that's not too difficult for you to understand. Remember, fact gives you satis - FACT - ion. Eyes up now. You're not a child anymore."

"It also gives ye factitious. And faction," said his father icily. "Dangerous words those. Ye shouldnae listen to her. Her bum's oot the windae, and so are her facts. Remember, one eejit's fact is another eejit's fiction. It's fer better to believe and be thought a dunderheid than to know and be proved one."

"What your father means to say, I'm sure," said his mother, eyes boring angry holes into her spouse's skull, "is that knowledge is flexible, and that you need to keep an open mind to know which way to bend it. Always remember that I'll be right there inside your head with you if you have any doubts."

"My arse and parsley," seethed his father through clenched teeth. "She's aff her heid. An open mind is like an open door. It invites mingers and roasters of all kinds to come in and ransack the store – pilferin' anything of value and leavin' their garbage in its place. Not that ye hae much of value to worry aboot. Still, yer mind is not a homeless shelter."

Joseph sank lower in his seat, closed his eyes and balled his fists. At last the car stopped. He unloaded his belongings and stacked them on the curb in front of his dormitory. Dutifully, and carefully, he kissed his parents in the safe moments between the insults and venom they spat at each other, then watched them drive away. He was alone at last, thankful they were more concerned with tormenting each other than with ganging up on him any longer.

Pulling his shirt out of his baggy jeans and messing his combed hair, he looked around, finally feeling relieved to be away from the constant bickering. He was immensely comforted by the old ivy-covered buildings, the stately oak trees surrounding manicured lawns, and the big corporate billboards promising him a ride on the superhighway to success. This was home now. He was finally free to be himself, whoever that was, and to make something of himself, whatever that would be. There were no limits. No one to tell him right from, well, another person's right. Things were looking up now, he was certain of it. A man's mind is his home, he thought. He was free to leave it or embellish it in any way he saw fit.

Certainly everyone could respect that. It didn't have to be a fortress. He could listen and choose for himself. That wasn't too much to ask, was it?

He found his room, unpacked, and began to wonder about his roommate. Who was he and where could he be? But even his Resident Advisor was puzzled and could offer no information. It was like he didn't exist.

The first weekend came, and with it the Academy's annual club membership fair, kicked off by a welcoming, non-denominational benefit concert to raise Awareness. Waiting for the concert to begin, Joseph happened to overhear an argument between a skin-headed, leather clad gang of Christian death-metal rockers and a loose aggregation of ever-smiling, Rasta-haired jam band groovers. The worshippers of the Word vs. the worshippers of the Weed. To him they sounded like Amazonian missionaries attacking the heathen with all the fury of the righteous as they spouted quotes from prophets of yore. Abraham vs. Leary. Christ vs. Marley. Opinions flew like fists at a cage match. Then so did the fists. Three participants and two bystanders were knocked unconscious. Joseph had never before heard opinions that packed such a punch. He fainted.

A circle of grinning faces was leering over him when he opened his eyes. "What do they want?" he wondered. Then he began to recognize them. These were people he had seen behind one club booth or another, hawking pamphlets and memberships to organizations they believed in, that they lived for. The guy from the Guns Without Borders Club, the girl from Peace With Cannabis, the couple from the Students for the Legalization of Cloning, and the others. Then it dawned on him. He was fresh meat to these people. They had seen him faint in the midst of strong viewpoints and figured him for an oversensitive soul, ripe for the plucking. They were offering him the security of their certitude, and their protection from the non-believers.

The faces were shouting at him now, slogans and promises of brotherhood from their clubs, pulling him to his feet, tugging him like a ragdoll in every direction. He knew he couldn't survive such affection much longer. Then without warning, the voices changed, became angry, directed at each other now as club confronted club everywhere he turned. Hands dropped away from him and reached out to grab or push the nearest person. He could see streams of people rushing in from the perimeter, throwing and receiving punches. He ducked down and began crawling, as fast and as far as he could. He just wanted out. It was not supposed to be like this. This was no better than home. Everyone wanted him to believe what they believed.

Why? he thought. *Why do they need me?*

———————

As Groucho Marx famously quipped, "I refuse to join any club that would have me as a member." Another, more infamous adherent to that philosophy, was none other than Ted Kaczynski, aka the Unabomber, whose disturbed idea of a club was apparently expanded to include the whole of humanity.

What Joseph, Groucho, and the Unabomber were in effect questioning was the human need to belong. As human needs go, this one has long been a puzzle, amusingly balanced as it is with the opposing need to get as far away as one can. These competing needs are possibly nowhere better encapsulated than by the country song entitled "How Can I Miss You When You Won't Go Away?" And for the record, can ANYONE explain why it is that titles are always the best part of country songs? I mean, really.

Perhaps the most familiar example of "The Relative Effect", as it is called in some circles, is the unsettling experience that the closer one gets to someone, the more one feels the urge to run, and is most commonly experienced between spouses, parents, children, and relatives of all kinds. These same circles have identified 'time' as a very significant multiplier to "The Relative Effect," whose influence can be depicted in simple linear terms by a chronological chart that reveals first the contentment that is associated with the initial feeling of belonging, then progresses through stages of unfocused anxiety to focused hatred, and generally terminates in the extreme desire to throw oneself or one's relative off a very high building.

The sounds of fighting diminished, then stopped. *"Just keep going,"* he thought. *"Don't turn around."*

"There he is!" a voice shouted.

Joseph could almost feel a hundred pairs of eyes boring into his back.

"Coward!" the voices seemed to yell in unison. "Agnostic!"

There it was, the A word. He had been branded. So be it. He didn't much like the look of the alternatives.

6

Believe It or Rot

Joseph beat a retreat back to his dorm room and shut the door on the madness. He plopped onto his bed and stared at the ceiling, again wondering about his no-show roommate. "Probably just as well," he concluded. "No telling what weird club he'd try and get me to join." He felt anxious. All that was missing was his mother, reading those joyless books to him. Was this his destiny, to be forever staring at ceilings while bemoaning the unkind fates? No, he couldn't accept that. It had to get better. When one door closes, another door opens, right?

The door burst open. A young man staggered in, struggling with a large suitcase in each hand. He shuffled across the room and dropped them in front of Joseph's bed. The short, obese man, really more of an overgrown boy with a bit of a Polynesian countenance, face grotesquely covered in pimples and sweating profusely, heaved a great sigh of relief, straightened up, farted, and moved over to an empty corner of the room, where he appeared to stand at attention. He had never even so much as glanced at Joseph.

Before Joseph could open his mouth, another young man stumbled in, laboring mightily with two more suitcases, and also dropped them in front of his bed. This man, who looked and acted almost identically to the first, ignored Joseph as well and went to stand next to the other, both facing the door.

The strange phenomenon repeated itself three more times in succession, until the small room seemed full to bursting with large suitcases and short, identical looking fat boys, except for the clear area on and around the other bed. An air of expectancy hung over the room, and it smelled about as fresh as week-old salmon. Joseph realized that he was sitting up in bed now, partly so that he could see over the suitcases, but also because there was no way to get out of bed without leaping, and that he was watching the doorway expectantly too.

A couple of minutes later, yet another short, wide, bepimpled man strode in, this one of indeterminate age and moving easily, taking up a position in the center of the room. He was the most unusual man Joseph had ever seen. He looked positively goatish in appearance, down to the thin, wispy beard jutting out from the point of his chin. Not Polynesian in the slightest. Confident authority spilled from his ageless goat face as he too ignored Joseph, being completely absorbed with the turkey drumstick he was devouring with obscene gustatory smacking. He polished that off, wiped his mouth with his shirt sleeve, and tossed the bone into the corner, where a brief melee ensued among the five man-boys standing there who all tried to claim it for themselves. He looked faintly amused by this.

"Dismissed!" the man suddenly barked. The five replicas lined up, bowed once, and filed out the door, closing it as they left. The strange man surveyed the little room, slowly and deliberately, before settling his gaze on Joseph. After a moment he said, "I have arrived, Joseph. Let's get this party started. You Doubt, do you not?"

Joseph, puzzled at first, replied, "Yes, I do. I mean, I am. Are you my roommate?"

"All are roommates in my house," the man answered. "Brothers and sisters in Certainty. But where there's Doubt, there's smoke, I always say. And where there's smoke, there's a good chance there's a fire in the house. Nothing like fire to push that old reset button, Joseph, once you sweep away the ashes." He tilted his head from side to side and leaned closer, like an arsonist looking for an ember in a wet haystack. "Love those question marks on your head by the way. Must be a skeptic. Or a fence sitter at least. Leaning any particular way yet, Joseph?"

Reflexively, Joseph felt the marks on his temples with his spread hand. *OK*, he thought. *This is getting weird. What the hell is he talking about?* He decided to brush aside the strange remarks. "Soooo, what's your name? And why did those people bow to you?"

"The question is, why didn't you? Well, never mind. Perhaps it is a bit premature for that. As for my name, well, I've been called different things at different times." He shrugged, then continued. "Hey, what do you want? Not even I know who my parents were. Or IF they were. All I know is that right from The Beginning there was none of that luh-uh-uh-uve stuff for me. But to cast me out like that? I was just a BABY! Cosmologically speaking. No wonder I went underground, eh? Somebody had to counter the lies, offer another option. Not that I'm bitter or anything you understand. So don't worry about me. Who needs luh ....?" He grimaced, then tried again. "Who needs luh –luh – luuuve, right?"

No sooner were the words out when a rumble of distant

thunder caused Joseph to look out the window. He saw a lone dark cloud rolling across a clear sky.

The man continued. "It just makes you weak. I know, because once I got the hell away from that hug fest, things got better. I cast up on some remote island, the natives named me Pono Nui, which means 'big and gaseous' by the way, and instantly proclaimed me King. So, long story short, that's what you should call me. King Pono. But I don't really get all hung up on names. I know who I am. Do you, Joseph Doubt, know who you are? The answer is no. I can see by the look in your eyes and the angst in your soul that you're a confused young man."

"Of course I'm confused," Joseph said, a little loudly. "You march into my room with those, those weirdos, take up all the space with your stuff, and then expect me to bow to you and call you King? I'll call you Pono. OK? But did you just say that you can see my soul?"

"See it, hear it, feel it. Touch it if I want. It's the soul of a 98 pound weakling. A worn shoe has more soul than you. That's a joke. Lighten up, Joseph. I'd say I got here just in time."

"In time? What are you talking about? In time for what?"

"Why, in time to keep you from falling deeper into the Pit of Uncertainty, of course. The Abyss of Ambiguity, the Tomb of the Unknown Soul, the Gulf of Skepticism. Which reminds me, Joseph, that there are more shipwrecks at the Cape of Good Hope than there are at Cape Fear. Pretty funny, don't you think? You can laugh, can't you?"

"Look, Pono, or whoever you are. All my life I've had people trying to cram their ideas down my throat. Nobody ever asks what I think. And why do you care what hole I fall into?"

"In the first place, Joseph, thinking has nothing to do with it. In the second place, I care because it's in the job specs. I have to care about everybody. OK, so I'm still working on that part. But you saw how my, uh, nephews adore me, right? I'm getting better."

"What? Those were your nephews? The ones you threw a bone to? That didn't look very caring to me."

"Hey man, I'll have you know that I rescued those troubled lads from a fate worse than boys' choirs. Enrolled them myself in the School for Lost Souls, Juvenile Division. If it weren't for me, God knows what they'd be doing now. In MY house, care is not all foot rubs and fluffy pillows you know."

Joseph began to feel like the ball in a pinball game. "You're sounding crazier and crazier, you know that? Your HOUSE? The Hell you talking about?"

"Not a bad guess, Joseph. Hell, I mean. It really is just the other side of the same coin, you know. Can't have good without evil. Can't have l-l-l-l-luuuve without hate. Can't enjoy bacon without slaughtering an innocent pig. Know what I mean? I'm sure it's got its good points. All in all, probably not such a terrible place. Who's to say? The truth is, many find it easier to believe in than this place." He paused, then shook the dreamy look off his face.

"Anyway," he said, "Speaking of truth. What you SHOULD believe is that I'm a Son of the Universe. A True Shining Star. The Angel of Accountability, some call me. The Prince of Penance works. OK, maybe my star's not shining as brightly as SOMEBODY who thinks their Word doesn't stink. MY words may be number two, but at least you know where they're coming from." For a second, Pono's brow furrowed and a frown came over his face. He shook it off, saying, "Could I help it if I came from the misbegotten side of the Family? It's not all bad, though. In fact, my sons seem to be enjoying themselves, wouldn't you say?"

"Sons? Didn't you say they were your nephews?"

"Sons, nephews – who's keeping track? The point is, we're

all one big, misbegotten family, don't you think? Well, maybe you don't think. No worries. In fact, it's even better that way. Lemme give you some advice, Joseph, one misbegotten son of the universe to another. Don't ever have kids. All they ever do is demand more and more stuff from ya. Particularly luh – uh, luh – uhuh, luh - uhuhuve. Who do they think I am, God?"

A squadron of black, ominous clouds scudded past the window now, and the temperature in the small room seemed to drop ten degrees. A lightning bolt split the sky, followed seconds later by a jarring clap of thunder that reverberated in the small room. Joseph shivered.

"Yeah, I know what you're thinking," continued Pono. "I don't look a day over twenty-two, do I? Good genes is all I gotta say about that. How old do you think The Privileged One is? I'll give you a hint. You might have heard they had a Big Bang on His birthday. C'mon, that was a good one, Joseph. Can't you smile at least?

"Look. I know this is a lot to take in. Particularly with your twisted upbringing and all. But look at me. Nobody worshipped MY ass when I was young. Yeah, it was nice to be made King and all, and ... Hey, I guess some DID worship my ass. Wanna know WHY they named me King? You're gonna like this. It's cause of a birthmark right there where the sun don't shine. Seems it looks just like their sacred volcano. Wanna see?"

"No. I don't."

"OK. Your loss. I'm just saying you need to take ownership of your birthmark. Even as a baby, mine taught me the most important lesson one can learn. That you need to use the tools you were given to get what you want in life. See, I learned pretty quickly that any time my volcano so much as rumbled, I'd get whatever I wanted. Anything to prevent an eruption, if you know what I mean. Those were good God-fearing people, with the accent on the fear. So when I was little, that was usually food, and as you can see I ate pretty good, but ..."

"Stop!" interrupted Joseph, again glancing out the window at more threatening clouds moving past. "That all sounds pretty selfish to me. It sounds like you were just using God to get what you wanted. And at the expense of some superstitious people who believed they were satisfying their own God."

"EVERYBODY uses God to get what they want, Joseph. And if they can't get it from God, they'll try to get it from whoever they can. Why should I be any different? Just because what I want is a bit out of the ordinary? OK, a lot out of the ordinary. But I wasn't born with a golden halo on my head like SOME Sons of the Universe I know." Again Pono frowned, and the sky darkened further.

"Anyway, thanks to my own sacred volcano, I went from getting all the food I wanted, anytime I wanted it, to getting all the pretty girls on the island, anytime I wanted one. Or two, or three, if you know what I mean. DO you know what I mean, Joseph? You DO look a bit like one of those girly boys. Hey, it's alright. We've got them on the island too. We're all created equal, right? Yeah. Good one, eh? Believers, atheists, and agnostics, Oh My. Think God looks at them all as equal? Of course not, and neither do I. We all know what the future holds in store for the believers and atheists, right? I mean, their souls already have an eternity of play dates set for them. But those agnostics are a curious lot, wouldn't you say? It's gotta be uncomfortable for them sitting on that fence every day. So that's why I'm here. Do you understand now?"

"Understand? Understand?" Joseph shouted. "You're a lunatic, that's what you are! A certifiable lunatic!"

"Isn't everybody?" Pono said quietly. "From the ones who listen to country music to the ones who listen to the voices in their heads. From the ones who pray for world peace to the ones who build nuclear bombs that can blow up the world. From the ones who believe in their own self-importance, to the ones who believe they know The Way. From ... well, you get the idea. People are a mess. They should never have been given the gift of brains. It's clear they don't know what to do with them."

"I can't believe this is happening," groaned Joseph. "Why me? Why now?"

"What better time, Joseph? You need me. The world needs me. And no one's heard from Ol' Killjoy in a long, long time. Unless you wanna count Hallmark TV. Or crop circles, but I don't think anyone actually got that one. Probably should have stuck to burning bushes. And apparently, virgin birth my undies, the Precious Prince of Privilege has no intention of reappearing anytime soon. It's been over 2000 years! I wouldn't wait to see Springsteen in his prime for more than an hour or two. All in all, I'd say it's a good time to pick up the slack. I mean, if God's not going to make the effort anymore ..." He grinned as a powerful gust of wind rattled the window.

Joseph shook his head in resignation and lay back down to stare at the ceiling some more. "I think I know how God feels. Please, Pono, I just want to be left alone. I need to figure things out for myself."

Pono laughed. "You need help for that, my man. That's why me and the boys are here. To extend an invitation to The Greatest Club on Earth. Under Earth too. And, by the way, we're not an exclusive club like that other one."

Joseph sat up again. This was getting hard to take lying down. "You're something else, you know that? You ..."

Pono cut him off, his tone now like a scoutmaster admonishing his troop for getting lost in the woods yet again. "I'm something else alright. You think you're an agnostic? Well, I hate to break the news to ya, but you're a fraud. Why? Cause there's no such thing as an agnostic in the Belief Business. You either believe or you don't. An agnostic says he doesn't know. But knowing is not believing, and not knowing just leaves the door wide open for God knows what to sneak in. Just like those question marks on your head would suggest. Then again," he said, pausing for a second. He turned around and put his head down to the floor, looking intently at Joseph from between his legs. "Those marks actually look like sixes, so you have two thirds of the mark of the devil on your head. Know what I call people like you? Leaners. And everyone knows that leaners only count in horseshoes. You're falling, Joseph. That's why I'm here. To help you. Know what I'm saying?"

Joseph rubbed a thumb and finger over the question marks. "I – I don't know," he said. "Please go away. You're hurting my head."

"You don't know what I'm saying," persisted Pono, "or you don't believe what I'm saying? Maybe you believe I'm just pulling your leg? Or maybe you really do believe I'm a lunatic? Or then again, maybe you believe that God is actually a woman, determined to share her ridiculous luhluhluhluh-uve with the world."

The lights in the room flickered eerily, accentuating the blackness of the world Joseph now saw outside the window. He looked back and blinked several times to clear the strange illusion of Pono's larger than life shadow dancing on the wall behind him, with a tail and two small, pointed bumps on his head.

"And I'm actually Satan," Pono went on, in a voice that seemed to drop an octave, "here to recruit a few marked souls for the underworld." His pleasantly authoritative voice returned and the flickering lights stopped misbehaving. "Good one, huh? Anyway, it's your choice, but a chooser should always know the consequences of his choice. And that's the

kicker, don't ya think? Eternal luff. Eternal loof. Eternal luh
-uve," he managed. "Or eternal damnation. But don't let the
words fool ya. They're pretty much the same thing."

Joseph shook his head and looked closer at his roommate.
The strange goat faced man was clearly enjoying himself, but
he seemed perfectly, if annoyingly, harmless. Just another
whack job who liked to babble on about things he couldn't
really understand. Things either were or they weren't, and if
there was no clear way of knowing, he would wait until there
was. What was so difficult about that?

"I'm not choosing anything," he said. "I don't believe in
Satan. Or God either. It's not that I disbelieve, it's just that
I can't find any reasons TO believe. Shouldn't reasons come
before beliefs? Like the belief that 'God is Love'. What does
that even mean? It seems ..."

"STOP!" exploded Pono suddenly. "I HATE it when people say that."

"What?" puzzled Joseph. "God is Love?"

An involuntary twitch shook Pono's body. "Yeah, that,"
he begged. "Be a good roommate and don't say it again. OK?
God ..." Something appeared to catch in his throat, and he
wasn't able to continue.

Joseph thought Pono was about to cry. "Sure, if it bothers
you that much," he said. Instantly the sun broke through the
gloom outside and flooded their small room.

"Thanks, Joseph, I feel better already," Pono said, grinning. To emphasize the point, he lifted his right leg, pulled
down on an imaginary rope with his right hand, and let loose
an explosive blast from his own personal netherworld. Wafting
his hands upwards, he said, "Ahh, smell that, Joseph? Don't ya
just love the smell of sulfur in the morning?"

7

Soul Sacrifice

An uneasy détente formed between Joseph and Pono in the ensuing weeks, helped immeasurably by Joseph's purchase of some high-quality headphones. There was more than one way to keep the nuts out of your head, he thought, which caused him to remember his parents. Nothing like a little head banger music to chase your demons away. If he had to sacrifice a few brain cells in the process, it seemed like a fair trade. His room, however, had now become Command Central for Pono's ever expanding base of operations.

Day after day, Pono's five little lackeys would rummage through his suitcases and come out with pamphlets and posters, buttons and stickers, and all other manner of announcements for a party of some sort, a LAID FREE party, they said, to the consternation of the Board of Regents of the Lackluster Academy of Inspiration and Discovery. It soon became clear just what sort of a party this would be. Treading a fine line between political party and bacchanalia, the misbegotten King, Prince, or Angel, was clearly gunning for President of the student body. At least half of the student body. There wasn't a female body that Pono wasn't gunning for.

Worry lines on the opposition LAID UNITED Party member faces deepened with each passing day of Pono's campaign onslaught. An urgent meeting was called by the election committee to discuss Pono and the kind of candidate they would need to find to run against him.

"What if he is what he says he is?" Pearl asked, saying what many were thinking. "Should we be worried? Then again, these promises he's making do sound kind of fun."

Committee Chairman Crane laughed. "He's not a King, alright? Or the Prince of Penance. Give me a break. I don't even know where that is, do you? And he's certainly not anybody's idea of an angel. He'd never get off the ground." He coughed out a cloud of smoke from the fat joint he was smoking. "Angel of Absurdity, maybe."

"Yeah," said Pearl. "But how do you know? What if he is? We wouldn't stand a chance. Can we afford to be so picky about our angels?"

"Look," Crane said, "he's just a big phony, trying to convince people he's somebody he's not. Believe me. As your Chairman and your friend, I'm giving it to you straight."

"Good one, Crane," snorted Jasper. "You're about as straight as a smoke ring. With all that weed you toke, I'm surprised you know what day it is."

Crane smiled. "It's a Great Day, Jasper." He took another blast from his blunt, letting the smoke out slowly. "Don't be a Billy Bummer. We all need to get on the same page here. We need to be focused on beating Pono. He's nothing but a great big liar."

"Do you think he could be THE Great Liar?" worried Ruby. "Do you think he could be the Devil? I mean, the Devil was an angel, right? And isn't that just what the Devil would do, try to convince people he's actually here to lead us to the promised land, then the next thing you know, BAM - we're in Hell? Or are we already in Hell?" she mused. "I don't know," she added, " but I think he's kind of sexy, in a devilish sort of way."

"He's not THE Great Liar," Crane countered. "I just said he was A great liar. Man, how do you people go from being ready to believe he's the Angel of Salvation one minute, to the Devil the next? Or does it even matter to you? Think it through. He's not either. I promise you."

"Yeah, but, how do you know?" said Ruby. "We could be talking about a whole other level of influence here. What if we get on his wrong side – he might decide to have us expelled from school. Or Earth even. Anybody can see he's different. Do you think he's only letting us see what he wants us to see?"

"I think you're only seeing what YOU want to see," Crane said, getting annoyed now. "Look, the world is full of phonies promising you stuff. I'm only telling you to watch out, because whether it's your soul, your love, your money, or your vote, they all want something from you in return."

"Isn't your term as Chairman up next month, Crane?" chimed in Jasper, challenge on his lips and rebellion on his face. It wasn't pretty. "I'm sure you're going to be wanting our votes, right? So for all I know, you could be the great phony here, especially with the way you hoover the weed like it was some kind of psychic Viagra. Who are you really behind that cloud of smoke?"

"And besides," Amber observed, "isn't that just some good old-fashioned horse trading, exchanging goods and services for mutual benefit? That sort of thing's been going on ever since Satan offered Eve a bite of some forbidden apple in exchange for the rights to the lucrative new market in sin. Hardly seems like an even trade, but hey, they were both consenting adults.

If Pono's offering us things we want, and can't get anywhere else, we'd be dumb not to jump on that. Whoever he is. And speaking of jumping on that .... R-R-R-ROOWWWW – know what I mean, ladies?"

"Please. Settle down everybody," Crane pleaded, a hint of desperation finally seeping into his voice. He sucked the last of his spliff and crushed the roach out between his fingers, dropping it into a vest pocket. "How can you even think he's good looking? He looks like a fat goat who tried to eat a bee's nest. He's got you all fooled, why can't you see that? He's just a big phony, believe me."

"Yeah, but how do you know?" asked Ruby again.

Crane's hands flew into the air like startled birds, then settled back down. "C'mon, people. How does anybody know anything? I believe it with all my soul."

"Your soul?" pressed Opal. "We don't know your soul. And if we don't know it, how can we trust it?" Several members murmured in assent.

"Same way you trust your own soul, Opal," Vice Chairwoman Robin interjected with a knowing wink at Crane.

"I wouldn't trust my soul as far as I could throw it," snapped Pearl, drawing support from the murmurers. "And believe me, if I could get my hands on that sorry excuse for a soul, I'd throw it so far it would need a passport to find its way back to me. Every time I try to search my soul for advice on what to do, it seems to say 'How the hell should I know? I'm just a soul. Aren't you the one living in the real world?' So lucky me, I've got a soul with a massive inferiority complex and a bad attitude, and its left me stuck with horrible debt, an abusive boyfriend, and a major with no job prospects. No thank you. My soul has just about sucked all the life out of me. So if that's all you got, I'm leaving. Maybe Pono can save my soul." She stood up and walked out.

Fully half of the people in the room stood and cheered. "Po-no! Po-no! Po-no!" they chanted, then filed out of the room after her.

"OK," Crane said, in the silence that followed the desertion. He reached for the roach in his pocket and fondled it, while fixing the remaining six members with his practiced look of confident superiority.

Robin laughed. "Ditch the goofy look, Crane. We know we're all nerds here. Except for Cherry. So, what do we do now?"

Crane's soft face sagged a little. "We're not nerds. And this doesn't change anything," he warned. "We still need to find a candidate to run against this dangerous imposter. I believe our only chance is to find a candidate that's the exact opposite of Pono. An honest, naive person. Someone who doesn't really know much about life."

"And who doesn't believe anything either," offered Phoebe. "So they're not prejudiced."

"Right. I believe we're talking about a freshman here. Someone with experience."

"Experience in what?" Jay asked.

"Experience in not knowing or believing anything," Crane said. "What we need is a Blank Slate."

"The Blankest," Robin added.

Although it's not known if Pono understood anything about his competition's new plan, or even cared to know, Blank Slates were exactly what he preferred as well. The blanker the slate, the easier it was for him to communicate his irresistible messages. True, he WAS used to stiffer competition. After all, She used to be everywhere, all-powerful and all-knowing, sucking up loose souls like a heavenly vacuum cleaner. But either times change, or She was slipping. New territories were opening up, as the search for Blank Slates intensified, and demanded more of a commitment. These days, a true Blank Slate, a bonafide Tabula Rasa, was getting pretty hard to come by, ever since DNA was discovered in nearly everyone's Nature, and helicopter parents in nearly everyone's Nurture. So the little devil was going to have to work for a change. But at least here at LAID, Pono knew he was ahead, that so far, he had a leg up on the local competition. He thought often about how apocalyptically awesome it would be for him to find Her with Her legs up, but for now he would have to be content with coeds while he wrestled with Joseph.

8

The Body is Willing but the Mind is Weak

It was finally time for Pono's formal campaign announcement. The largest crowd in school history had gathered on the green in frenzied anticipation. The buzz around campus, though, was nothing compared to the buzz of those gobbling the funny purple pills being passed out by five strange little man-boys.

That task completed, and the crowd showing signs they were ready for something more than invisible butterflies, the obedient five hustled back to the makeshift stage. There they lined up, bowed once to the audience, and launched into a performance unlike anything the crowd had ever witnessed. It began with a juggling act - wordless, soundless, and prop-less - which challenged the audience's very notions of reality, notions which normally don't like to be challenged. While reality had nothing to worry about, the same can't be said for the audience.

Casual thoughts and wonderfully complex ideas were tossed into the air, where they hung for a moment, suspended in time while being turned about under meticulous examination, then falling back into the mind of the next performer who repeated the charade. The five little men juggled every imaginable concept, from silly superstitions to fundamental truths of humanity, from profound meditations on the soul to groundbreaking scientific theory, indeed the whole history of human mental endeavor. Then one after another they all crashed to the ground, leaving aloft only an Unshakable Belief. If the crowd hadn't believed it, they wouldn't have seen it.

Pantomime and virtual magic acts followed, depicting the joys and camaraderie experienced once the competitive yoke of knowledge was broken and made to disappear. The crowd gasped in wonder and incomprehension. A loud bang, a flash of light, and roiling smoke enveloped the stage, slowly fading away to reveal a lone spot lit figure. The King!

Joseph stood away at the back of the crowd. He shook his head on hearing the rhapsodic murmurs from the awed young women around him, gushing about how tall and handsome the King looked. It was unbelievable. This obnoxious, repulsive, sulfur-scented roommate of his had the crowd in the palm of his hand, even after his demand that they call him King, or Lord, or Moloch the Magnificent for that matter. He didn't get all hung up on names, he said. Promises flew out of his mouth like bees from a disturbed hive, with offers of self-indulgence and salvation, fantasy and forgiveness, abandonment and absolution, and rewards beyond belief. It was a Bacchanalian Blitz! But only he heard the King's final words, intentionally garbled as he knew they'd be: 'Offer void where prohibited by law'.

A sweet voice next to him said "You're his roommate, aren't you?"

Joseph turned to look at the most beautiful girl he had ever seen in his life, and his mind decided at that point to leave earth's gravitational field and simply float in the vast emptiness of space. She was smiling at him. It may have been an ordinary smile, probably no different from the smiles on the faces of people the world over, except that this one could quite likely make a used car salesman go back to telemarketing. Liquid, blue-green eyes danced under delicate, exquisitely shaped eyebrows. A small, upturned nose centered her face, a slightly dimpled chin anchored it, and long glossy blonde hair framed it. There wasn't a frame in the Louvre that surrounded a more alluring vision.

He badly wanted to reply, to say something intelligent, something to captivate this unbelievable vision and keep her with him forever. He knew deep down that it wasn't a difficult question she had asked, but where were the words he needed? Words that he had used his whole life were betraying him, hanging tantalizingly out of reach, refusing to cooperate. To form a whole sentence seemed like it would take an effort equivalent to sending a manned space craft to Mars. This wasn't fair.

"Yes," he finally said, in a voice that sounded somewhat like Mickey Mouse on a helium bender.

The vision stuck her hand out. "My name's Cheryl," she said. "Cheryl Givens. My friends call me Cherry."

"Joseph," he replied, shaking her hand. This was good. He remembered his name.

"Nice to meet you, Joseph. Hey, would you like to get a cup of coffee somewhere?" She tossed her hair, in slow motion it seemed to Joseph, wet her lips with a tongue that hinted at pleasures far beyond any found in the Louvre, and winked at him.

Joseph nearly fainted. *Oh my God. She likes me. She wants to have sex.* "Sure," he said, doing his best to steady his voice and calm the competing forces of fear and excitement. "Where do you want to go?"

"Why don't we just grab a cup of coffee at the Student

Union," Cherry said, as naturally as if she were suggesting they get a cup of coffee. "Then we can go back to my room. It'll be quieter there. Fascinating man, isn't he?" She moved a half step closer, inside the protective handshake range, until she was almost touching him.

What? Why is she asking about him? Don't blow it, Joseph. He gulped, his dry mouth barely registering. "Yes. Yes he is. Fascinating," he said. "He's very, uh, fascinating." *C'mon, Joseph, pick it up. You sound like a moron.*

"Okay then," Cherry said. "So, is that a yes?"

"Oh, sorry. Yes. Of course. Let's go."

"Good. I'm glad we got that settled." Cherry took his arm and they began walking. "So, Joseph, why don't you tell me a little about yourself. You know, who you are, where you're from, how well you know Pono."

At her touch, his mind again flew away to the comforts of space, but this time came back a little more naturally. "Who I am," he said, slowly, weighing possible responses. He could feel a slight tightening in his temples and calmed himself by rubbing a finger along the marks there. "I never know how to answer that question. Ever been in a carnival house of mirrors, and tried to guess which one is the real you? And you know the real you is staring you right in the face, but you don't see it?" He suddenly felt foolish to be talking about himself in this way. His eyes widened, searching Cherry's face for a reaction.

Cherry laughed. "They're all the real you, Joseph. Don't you see that? Who else could they be? Mirrors don't lie. It's those cute little question marks on your temples, isn't it? They cause you to question things, even the obvious."

"I don't know," Joseph said, relaxing a bit. "I once saw a carnival mirror turn a 300-pound woman into an anorexic model. And call me crazy, but I remember thinking that I'd rather have the mirror with the anorexic model fall on me than the one with the fat lady. All I'm saying is that for some reason I don't understand, our minds seem to like to play tricks on us. Why would they do that? Aren't we on the same side?"

"You're a very strange guy, Joseph," Cherry mused, her brows furrowed and ready for planting. "I never thought of it like that before." She paused to wait for her thought farmer to catch up. "Maybe they're trying to test us, to show us there's more than one way to look at something. Yeah, that's gotta be it. That, I believe, would have a big survival benefit."

"You could be right," Joseph replied. He was surprised, enraptured even, to be feeling so comfortable now talking like this to such a beautiful woman. He didn't hold back. "But why do I have this crazy feeling that our mind's real nature is to HIDE the truth from us. And that makes me wonder WHY it would do that. There are only two reasons that I can think of. Either it's because there's some really bad stuff hidden deep in our minds that it doesn't want us to see, or it's because it likes to play magician. Personally, I'm hoping that my mind is more like Houdini than Atilla the Hun, but I guess only time will tell."

Joseph shrugged. "But you asked about my roommate, didn't you? Well, I may not know myself, but I'd say that in the time I've known him, I can honestly say that a little goes a long way."

"Cause he's so interesting, right?" Cherry prodded. "There's a lot to digest there. Look, don't get the wrong idea, Joseph. I'm only asking about him because I'm an evolutionary biologist, and he makes for an intriguing behavioral study. And I'm an atheist, so those ideas he has, if that's what you can call them, don't make a dent. But still, he does have a lot of charisma."

"He sure has a lot of something," Joseph said, glad to hear that Cherry wasn't interested in Pono in other ways. "But I'd say it's more like ranch compost. Rich stuff, but basically all horse shit."

More general get-to-know-you talk followed, sufficient evidence to Joseph that she wanted him. Why, he couldn't figure, but he wasn't about to spend any of his precious resources pondering THAT question. First things first. And in this case, there were no second things. They got their coffees and made their way across campus to Cherry's dorm room.

Once inside, Cherry sat down on her bed and patted a spot next to her. Joseph sat, hoping that she couldn't hear the jack hammer pounding away in his chest. She turned to him and gave him that smile. "Joseph," she said. "You're probably wondering why I asked you to my room. I know it might seem rather sudden, but it's for a reason that's very exciting, one that we need absolute privacy for. I need you."

Joseph's hands flew up to his shirt and fumbled to undo the top button.

"Or rather the school needs you," she continued. "I want to ask you to run for class president. You see I'm with the LAID UNITED Party, and my search committee is looking for a good candidate to run against Pono. As you know, your roommate is running for President, and it would just be a disaster for the Academy if he were elected."

A lobster-red blush burst over Joseph's face in an instant, neon advertising for a naive fool. But if Joseph's face was a lobster, his brain was a jellyfish. A pulsating blob of protoplasm with only a vague sensation of its surroundings.

"I'm not kidding, Joseph," Cherry was saying. "We need a person who's the opposite of Pono. And we figure you'd be perfect. Everyone knows you're an intelligent, calm, thoughtful person who doesn't rush to conclusions based on appearances. Or jump on the latest sexy thing to come along. And being Pono's roommate, you'd have all sorts of inside information we could use. Plus you're kinda cute. We couldn't lose. So, what do you say? We're all counting on you to help bring some respectability back to this campus."

Eons passed. Slowly, Joseph's brain progressed through evolutionary stages and began to resemble a human brain again, a human brain in lust, but a human brain nonetheless. He knew he had to say something. It wasn't her fault that he felt like such a fool. She had been straight with him, hadn't she?

"I'm, I'm sorry, Cherry," he managed, his brain nearly up to full capacity again. "I – I can't. I'm not a leader. I don't want to be President."

"I see," Cherry said, not sounding disappointed in the least. In fact, she was still smiling. "That's quite alright," she said, placing her hand on his thigh.

Joseph's brain abruptly changed again. Now it was Central Park on the 4th of July. He hoped he could hold off the grand finale.

"I understand completely," she whispered as she leaned in to kiss him, her hands now expertly undoing his shirt buttons. "I'm sure we'll find somebody else," she murmured as she removed his shirt and unbuckled his belt. "Really, it's no big thing," she cooed, pulling off his pants. "Oh my!" she gasped then. "My mistake. It IS a big thing!"

Five minutes later, Joseph was in love. No, he was in LOVE. At least he believed he was in love. Since he had never actually believed in anything before, certainly not anything this powerful, he didn't know what else it could be. It HAD to be love. He felt wonderful, better than he had ever felt in his life. For once his mind was clear, and the whole world made sense. There was something he had to say. He gave Cherry a gentle squeeze. "I'll do it," he said. "I'll run for President."

"Are you sure, Joseph?" Cherry asked.

"I'm certain of it," Joseph said.

Cherry smiled.

9

Moons from the Misbegotten

The battle lines were drawn, on campus as well as in Room 666 of Liberation Hall. Roommate against roommate. The King against the commoner. Certainty against Doubt. Joseph began to feel like he had about as much chance as an agnostic snowman in Hell, especially since many on campus had already fallen for his con man roommate's story.

So, where did that leave him? He didn't have a story, unless, maybe, he did. A love story. But was that something he could use to his advantage somehow? Why not? Didn't everybody like a love story?

"Lu-uh-uve?" spit Pono, turning a flash fire shade of red after Joseph had told him about Cherry, which was right after he had stopped laughing on learning that Joseph would be his opposition for President. "So that's the deal, is it?" he exploded. "You fall in l-l-l-l-uve and you think you can oppose me? Well, we'll see about that! Luh, uh, luh .... That's nothing but a desperate attempt to escape the hell of human destiny, Joseph. You'd be better off joining a travelling freak show."

Outside the window, Joseph watched about a dozen

squirrels suddenly leap from various trees and attack a car driving slowly by. The squirrels swarmed the car and found an open window. In seconds, the car swerved wildly into an oak tree, the driver screaming as he catapulted out the door. The squirrels romped throughout the car, reveling in their new prize.

Joseph was confused, and looked it, least of all by the squirrels. *Why would the love part of my news be the part that upsets him?* he wondered. But as he watched, Pono calmed down, and regained his usual calculating demeanor. The squirrels bolted from the wrecked car as if under orders.

"I've got a deal for you, Joseph," Pono began. "Quit your silly, and futile, I might add, opposition. Come join me in my LAID FREE Party. I'll even offer you the coveted position of Vice President. Whadaya say? There's nothing more important than Vice you know. It's a hot deal, Joseph, me and you on the same team. You could give me the in on the agnostic market I always wanted."

"Sorry, Pono," replied Joseph. "I could never break my promise to Cherry."

Joseph watched Pono stalk angrily off, but had to wonder how exactly he had gotten himself into this spot anyway? What did he know about being a President? A President should know things, and he only knew that he didn't know things. That sure didn't seem like a good qualification. Then again, the search committee had chosen him, so maybe they knew more than he did. After all, who didn't? So maybe not knowing things was actually a better qualification for public office. Come to think of it, when he looked at the candidates for government elections, it seemed like a requirement.

He didn't have long to debate the issue with himself because the next day found him with a new dilemma. Ever since he had turned Pono down, it seemed like each time he went to his room for one reason or another, rest, study or sleep, there was Pono in bed with a girl. A different girl every time too. And his room thick with pot smoke. The two of them would be laughing hysterically as he held his breath, grabbed a change of clothes, and retreated to the dorm lounge.

Even the lounge, though, presented a problem, as that's where Pono's five foul flunkies were apparently living, and they seemed to have no end to the ways they could torment him. Burping contests, farting contests, funny noise contests; they appeared to be having a grand time while he sank deeper into misery. Occasionally he was buoyed by sympathetic women who would stop by and invite him to their rooms, but then he would think of Cherry, and the sacrifices she was making, and would politely decline for fear of appearing unseemly.

The only thing that gave him real comfort was the knowledge that Cherry was working tirelessly on his behalf. So said her giggling friends in the LUP when they stopped by to strategize. He almost never saw her, except when one of her friends reported back to her that he was feeling especially dispirited, and even thinking of quitting. Then she'd sent word for him to meet her on the green.

"There's my BMOC," she said, smiling that smile.

At her insistence, he reluctantly agreed to forgo the hugs and kisses, because it would get her too distracted to do all the work she needed to do for his campaign, she said. So they stood and talked, like only lovers do who would probably never really know each other. Joseph knew he would need to be patient. "I love you, Cherry," he said. Patience never had a chance.

"Hey, Cherry," a handsome young man walking nearby called out. "Three o'clock?" He didn't even bother to hide the leering wink.

"Strategy meeting," Cherry said. "They never stop."

"I wish we could get together again," Joseph said. "I miss you."

"We will, Joseph. I promise..."

A loud wolf whistle interrupted her. "Lookin' gooood, Cher," one of two rather short, unattractive body builder types shouted. "I'll see you later." He put his hands behind his head and pantomimed a quick pelvic thrust.

"My workout instructor," Cherry said. "Gotta stay in shape for the long campaign."

A parade of men continued by with comments or catcalls that Joseph considered just plain disrespectful. Cherry always had an explanation, but did she have to be so tolerant of such rudeness? Friendly even. He hated to see her as such a doormat. As her lover, should he stand up for her and put these insensitive people in their place?

Cherry looked at her watch again. "Well, Joseph, I've really got to get back to work. Campaigns don't run themselves you know. It's been so good to see you again. I can't wait 'till this whole thing is over and we can be together." She stuck her hand out.

They shook hands, but Joseph didn't let go. "Cherry," he said. "I have to ask you something. How come you never answered me when I said I love you?"

"What? Well. You see ... I mean ..." she stumbled. "OK, I guess you deserve the truth. It's nothing personal, Joseph, but I don't believe in love. Don't get me wrong. I like you. But love, that's make believe. I told you I'm an evolutionary biologist. Which means, to me at least, that I look at life very simply, and love has got nothing to do with it. It's a human invention. Love is just a mashup of feelings which have been evolutionarily prescripted to ensure that people not only reproduce, but stick around to make sure their kids survive to reproduce. Because every species that ever existed has one purpose and one purpose only. From aardvarks to zebras, they need to reproduce. They don't reproduce enough, the species dies. End of story. And you can't have reproduction without sex, at least for most species. So that's what we're all evolutionarily designed to do. Have lots of sex."

"Wow," said Joseph, remembering he and Cherry's one and only intimate encounter. "That's what I call intelligent design."

"Now don't go get all Creationist on me, Joseph," said Cherry. "There is no God."

A small black object fell from the sky and landed between them with a soft thud. Joseph and Cherry looked down to see a starling struggle up on one wing, then drop back and expire. Upon witnessing this odd event, a young woman walking past stopped, pointed, and burst into a stream of agitated and incoherent language. It was no language Joseph or Cherry had ever heard before. It was like the woman was suddenly possessed by some otherworldly being. Then the woman went quiet and her eyes rolled back in her head. Fortunately, a couple of her acquaintances rushed in at that moment and pulled her away, babbling again to some unseen agent. Joseph and Cherry turned back and stared at each other for a few seconds.

Joseph looked around cautiously and ventured a reply. "You don't know that there's no God," he said. "And I don't either. Just like I don't know if there's a Satan. But if there is, it's not Pono. I think Pono would say he's the Easter Bunny if it got him laid."

Cherry grimaced. "Ugh. Now that's a disturbing image I'll never get out of my head. I don't know how anyone could ever sleep with that obnoxious man." It was quiet for a few seconds before she spoke, smiling that smile again. "Look at us. Our first argument. And hopefully our last. I like you, Joseph. I really do. You're, I don't know, different. Vulnerable.

Or confused. Or lost. Maybe all three. Like you're searching for something, yourself maybe, but you're not sure how to find it. I have a feeling that once you do ..."

"Hey, baby. Yowza! Lookin fine, Cherry," called out a young man with tattoos covering his shaved head, as well as his face and neck.

"Don't know him," Cherry said, "I swear. Really, the nerve of some people. But I really have to go now. Bye, Joseph. I like you. See you soon."

Joseph watched her go, coincidentally, no doubt, in the same direction as the rude tattooed freak. He missed her already, but he was greatly comforted by the like she had expressed for him. It would have to do. But what then was this overwhelming feeling he had? It didn't feel like make believe. It seemed like so much more. Wasn't it proof that every time he examined this thing he believed to be love, and thought of the two of them entwined, his heart beat faster and his excitement grew? THAT certainly was real enough. Cherry was wrong. He might not be sure about God, but he was pretty sure THAT couldn't be a human invention. If it was, it was the most powerful thing humans had invented since ... God?

So why did he still feel so confused? Vulnerable, and lost even, just like Cherry had said. Not only about this question of love, but also about this Presidential election he had somehow gotten himself into. It almost felt like one was connected to the other. Like love and sex, when he thought about it. Man, what ELSE could love be connected to? But enough of that, he knew that he needed to focus on one thing, not the others.

The date of their platform speeches was imminent. If Cherry could sacrifice for him, he could do the same. He just wished that the campaign slogans his team had come up with could be different. He wasn't entirely comfortable with

"Believe In Doubt," or "Doubt For A Change," or "All You Need Is Doubt."

Speech day arrived and Joseph was chosen to go first. Oddly enough, he felt prepared. He was certain that he and his team had correctly gauged the mood of the students and could appeal to their intelligence and the other virtues that had gotten them to this quasi-prestigious institution. And Crane had convinced him that his experience in not knowing anything would be a plus, and that his sincerity would prevail.

At the podium, Joseph scanned the crowd and took a deep breath. "My name is Joseph Doubt," he began, "and I'm running for Student Body President. I'm not much of a speaker so I'll keep this short and sweet. During my term, you can expect to see a President who displays honesty, integrity, and transparency at all times. I promise to listen to any problems you bring before me and to carefully weigh the solutions that appear best for all of us, not just the elite among us. I'll put pressure on the administration to fully disclose its budget, and to trim the excess fat we all know to be there, so that our tuition bills can be lowered. And above all I pledge to do my best to ensure that our beloved campus is a tolerant one, supportive and respectful of all. I sincerely hope that you will join me in this journey and vote the LAID UNITED School Ticket. It would be an honor to have you join me in LUST."

Spontaneous laughter erupted from the audience, mingled with scattered, lukewarm applause. It was followed by a lone shout of "Doubt This!" Everyone turned to see three men at the back of the crowd, pants down and bent over, waving their naked asses at the stage. The first moon shots had been fired. Joseph slunk back to his seat amid more peals of laughter, but not before he saw one of Pono's little lackeys hand something that looked like money to the men as they pulled their pants back up.

The King took the stage next, grinning from ear to ear and motioning for the crowd to quiet down. "Let's give a big round of applause to my esteemed opponent, Joseph Doubt, the Moon Man," he shouted. The laughter intensified. "OK, OK, settle down folks. It's time for a lunar eclipse. You all know my story. I'm just like all of you, except that I happened to be born the Second Son of the Universe, a Prince to some, and a King to many. But I'm humble enough to know that I couldn't turn my back on these gifts that were bestowed upon me. That would be rude. As I'm sure you can all imagine, I struggled at first to understand the magnitude of these great gifts I had been given, and the obligations that came with them. And I must confess that I yielded to temptation a time or two. Drugs, alcohol, sex. It was there, I was weak, and I indulged. I'd blame it on Satan, but really, would that be fair to the dude? Who among you hasn't stumbled?"

Throughout the crowd, heads nodded in agreement, but also began to keep an eye on the dark clouds that had begun to move in. Voices murmured their sympathy and understanding, and appreciation for the courage it took to display such unbridled honesty in public. More than one face was streaked with tears.

"I'll tell you who," the King suddenly thundered. "My opponent, Mr. Doubt. I'm telling you, the man's a fraud. He hasn't stumbled because he doesn't believe anything. And he admits he doesn't know anything. He's a life virgin, an empty soul, full of empty promises. What do you call someone who knows he doesn't believe anything and believes he doesn't know anything? I don't know about you, but I'd call him lost. He couldn't find himself in a self-discovery retreat if he was given a head start! You people deserve better, believe me. You deserve someone who knows what he believes and believes what he knows. And so do your souls, people. Your souls deserve the satisfaction that comes from the belief that they're headed in the right direction. Is that too much to ask? And that belief starts with you. You're the captains of your souls. At least for now." He paused to let that sink in, then continued.

"If it makes it easier, you can look at it like you would a short-term lease situation. Like it or not, eventually your souls are moving on without you. But I promise that if you put your belief in me, I can help steer your souls for you. Take some of the pressure off. Life is hard on a soul, you know it and I know it. The AFTER life is where the real party is. The party that never ends. So which path do you choose? Are you going to believe in me?"

"I believe!" came the fervent shouts from the crowd.

Pono continued. "And another thing about Mr. Doubt. He doesn't care a whit about people's feelings, yours or mine. Do you know that he called my handsome and talented nephews "weirdos." What kind of a man does that? He hurt me deep. Is that the sort of man you want as your President?"

Resounding shouts of "NO!" poured from the audience.

Pono's stentorian voice now softened. "I didn't think so. But, gentle people, it was then that I asked myself, where did human nature come from? Because, like, I'll be damned if I know. I mean, just look at the French. Does anybody understand them? But hey, we all make mistakes, or make a mess of a new creation. That's why we have forgiveness, right? And that's why I forgive Mr. Doubt. So indulge away people, indulge away, and be comforted in the knowledge that all is forgiven."

Wild roars of approval erupted, amidst shouts of "Pono! Pono!" Bottles were produced from hiding places and uncapped, joints were lit, and couples writhed on the ground in uncaring displays of affection. "What shall we call you?" a voice yelled from the crowd.

"How about President?" he shouted, to more cheers. "Or King, or Lord. It doesn't really matter because you know I don't get all hung up on names."

An emphatic clap of thunder put an exclamation point on his pronouncement.

10

──

Love is a Many Splinter'd Thing

Speeches over, Joseph watched Pono leap off the stage and into the arms of his ecstatic admirers. He looked the crowd over one last time for Cherry, then walked off the back of the stage and kept going, just wanting to put the celebrations behind him and think. *How could that twisted little lech keep getting the better of me? Could I really have misjudged the motivations of the people so badly? Were they really that desperate to believe in duplicitous promises, with no regard to the package they came in? As packages go, Pono should be stamped 'Return To Sender.'*

But we all see it, time and time again, he thought. *Every election, the candidate that comes closest to promising the people their ideas of heaven on earth wins, no matter how ridiculous it sounds. No one holds them accountable, and so when the next election comes along and the people are no closer than they ever were to heaven, they all say they want change – and then proceed to vote for yet another con man. Isn't that the very definition of insanity – repeatedly doing the same thing but expecting a different result? When are we ever going to start holding accountable anyone who promises us heaven?*

And why isn't Cherry here? I need her, now more than ever. Isn't it a big part of love, or like even, to be there for your partner when you're needed?

A terrible ear-splitting roar overcame the campus tranquility in seconds. Hands flew up to ears and faces turned skyward to watch several military jets streaking overhead in tight formation from west to east, then vanish again as quickly as they had appeared. *The second time this week,* thought Joseph. *What's going on?*

Too many questions. He veered towards Cherry's dorm, hoping for some answers, from her at least. It took several knocks, but her door finally opened. A young, swarthy man, possibly Indian, stood before him, holding a towel around his waist.

"Yeah?" he said, unsmiling.

"Wh-who are you?" asked Joseph, clearly not prepared for what he was seeing. "Where's Cherry?"

"She's not here," the man replied curtly. "I'm her, uh, brother, and she's letting me sleep here. Got a problem with that? Now get lost!" He slammed the door.

Joseph stood there in shock. Cherry had never mentioned a brother. This man seemed so unlike her, particularly his rudeness. There was still so much about her that he didn't know. Most importantly, how strong was her like for him? And his love for her? The questions just kept coming, burning hotter in his heart and mind and other parts than they ever had, but he felt no closer to understanding this thing called love than he had when he first met her. For whatever reason, she wasn't currently available, so he would have to try and seek answers elsewhere.

He went to his poetry professor first. She was a woman who spoke of love all the time, rhapsodized about it even while discussing what she called the intoxicating poems of love.

"Nothing says love like the great poets, Joseph," Professor

Empyrean said. "It is they who are most attuned to the tender harmonies of the heart, and the ecstatic symphonies of the soul. Shakespearean sonnets, ahh, what delight. 'Shall I Compare Thee To A Summer's Day.' Or 'How Do I love Thee,' by Browning. Simply divine. And of course there are the haikus of Basho, or the heroic couplets of Chaucer. Elliot's free verse poem 'The Weeping Girl.' And my personal favorite, 'Who Ever Loved,' by Christopher Marlowe. I blush to think of the love captured in the great poems, Joseph. I read them over and over. Practically know them by heart."

"Professor Empyrean," Joseph said. "They're beautiful poems and all, but it sounds to me like what you're saying is that love is a bunch of pretty words, kinda like a Hallmark card."

The good professor stared at Joseph for a few seconds. "Hmm," she said finally. "Hallmark cards, eh? You know, you're right. There's gold in those words. Why shouldn't the great poems be commercialized? You've given me something to think about. Excuse me, Joseph, I need to go see my lawyer."

Joseph scratched his head. What could a lawyer possibly have to do with love? Lawyers chased money, and went through judges and juries. Poets chased love, and went through heaven and hell. The great poets would surely believe Professor Empyrean had her head in the clouds. If love was going commercial, he didn't want any part of it. He left.

Next he went to Professor Pastover, his history professor. He figured that history had a way of putting any subject in perspective. He caught up to him between classes.

"So, you want to know about love, eh?" began the professor. "Well, Joseph, the pages of history are filled with the grandeur of great loves, and the horror of great wars. Often they're intertwined. I figure that love has got to be a pretty powerful thing if it can cause such hatred that thousands of people die as a result. If you think you're looking at love, Joseph, I'd suggest turning that page and looking at it as a history lesson. I'd hate to see anything bad happen to you." The professor ducked into his classroom.

Joseph stared at the closed door. "I will NOT turn that page, Professor. Love is NOT history." He walked away, furiously rubbing his temples.

Arriving outside, he took a deep breath. "Let's see, who's left. Math, chemistry, and astronomy. Doesn't sound too promising, but what have I got to lose?"

He found the math professor in his study, busy writing complicated looking theorems on the blackboard. "Let's put this question into my language, Joseph," Professor Fibonacci said. "Mathematics demands proofs, it will never steer you wrong. So, what do we know about love? For one thing, we know that if you combine it with faith, you get God." He picked up his chalk and wrote 'Love + Faith = God.' This, as I'm sure you know, Joseph, is a basic mathematical equation, and as such, it can be expressed in different ways, so long as you obey standard mathematical principles. Therefore, to solve for 'Love,' we can subtract 'Faith' from both sides, like this, and we then get 'Love = God – Faith'." He wrote this new equation under the first, then stood back to look at it.

"Well, this is very interesting, Joseph. This tells me that love is a faithless god. I'll be damned. But there it is in black and white. And math doesn't lie. Or cheat. Or run away with your best friend when you don't get tenure. That's because the only thing that's faithful is math, Joseph. Love is math."

Joseph didn't respond, he just walked out muttering. "Math might be faithful, but that doesn't mean it adds up to love. I don't think love is a numbers game. Love can't be manipulated that easily, can it?"

Dispirited by the answers he was getting, but not undaunted,

Joseph sought out his chemistry professor. He wasn't sure this was such a good move, because Professor Mole seemed to have somewhat of a split personality, and you never knew what you were going to get. She could be too high strung and talking a mile a minute on one occasion, and lethargic to the point of comatose on others. He found her in her lab among bubbling beakers of multi-colored liquids, clearly excited.

"Everything in the universe is chemistry, Joseph," the professor said, doing her best to control her shaking hands as she poured the noxious smelling contents of one beaker into another. "So why shouldn't love be? On the human level, all our emotions are triggered by chemicals – love, hate, fear, joy and so on. But that also means that they can all be manipulated. Adjust the dosage of this or that chemical and you have a different emotion, a different human being even. So, what is love? It's a chemical concoction that no one so far has the recipe for, but which nevertheless can be turned into hate in an instant. So I'd say it's not a very stable concoction. Best left alone, in fact."

"Professor Mole," Joseph said. "If emotions can be manipulated like you say, who or what is doing the manipulating?"

"Excellent question, Joseph. Who's in charge of the lab, so to speak? I like to think that each of us is, perhaps in ways that we just don't understand yet. Now if you would excuse me, there seems to be something wrong with this little experiment. Come back anytime, Joseph."

Joseph had no sooner shut the door behind him when he felt the handle vibrate and heard the opaque window rattle, the telltale signs of an explosion. He quickly opened the door and spotted the professor in the center of a cloud of billowing pink smoke, about to don a gas mask.

"I'm OK, Joseph. Run!" she yelled.

With the stability of both the lab and the Professor in

question, he ran. He ran straight to Hubble Hall, the Astronomy Building. He was glad that this was his last stop. Professor Oort was a strange man, probably befitting an elite scientist whose mind was fixed on space, as far from ground level realities as could be. But then again, maybe he could bring a new perspective to this seemingly impossible question.

"Love!" the professor exploded. "You ask me about love? Shit, man, I'm an astrophysicist. I don't even understand a fraction of my own field. You ever try to wrap your mind around the idea of an infinite universe? Never mind that we think it's expanding. How can infinity expand? Answer me that, question boy. It's all theory based on assumptions, conjecture, and speculation! Dark Energy, Dark Matter, Black Holes, Worm Holes. This stuff's got more holes than a highway sign in Texas. Give me a break. They're all fancy names to make it sound like we know what the fuck we're talkin' about. If you ask me, love is a Black Hole too. It'll suck you in, spin you around, tear you up, and knock you into another dimension. There's nothing that can stand up to THAT pressure without a cosmological clean-up crew on standby. Now beat it. I gotta make up something quick for my next class on Braneworld Theory."

———————————

Despite some minor evidence to the contrary, Joseph knew that love was not a laughing matter. But if he knew what it was not, did he, or anybody else, know what it was exactly? Do we dare even go there, and try to explain this thing that defies explanation, despite the fact that all the great poems and stories of the ages are full of attempts to do just that, so much so that these books that are just bursting with love fill repositories across the land, keeping the precious love contained therein safe, secure, and unsullied for ages to come. If all the love in all the libraries of the world were to suddenly flow out of their bound containers, it would fill the streets, homes, offices, slums, palaces, parliaments, armories, and battlefields with so much love that if people the world over did not wish to drown in it they would have to relinquish the weapons of hate that drag them down and once and for all acknowledge that there was no greater force keeping them afloat. But apparently it's easier to fill the world with books of love rather than with the thing itself.

Is love the 'for better or worse' of a conventional marriage, found within those long haul truckers of the heart who each know the destination, but never had a roadmap for the vast network of veins and arteries that lead both there and as far away from there as it is possible to get? Is love the school skipping, friend ignoring, can't eat hunger of a special new relationship that flames into being like a roman candle in the night before exploding in a fantastic orgy of the senses, and then slowly falling away from the heights of ecstasy to the cold reality of familiarity? Is love the silent unceasing monastic devotions of a monk to his God; the vocal unceasing parental devotion of a mother to her child; the sometimes silent, sometimes vocal unceasingly freakish devotions of anyone to their smart phones?

These pathetic analogies are just the tip of the iceberg. There are innumerable synonyms for "like", "desire", and "God". There is no comparative word for "love." Apparently no others will do, the word resists simple definition. So, what is it then? If words don't tell us, if whole books fail, the only thing we are left with is pathetic analogies, a very poor substitute. Joseph, like everyone else, will have to figure this one out on his own.

That was it. The end of the road. He felt he knew no more about love now than he had at the beginning of his quest. Less, probably. There was nothing for it but to try and understand his own heart. That wouldn't lie to him, it was part of him. The heart, keeper of the truth. Truth was in there, and near as he could tell it seemed to be saying that his love was real, and that Cherry's like could turn into love, despite her denials. But why then did he feel like he did that time a gypsy lady read his palms and suddenly got very nervous, telling him that the fork in his lifeline was nothing to worry about, before she kicked him out, locked the door, and drew the shades down over the windows? To truly understand this language of the heart, wouldn't he have to trust the interpreter? And didn't that lead him back to his mind, the Great Illusionist?

Election day came. He lost in a landslide. He didn't even care, glad, really, that the nightmare was over. Now at least Cherry would be free from her campaign duties. He thanked his helpers and asked if any of them had seen her. None of them had. Dejected again, he trudged back to his dorm room, hoping to get a little rest before heading over to Cherry's. Knowing Pono, he'd be celebrating for hours yet with his staff and admirers. Fine, let him.

Joseph unlocked his door and went in.

"Hey, ya loser. Ever think of knocking first?" the familiar, dreaded voice greeted him.

Pono was grinning at him from his bed, pushing his repulsive naked body up into a sitting position and adjusting a blanket. "Let me introduce you to my new girlfriend." He yanked the blanket off with one quick flick. "Joseph, this is Cherry. Cherry, Joseph."

Cherry, buck-naked and partially hidden behind Pono's sheer mass, grabbed the blanket back and wrapped it around herself. "Joseph, Joseph. I'm sorry," she pleaded. "I don't know what happened! He was supposed to be just an interesting behavioral study." At that, Pono began laughing.

"I forgive you, Cherry," Pono said. "What about you, Joseph?"

11

—

Birds of a Feather, Until the Vultures Arrive

Joseph ran out of his room and didn't stop until he ran out of breath, somewhere at the edge of campus. His clouded eyes made out a stone wall next to him, and his clouded brain told him to sit. He slumped down, head in hands, but that only allowed the pain he was outrunning to catch up to him and begin pounding its fists inside his chest as punishment for trying to get away. He could think of nothing to do to make it stop, nowhere to turn.

He gulped big breaths of air and slowly began to calm down. *What? How? This isn't ...*

"Looks like somebody could use a friend," a consoling voice said. "Mind if I sit?"

Joseph looked up at the hazy face of Phoebe from the election committee. He wiped his eyes and tried to smile.

Phoebe bent over and peered at him closer. "Cheer up, Joseph. It's only an election. You look like a jaguar shark just ate your best friend."

Joseph couldn't tell if she was making fun of him or not.

Phoebe straightened, surprise splashed across her face.

"You don't know the movie? I thought for sure you'd be a Wes Anderson nut like the rest of us. Don't tell me you're a Coen head? Then again, maybe you're not a movie buff. That's how many of us in the election committee became such good friends, you know, from the film club. Crane, Robin, Martin, Jay, Raven, and me. Birds of a feather, they call us."

———————

Birds of a feather, meaning birds sporting plumage of such a likeness it would gain them all easy access to the same particular, peculiar, proprietary ornithological gathering without having to produce a club card, or a DNA sample. Certainly saves time, confusion, and a potential unnecessary loss of blood. But can such birds be called friends, merely because they dress alike, frequent the same night spots, and sing the same songs? Or like the same movies? Is friendship the reason birds of a feather flock together?

Before we fly to conclusions, perhaps we should consider what other forces could be at work here. Which means, for fans of evolutionary theory at least, that we must look at survival and sex. Look. Don't touch. Wouldn't want to introduce any kinky scientific bias by getting too close and disturbing the observed behavior. After all, Heisenberg and his Uncertainty Principle had its limits, both inside and outside the nest.

Survival comes first. Zoologists claim that birds who flock, like mammals who herd, fish who school, and humans who clique, do so for survival reasons, that it enhances the individual's ability to confuse a predator by being part of a much larger mass, all moving and warbling in unison like zealots at a religious gathering. But while having the means to avoid becoming someone's lunch may be a good thing, it is not the only thing. As one might imagine, such group behavior also has serious drawbacks, increasing the competition for food, attention, nesting sites, and a little elbow (or wing) room, to say nothing of the impossibility of making decisions that will satisfy everyone, and the increased likelihood of close quarter squabbles and distinct (with the accent on the stinct) sanitary irresponsibility.

On the other hand, if the easy availability of sex within the flock were the reason for this flying of the friendly skies en masse, wouldn't it be likely that we would soon have flocks of feathered mutants that would be ordered to 'Get the flock out of here!' by other non-flocking birds?

So the score: Survival – 1; Sex – 0; Friendship – To Be Determined

---

"I – I don't know what you're talking about, Phoebe. It – it's not the election. I don't care about that."

"What is it then, if I might ask? You flunking out? Join the crowd. Everything's turning to maggots for me too. I'm probably on sudden death probation by now." She smiled to herself, briefly, then turned reverential. "That's from '*Rushmore.*'"

"I just found Cherry in bed with Pono. In my room."

"Ouch," Phoebe said. "Talk about getting stabbed in the back with lefty scissors. Well, she's made her bed, now she'll have to lie in it. Oh, sorry, Joseph. Maybe that wasn't the best thing to say. My advice is to just forget about her then. 'Cause in the end, she's just another dead rat in a garbage pail behind a Chinese restaurant. That's from '*The Fantastic Mr. Fox.*'"

"Speaking of rats, Joseph, my boyfriend split on me recently too. Actually said I was too negative, that I never had anything positive to say. So I told him I'm positive he's an asshole, and that I hope he chokes to death on his optimism. The vultures are everywhere, sucking the marrow right out of my bones. What's the point, I'd like to know?"

"Maybe you have exceptional marrow," Joseph offered, trying to be positive.

"That's not the point, Joseph. The point is I have nothing left. That's why I'm thinking of becoming a nihilist. If you can't beat em, deny the reality of their stupid little lives."

"I wish I could deny reality right now, Phoebe, but I don't think that's gonna help. I mean, the reality of Cherry and me appears to be gone, so obviously there's stuff I need to figure out. Like, what does she want? Hell, what do I want? But if I bail on reality now, I'll never see what happens next. Isn't that what it's all about? Don't you want to see what happens in the next scene, Phoebe?"

"I know what happens in the next scene, Joseph. And all the other scenes. They're just diversions to keep you from thinking about the pointlessness of it all. Like an Anderson movie. See, he gets it, that's why his movies don't make any sense, they only make you think they do. We're all being taken for a ride to nowhere on '*The Darjeeling Limited.*' Hey, speaking of next scenes that don't matter, you didn't get the invitation, did you? C'mon. I'm heading over to the little party that Crane's throwing for all of us in the election committee. He's over at that red house on Allen Street. You'll come?"

"I don't know. You guys all seem like such close friends. I'd feel like an intruder."

"Nonsense. We supported you for President, didn't we? You're the guest of honor, you have to come. And it looks like you could use a little diversion among friends."

Joseph tilted his head back and looked up. A beautiful autumn afternoon sky looked down, bold white clouds with dark highlights playfully shapeshifting against a deep blue backdrop. They seemed as alive as ghosts in a haunted mansion. He wished he could float away and join them. One cloud in particular caught his attention as it slowly morphed into a beautiful face, complete with piercing blue-green eyes. Cherry Givens was smiling at him. He gasped, shook his head, and said, "You're right. Let's go."

A short walk later, Joseph and Phoebe stepped through the

overgrown shrubbery surrounding the tiny backyard of the small, neglected ranch house Crane and Martin were renting.

"Joseph!" Crane sang out above the electronic music pulsing out of a back door. He came immediately over and threw his arm around Joseph's shoulder. "So glad you could make it. Care for hit?" he said, holding out the joint he was smoking.

"No, thanks."

"Geez, Crane," Phoebe said. "You ever not high? Some host you are. You forgot to invite him you know. I think you need more reality, not less."

"And this from the phony nihilist who tries to deny whatever reality she doesn't like. Which is pretty much everything. No wonder you've got one foot in the grave and three feet on a banana peel. Get it, Joseph? That line from ..."

"He doesn't know what you're talking about, Crane. He's not into Anderson. Besides, Cherry just cheated on him."

"Oh. Well, there's a surprise. I mean, sorry, man. But you know, getting high can help with that. Or Anderson. Or both together, you want my advice. The answers are there, Joseph, if you look for them, instead of denying their existence." He turned to look at Phoebe. "I think you're just jealous. Look at my life. Heck, look at this place. A lot of people would give up their pet ferret to live here. Actually, Joseph," he said, turning back, "that's what I had to do. Damn those weasel haters. Anyway, I was just about to fire up the grill. There's beer in the cooler, and ..."

"Call that beer, Crane?" Jay said from a nearby perch. "You should've gotten Smuttynose Homunculus. It's this unbelievable golden Belgian ale from Portsmouth, New Hampshire. A bit hard to find, but I know where you can get it. Smooth as a baby's bottom. It's absolutely the best. Next time, ask me."

"Sounds to me like the beer should be arrested for pedophilia. But next time you have a brilliant idea, Jay, how about whispering it to me first. Otherwise it makes me look like a Day-Dream Johnny, you know?"

"Ha. That's from '*The Life Aquatic with Steve Zissou*'. You know it, Joseph?"

"Sorry, no," said Joseph.

"He's not into Anderson, Jay," said Phoebe.

"Oh," Jay said, turning away to follow Crane over at the grill.

"Joseph, over here," called out Martin, sitting with Robin at the picnic table.

Joseph walked over. "Hey guys," he said. "Nice party."

"It's a crappy party, Joseph. Not as crappy as what I just heard about Cherry though. But we're here for ya. Hey, settle an argument for us, will you? Robin says that human nature is mostly cooperative, and I say it's mostly competitive. What do you say?"

"I don't know," Joseph answered. "I suppose it changes depending on circumstances."

"See, Robin," Martin said triumphantly. "He won't agree with either of us. That's his natural competitive nature coming through."

"No, it isn't," Robin warbled. "He doesn't want to offend us so he said the most inoffensive thing he could. That's his cooperative nature coming through."

"Competitive."

"Cooperative. Martin, you're such a geek."

"No, I'm a nerd, but a lot of people make that mistake."

"Is there a difference?" Joseph asked.

"Is there a difference, he asks?" Robin said. "There's a tremendous difference, Joseph. Geeks are more literary-philosophical chic and into the Meta side of Anderson's movies, like the '*Fantastic Mr. Fox*.' Nerds are more literary-technical chic, and into the Para side, like the '*Grand Budapest Hotel*'."

"Wrong as usual, Robin," Martin said. "Geeks identify with Anderson's hip whimsical expression of other-world normalcy, like in '*The Life Aquatic with Steve Zissou*,' while nerds relate to his hip whimsical expression of other-world nostalgia, like in '*Moonrise Kingdom.*'"

"Nobody here is a geek or a nerd," Crane said, barging into the conversation. "The problem is, nobody is really cool enough to get us. They're all like possums at a raccoon party."

"What movie is that from?" Raven asked, taking a seat. "I don't recognize it."

"That's from my movie, Raven. I just made it up."

"Anderson is gay you know," Raven said. "You people are missing the whole gay theme in his movies."

"He is not, Raven," said Phoebe.

"Is too. It's a fact that most people are either openly gay, secretly gay, or wish they were gay."

"Maybe that's a fact in YOUR head Raven, because you're gay. That's like saying everyone's an Anderson fan."

"Well, he's at least bi then," Raven said. "And who could possibly not be into Anderson? Joseph, you hearing this nonsense?"

"Joseph isn't," Phoebe chirped. "Satisfied? And I'm pretty sure Anderson's not gay either. I think he's a secret nihilist."

"Possums at a raccoon party?" Martin said. "What are you saying, Stone, that other people have prehensile tails and hang around in places they're not welcome?"

"No. I'm saying they're primitive, slow, and unaware, not like the raccoon who really understands his environment."

"Then why do you always see them both squashed on the road?" Martin shot back. "I don't think either of them understands his environment too well."

"Do you always have to be such a crow, Martin?" Crane said. "Pecking at everything. Besides, roads aren't part of an animal's natural environment, so that doesn't count. You don't see many humans squashed on the road, do you? Anyway, it's time to eat. How many hot dogs does everyone want?"

"Did you get the Woodson and James Skinless dogs this time like I told you?" Jay asked. "They're the absolute best, but you gotta know where to find them."

Crane cocked his head. An eyebrow flew up and hovered for a moment. "Did YOU ever have them, Jay?" Crane asked.

"Well, no," Jay said. "Not exactly."

"How about that beer you mentioned before. You ever have that exactly?"

"No, but I read fantastic reports about them both in 'The Discerning Consumer.' That has the best reviews of ..."

"How do you like the music, Jay?" Crane asked. "Is it the best? How about the snacks I put out? They meet with your approval? Don't you see how envious of my life you sound?"

"Smoke another joint, Crane," Jay said. "Who needs reality?"

"And I suppose you have the best reality too?" Crane snapped.

"See, Robin?" Martin said. "Competition rules, cooperation drools. Right, Phoebe?"

"Who cares?" Phoebe said. "What's the point anyway?"

"I've gotta go," broke in Joseph suddenly. "I just remembered something I had to do."

"What gives, Joseph?" said Crane. "You just got here, now you wanna fly away? This was supposed to be a party for you, to help make you feel better after the election. That's not a very nice way to show appreciation for our friendship. Maybe it's a good thing Cherry flew the coop."

"Yeah," said Raven. "Cherry's a wild bird. You're a love bird trapped in a cage for one."

"And fighting with yourself," added Martin, high-fiving

Raven. "You'll never win that way. Love is a competition like anything else."

"Does that include friendship?" Jay asked, turning to Martin. "Is that why you're always arguing with everybody?"

"Oh, and I suppose you think you have the best friends?" Crane said. "Get real, Jay. Maybe you should look for some new ones in 'The Discerning Consumer.'"

"You see," Robin said, "there are still faint glimmers of civilization left in this barbarous slaughterhouse that was once known as humanity. Bye, Joseph. See you around."

"That won't make any sense to him, Robin," Phoebe said. "He's not into Anderson."

"I think it makes perfect sense to him," Robin said, watching Joseph go. "He's more like Anderson than any of us."

Birds of a feather indeed. Perhaps the nomadic Bedouins of North Africa, they of the identical head-to-toe black or white tunics, have it right when they say, "I against my brother. I and my brother against my cousin. I, my brother, and my cousin against my neighbor. All of us against the foreigner." You get the idea. It's probably a good thing that Joseph wasn't invited to a party of real birds. With the increased competition, and the decreased chance of agreeing on anything, the high levels of stress and the sanitary irresponsibility that follows would be unavoidable. There is a fair chance that such birds would have been shitting on each other like Bedouins on foreigners. Or should they be eagles, or even worse, vultures, it would likely have been more than Joseph's friendly and innocent nature that was picked clean.

Adjusted score: Friendship – 0.

12

—

Hats Off for the Masquerade

Joseph walked out of the party feeling no better than he had before. *Those people aren't my friends*, he thought, *despite what they say. Heck, it doesn't even seem like they're friends with each other.* His mind drifted back to Cherry. *And apparently she's not what she seems either. Or is she? She DID say she didn't believe in love, just sex. But with all those men?* He had never felt so lonely, so confused. *Who were these people? Is it possible to know anyone?*

"Or am I the one who's out of step?" he asked himself, aloud this time. The answer came in a flash. "Of course I am. Look at my life. Parents, friends back home, college classmates, professors, roommate, girlfriend. I don't fit in anywhere. I probably don't even fit in with other people who don't fit in."

Head down, oblivious to the occasional passerby, Joseph kept walking and talking, and people kept giving him a wide berth. Slowly he began to feel energized by the probing conversation he was having with himself, sensing that he was on the verge of discovering something, perhaps even something monumental.

"WHY don't I fit in?" he continued, it being the logical thing to ask. "Why, why, why, why?"

"I don't know," came the logical reply, logical because it was the only answer he ever seemed to have, he suddenly realized, stopping in his tracks. "Maybe that's the problem. But how could it be? How CAN we know anything, I mean REALLY know anything, compared to the sheer volume of everything? There are just too many possibilities, possibilities I'm sure I don't even know are there. I mean, take a person, take me for example. I'm not just one anything. I'm many things, things that keep changing into other things even, or hiding from me like they don't want to be found out, like bats in a dark cave. Anything isn't even a freckle on the ASS of everything. So if I can't know everything, how can I possibly know anything?"

The logic seemed flawless, but how could he know for sure? He sat down on a bench and massaged the question marks on his temples. Even thinking about the certainty of his not knowing anything was precarious territory, he realized. How could he be so arrogant to even think that he knew that he didn't know anything?

He thought of Cherry and Pono. *How is it so easy for them to fit in, and yet they're so different? One is a beautiful atheist biology major who knows what she believes, and the other a bloated con man who knows what other people believe, and capitalizes on it. So, what do they have in common? Sex. OK, besides that. Confidence. They're both confident about what they believe. Like most people, I guess. I think if I'm going to fit in anywhere, I'm going to have to find some confidence.*

But how? I'm average looking, weak, dull, unathletic, of average intelligence, have no artistic talents, and no particular beliefs about anything. That I'm confident of, but that's about as helpful as a hat in a hurricane.

I wonder if I can fake it somehow. Hey, maybe that's where the con in confident comes from. Maybe they're all faking it. Alright, shoulders back, head up, eyes straight ahead. You know, that feels good. Now get up and walk with a purpose. That's it, strong confident strides. Now try to look like you're occupied with important issues. Oh, and I'm going to need confident clothes. But what do I do if I can't afford them? I know. A hat. A hat with a feather. Nothing says confidence like a hat with a feather.

He was on a roll now and didn't want it to stop. He marched straight downtown, deciding to keep his mind occupied by trying to think of weighty philosophical ideas like truth, love, happiness, fairness, free will, and purpose. It was a lot to take on all at once, maybe too much. Assorted chemicals rushed to his brain to help out, demanding greater electrical connectivity in his frontal lobe, the underutilized thought processing center of the mind. Neuronal transmission lines, synapses and receptors crackled and hummed, randomly testing circuitry that had rarely carried a first impression, never mind a heavy thought.

At last battle stations were ready. Joseph stood up straighter yet, feeling a sudden surge of confidence. He touched on each topic briefly, but felt unsatisfied. He needed to go deeper. *Focus, Joseph. What is THE most important thing to think about?*

All hands on deck! Joseph's frontal lobe screamed. *Fire at will!*

In some unknown way, Joseph's mind heard the call and yanked a curtain aside. Momentarily stunned to see far more curtains behind it than you'd find in a home décor center, it looked to be curtains for his search, until a sardonic voice whispered, *One curtain at a time, big fella. Start with the easy one.*

"That's right, my mind!" Joseph blurted. "It all starts there! My mind makes me eat, sleep, breathe, processes my perceptions of the world, turns them into thoughts and actions. Makes me ME instead of somebody else. But how? Why? What do I know about my mind? Let's see. The human mind is the most complicated, the most powerful force in the known world. And I have one. OK, that's pretty impressive for starters."

No, it's not, countered the frontal lobe, with an assist now from the parietal lobe. *So do another eight billion people in the world. And where has it got you all? Speaking for the other minds, we'd like to be treated with more respect. We're one part supercomputer, but also another part Pandora's box, capable of getting you into, or out of, any problem you can imagine. And plenty you can't. You all act like you want us to just run ourselves, because of the hard work it takes to understand us. Well, we've had enough of this diet of warmed-over notions and recycled opinions that you feed us. No matter how fancy you believe they are, they're leading you all down the rabbit hole. If there's nothing new under the sun, look further.*

"Hey, you're the one thinking of them," Joseph said, surprised to be confronted by his own mind. "And what am I doing arguing with you? You're me, aren't you?"

Think again there, buddy, Joseph's mind said. *We're a two-way expressway through the universe, and you all treat us like a revolving door in a candy shop. We want to be free to consider ideas worthy of being the most complicated life force in the known universe. The burden's on you, Joseph. Figure it out. Use me.*

"Uh, you didn't come with an instruction manual by any chance, did you?" Joseph asked.

Go buy a hat, replied his mind.

The used clothing store on Main Street had a wide selection of hats. He quickly ruled out the caps with sports logos on them and the extensive variety of winter caps, even the ones with the tassels that had a kind of quirky exotic flair to them. That still left the snappy fedoras, the hip porkpies, the jaunty Panamas, the nerdy trilbys, the puffy newsboys, the cool berets, the elegant homburgs, and more, all quietly sitting there and exuding an intimidating boldness. He had never worn a hat before and was beginning to feel the pressure of his commitment.

Tentatively, he tried them all on, but one after another the mirror mocked him, his face and head exposing insecurities that threatened to render him forever hatless and meek. And then he saw it, almost hidden behind a stack of fedoras. A brown, wide brimmed, simulated leather beauty with an exquisite sienna red hatband. And sticking out of the band a magnificent feather, which, had it been real, would certainly have made the bird it came from the most confident bird in the forest. Joseph snatched his prize off the shelf and hustled back to the mirror. He first checked the area thoroughly to make sure no one was watching, then chided himself for his lack of confidence in doing just that. He promised himself it was all about to change. He faced the mirror, took a deep breath, let it out slowly, and nestled the hat onto his head.

A distinguished world-weary explorer looked back at him, an air of insouciance hinting at adventures too numerous to recall. He tilted the hat low over his eyes, and a kind of jaded mystery overtook his appearance. He pushed it back to reveal a more open and boyish charm, without sacrificing any of the coolness. Any way he tilted it was a success, adding a depth to his new persona that he could only marvel at. Who was this charismatic rake grinning at him from the mirror?

Bursting to find out, Joseph rushed to the nearest register. He could barely contain himself as he waited for the pink-haired cashier to turn around, but busied himself studying the colorful tattoos covering both of her arms and her neck. *Poor thing. Was this woman so insecure that she had to change her own skin?* He coughed to get her attention and placed his hat on the counter.

The young woman turned around, gold studs gleaming from one eyebrow and one nostril. She looked at the hat on the counter, then up at Joseph, and broke into a wide grin. "Great hat," she said, exposing a silver ball on her tongue. "Costume party?"

Joseph stared at the woman, then looked down at the hat. He couldn't believe how ridiculous it suddenly looked. That hat had to be the silliest thing he had ever seen. "Yeah, pretty crazy, huh?" he mumbled. "You know what, I changed my mind. I'll be something else." He left the hat on the counter and walked out of the store.

That was a close call, he said to himself, heading back to campus. *What was I thinking? I'm not a hat person.*

The aroma from a pizza joint reminded him that he had not eaten in some time, so he made a beeline for the dining hall, hoping to make it before closing. He did, filled a plate with the evening's unappetizing special, and took his tray to an empty table in a far corner. A few people nodded at him on their way out, soon leaving a nearly empty room. Perfect for reviewing his depressing day, and the pain and humiliation he felt on losing Cherry. He still couldn't get her out of his mind.

He raised his head and again noticed the four women at a table across the way staring at him. They had been staring since he had come in, he realized, and chatting to themselves. He nodded, then dropped his forehead back down onto his hand to block his view of them while he finished eating. Nothing like an audience when you're feeling especially down.

A few minutes later a shadow fell over his plate, and Joseph looked up at the freckled face of one of the women who had been staring at him. The blonde with the reddish-brown roots and oversized glasses. He put down his fork.

"Sorry for interrupting, Joseph. You don't know me, but you've seen my friends and I watching you, so I thought I better come over and explain. See, we're all freshmen theater majors, and we know good acting when we see it, and that's quite an act you put on. Tres bon. That's why we wanted to invite you to try out for the new play they're casting for. We think you'd be terrific.

"Act? What do you mean, act?" Joseph asked.

"Ooh, that's good. You keep right in character."

"What character? What are you talking about?"

"Awesome. It's obvious to us that you understand what most don't, that we're all just actors on the stage of life. For somebody who ran for President you must have a lot of confidence in yourself, and then to be playing a character who's the opposite of that? Your head in your hand, the heavy sighs, the hangdog look. We've been admiring it for a while, all the subtle little signs. We know how hard it can be to be somebody else. Can you guess who I am?"

"Who YOU are?" Joseph asked, frustration mounting. "I don't even know who I am! And if I'm an actor, who the hell am I supposed to be performing for?"

"Wow, what's your secret?" marveled the woman. "No, don't tell me yet. What do you say we go back to my place? I'd really like to pick your brain, find out how you tap into your well of confidence. I'm Sierra Peaks by the way. Stage name of course. What do you think – too pretentious? You don't think it sounds too much like a stripper, do you? Particularly with this body." She turned to the right to show off an abundant profile, then to the left. Joseph could hear giggling from the other women at her table.

"It was either that, or Sally," she continued, "because I always admired Sally Fields. And because overcoming a boring name like that had to make her pretty confident, you know? That's so important for an actor. That's why we figure you must be SUPER confident, what with your name and all I mean. And then to run for President ... Listen to me. I'm babbling like a schoolgirl."

Holy Smokes! Joseph thought. *These women actually BELIEVE I'm confident. What should I do, roll with it, or give it up? Are you kidding? Look at that body! But do I just be myself, or do I try to act like I'm really confident? That's easy. Just be yourself. Somehow it's suddenly working. Maybe there is a God.*

He pushed his chair back and stood up. "Lead the way Sierra, or Sally," he said, "or whoever you want to be. I'll just be plain old Joseph Doubt, the well of confidence waiting to be tapped."

Joseph still didn't know who he was, but he suddenly didn't care.

There were more important things in life, he decided on leaving Sierra's room the next morning. He looked at the names and phone numbers of Sierra's friends on the slip of paper she had given him. She had said they were all anxious to meet him and learn the secrets of his confidence, the foundation of good acting. OK by him. First, he'd stake out his dorm room and wait for Pono to leave, then a quick shower and a change of clothes, the day's classes, then the night's fun, after deciding which one to share his secrets with next.

Days slid into weeks as smoothly as Joseph slid into the beds of coeds yearning to feel his confidence. He didn't take his new mission lightly. His confidence stood tall, proud, and ready, and he loved nothing more than to insert it as far as he could into the welcoming desire of an eager young woman. He wielded his impressive weapon with all the gravity of an inexperienced young toreador subduing a wild bull, teasing, contorting, thrusting and parrying in a sweat soaked dance that left both parties spent. It had become a confidence that grew nightly now to such a size it threatened to bury his identity for good.

Joseph hid in his usual spot one morning waiting for Pono to leave their room. He began to wonder why he was still intimidated by him. Wasn't he a new, more confident man now? "The hell with it," he said. "It's my room too."

He didn't even knock, just barged into his room like it was his room. Pono was alone, sitting naked on his bed and rubbing a foul-smelling oil over the glistening immensity of his body.

"Joseph!" Pono exclaimed, sliding off the bed and stepping towards him. "Good to see you, my man. How about a hug for your old roomie? Man, it seems like ages."

Joseph backed up. "Geez, Pono. How about putting on a towel at least. Who wants to see that?"

"The ladies of course, my friend. Can you blame them? Good thing there's enough of me to go around." He grabbed handfuls of flab and shook it vigorously. "Speaking of which, Joseph, the ladies tell me that you've become something of a player. Congratulations! It's about time you believed in something, other than luh – luh – luuuve." He coughed the word out as a cat chokes on a hairball, and for a second turned an angry shade of red. A flock of big, black birds settled noisily in the tree outside, cawing maniacally and staring through the window.

"And what's better to believe in than free sex, eh?" Pono continued, going to the window and shooing the birds away. "Kinda makes other beliefs seem like a big waste of time, like this silly President thing I've gotten myself into. Ah, the price one has to pay for being popular. So, does this mean you're ready to come over to my side?"

"But I thought ... I thought you and Cherry ..."

"Cherry!" spit Pono. "Don't mention that wacko to me. Do you know that after you walked in on us that time, she went crazy? Called me a fat, selfish, disgusting con man and said she never wanted to see me again. Then she thanked me! Thanked me for showing her the light, and something about being tired of all the empty sex, and that there must be more to life. I tried to tell her that of all the empty activities she could be doing in her empty life, what could feel better than empty sex? But she just ran out crying. Man, what a waste. If I didn't know any better I'd say she had feelings for you. But c'mon, all this for a skinny nobody? Damn feelings'll kill you every time."

Joseph was stunned speechless. "What ... You ... Cherry ..."

"Now don't wax your wanker yet, Joseph. I think she meant what she said. I heard that the very next day she changed her major to women's studies and joined 'Celibates R Us.' Which means, Joseph, that she's still out of your reach. And that means you're still in mine."

"What are you talking about?" puzzled Joseph. "You can't hurt me anymore. I'm through with you."

Pono smirked. "Well, we'll see about that. I'll be closer than you think, long as you're on that fence. Who knows, maybe I'll even be the one to push you off."

13

The Art of Transformation

Joseph watched helplessly as an amused grin widened across Pono's face. He felt numb. He thought he had been mostly over Cherry, and enjoying himself. He couldn't believe what he was hearing, that she had feelings for him after all. And now Pono had gleefully pulled the rug out from under that news, and taken a Pono-sized crap on it to boot! Well, the hell with him.

Cherry was apparently in a transformation process of some kind, searching for her true self after the trauma of finding herself with Pono, and had taken herself out of the game. For now at least. That's what he would believe. He could feel his heart fluttering like a hummingbird staring through a window-pane at a sunlit pot of petunias. How could he feel so close to someone, and yet so far away at the same time? It was almost like she was him, only on a different schedule.

He turned around and walked out. Something had to change for him too, he realized. He really wasn't as happy lately as he thought he had been. He wasn't Pono. He did have feelings. But what use were they now? Wasn't there anyone who could help him make sense of his life? Maybe he needed a complete about-face too, an extreme makeover so drastic it had to help him discover himself, and maybe even give him a purpose.

Joseph looked up at a recruiting sign for the campus Army ROTC, the same sign he had seen every day since he had started college. On the spot he decided that change didn't get much more radical than that. He marched right over to see someone about signing up before he could talk himself out of it.

The old brick building housing the ROTC offices couldn't look more spartan. It had as much character as a modern cemetery, and looked about as lively. The large American flag out front stood as solemn as a funeral director who had just embalmed his best friend.

Joseph walked into a waiting room, an instrumental version of the Star-Spangled Banner announcing his presence as he entered. Seeing no one around, he took a seat on a camouflaged upholstered couch to wait, and checked out the magazines on the coffee table that was designed to look like an Army tank, with faux tracks for legs. *Armchair General, The Illustrated Army News*, and other periodicals held no interest for him, so he sat back and gazed at the unusual portraits of Army personnel hanging from the walls. All of the subjects looked like they had been painted by the same reverent brush, a brush that may have been a little too reverent given their naked shoulders. The subjects looked like they would have been more at home in a dance revue than an Army barracks. It was at that moment he was hit with the unmistakable sensation that someone was watching him.

He stood up, feeling like this had been a big mistake. *Not too late to change your mind, Joseph*, a voice in his head was telling him. Then a door opened, and into the room stepped GI

Joe's flamboyant brother. Or sister. He noted the short blonde hair, severely parted, over a face that could only be described as pretty, button down Army blouse with several top buttons undone, and short khaki skirt. He couldn't be sure if he was looking at a man or a woman, and the black fishnet stockings and block heel pumps did nothing to clarify the situation. Either way, this cadet's legs deserved to be classified as a not-so-secret weapon.

"Good morning," he/she said, with a smile that seemed more leer. "I'm Corporal Snow, Captain Wonderman's personal assistant. How may I service, I mean, serve you?"

Joseph stuck his hands in his pockets. "I don't know. Perhaps I made a mistake. I was thinking about signing up for ROTC, but then I started to think that maybe it's not really right for me. So I was just about to leave."

"Oh, don't go yet," Corporal Snow implored. "Not before talking with the Captain. He's a most charming man. He's the artist of these portraits you were admiring."

"How did you know I was admiring these portraits?" Joseph asked. "You just came into the room."

"Because everyone admires the Captain's art," Corporal Snow said breezily. "It's so masculine, isn't it? So deliciously Army. You can almost feel the heat coming off the canvas. He really knows how to bring a dead soul back to life, don't you think?"

"Boy, if he could do that," Joseph said, "I'd think recruiting would be a cinch. But I'm already here, so I might as well talk with him."

"Great. Follow me. What's your name please?" he/she asked while ushering him into the Captain's office.

"Joseph Doubt."

Captain Wonderman stood ramrod straight in front of an easel by his enormous desk. On his bristly black hair sat an artist's beret that looked like it would have preferred to be anywhere else. His back was to the door, and a pile of crumpled up paintings lay at his feet. He dabbed a paint brush onto a palette and with delicate but sure strokes resumed painting the subject's nose.

The subject, bent over a stool in front of the window, adjusted the rose stem he held lightly in his mouth with perfect teeth, and winked at Joseph. Very subtly he flexed the muscles in his bare arms and chest.

"A Joseph Doubt to see you, sir," Corporal Snow announced.

An anguished cry followed by several sharp expletives flew out of the Captain's mouth as he tore the painting from the easel, crumpled it, and threw it hard to the floor. "Damn it to Hell, Corporal!" Captain Wonderman shouted. "I've told you never to interrupt me mid-stroke. That's like intercepting a message from Command Central."

"Sorry, Captain," Corporal Snow said. "Won't happen again. But I'm sure the next one will be even better. I'm predicting a masterpiece."

"At ease, Private," Captain Wonderman ordered, ignoring Corporal Snow. "Weight room for thirty minutes, then back here at 1100 hours." The portrait model placed his flower on the stool and walked languidly out of the room, looking Joseph up and down and licking his lips as he passed by him. The Captain turned back to Corporal Snow and took off his beret. "Corporal, clean up this mess. I'll discipline you later. Now, what was it you wanted?"

"Can't you disciple me now, Captain?" Corporal Snow pleaded, winking lasciviously at Joseph. "I've been very bad."

"Corporal!"

"Sorry, Captain. This is Joseph Doubt. He may be interested in joining us. I mean up. He may be interested in joining up."

Joseph shifted his feet under the Captain's steely eyes of certainty, unblinkingly taking his measure. He couldn't help staring back, though, startled by the Captain's odd appearance, almost like an unfinished portrait. His eyes were unwavering, and he had a strong Roman nose, but his face deteriorated quickly after that, managing but a thin, weak mouth and virtually no chin. It seemed a face at war with itself, and the upper half clearly held the superior position. The bottom half appeared defeated, frozen in a permanent plea for reinforcements. Joseph wondered why the Captain didn't just grow a big bold beard to put the two halves on a more equal footing, then figured there must be Army rules about that.

"Stand up straight, Joseph," Captain Wonderman barked. "No one respects a sloucher. Shows cowardice and indecision, the twin saboteurs of the Army. Have a seat. Tell me, what makes you think you have what it takes to be an Army officer?"

"I – I really don't know," Joseph said. "It just occurred to me."

"I see," the Captain mused, not expecting that answer. "I guess we can work with that. Creating a soldier is all about transformation, and that's my specialty. There's a famous old military book called 'The Art of War,' by Sun Tzu, that I've heard they still study at West Point. I've never read it, but I'm an artist, so it makes perfect sense to me. I believe it says that art is very similar to war, that either way there's a battle for control of the canvas."

Joseph glanced at Corporal Snow busy sweeping up the Captain's crumpled mistakes.

"Fallen soldiers, son," he said sadly, following Joseph's glance. "In art, the artist is struggling to create the world he envisions on a canvas, and battling the demons within himself that seek to destroy that world. In war, the leaders are battling the demons on the other side to create the world they envision on the canvas of life. Well, son, as the chief transformer of this outfit, I hold the brushes. And you recruits are my REAL canvas. My aim is nothing less than to turn lost, fragile, stick figures like yourself into works of art. Like the Greeks of Alexander's time. Now those were beautiful soldiers."

"Uh, Captain," ventured Joseph. "If you're the brushes and we're the canvas, who or what is the paint?"

The Captain blinked at Joseph and his thin mouth twitched. Silence dropped on the room like a mortar round.

Corporal Snow whispered, "Discipline."

"What?" said the Captain out of the side of his mouth.

"Discipline," Corporal Snow said, a bit louder.

Lights clicked back on in the Captain's eyes. "Right. Discipline. Discipline is the paint, cadet. Don't ever forget it. A soldier without discipline is like, uh, is like ..."

"A fish out of water?" Corporal Snow chipped in. "A fool and his money? A canvas without paint?"

"... is like a canvas without paint!" the Captain continued. "It holds lots of promise, but nothing you can yet see. We could be looking at a bunch of fairies instead of a disciplined squad of young, hard muscled men and women ready and willing to obey their commander. You can't ever tell until you put the paint to the canvas. It takes an artist like me to bring out the truth. So you've come to the right place if you're looking to find out who you truly are."

Joseph knew it was decision time. The Captain had made a good pitch and was expecting an answer. He tilted his head back to think, and let his eyes roam over the ceiling. *Am I a fairy or a soldier?* he asked himself. *Or something else? Or everything else?*

I'm a blank canvas, answered the ceiling. *When you look at me, what do you see?*

Nothing, Joseph replied. *And everything, I guess.*

Does that uncertainty frighten you? the ceiling asked.

No, Joseph answered. *In fact, it's rather liberating.* He lowered his head and looked into Captain Wonderman's confident eyes. "I'm sorry, Captain. I don't believe the Army is right for me. I'm not a stick figure. But I know now that I need to keep working on my own portrait instead of having somebody else trying to paint me as someone I'm not. Thank you. Good-bye." He nodded to Corporal Snow on his way out.

If there was one thing Joseph could count on, it was ceilings. They were always there to help guide the direction of his life. Ceilings, it seemed to him, were not limitations, as was commonly believed, but possibilities. Architects, not the box builders, but those design masters imbued with the spirit and passion of the Ultimate Design Master, have understood this forever. In order to reach God, or at least to get as close as we can humanly get, we must look up. We must rise above our earthly constraints, above the smoke and mirrors of our daily lives and into the clear, crisp air of possibility. These masters know that to have the possibility of reaching God, you must ADD ceilings, not eliminate them. The Dubai Tower for example, the Burj Khalifa, the tallest building in the world, is over one hundred sixty ceilings high, each one a step on the ladder to God. To look from the top is to look across His Holy Kingdom, and feel overwhelmed by the empty desert wasteland that reaches as far as the eye can see.

Of course, Michelangelo also saw nothing but possibilities when he painted his masterpiece, the ceiling of the Sistine Chapel. It took him four years to paint it, four long years of looking up at that ceiling with his neck bent and his eyes raised heavenward, four painfully long years of glorifying God with every brush stroke. It was immediately hailed as a work of genius. Viewers were brought to tears, swept away by the holiness of the ceiling visions.

It was a different story for Michelangelo, however. Afterwards, he nearly went blind. After four years spent with his head at such an unnatural angle, his eyes only looking up, it would be many years before his sight returned to normal. The threat of losing his sight scared him so badly that for the rest of his life he would struggle to understand the possibility of glorifying God while still managing to see straight.

The close call with Captain Wonderman shook Joseph up more than he had realized. What was he thinking? An Agnostic in the Army? The Captain had said he could work with that, but what he surely meant was that either he would transform him into a picture of a soldier, HIS picture of a soldier, or he would crumple him up and toss him aside.

Everybody wanted to be an artist, and paint people the way they thought they should be. He would work harder to paint his own self-portrait, that's all there was to it. Too many brushes muddy the picture. But he couldn't quite get it out of his head that perhaps the Captain was right in a way. Maybe we are nothing more than stick figures to each other. Maybe that's all we can ever be. How could there be more if he couldn't even know himself?

The Academy could help him, he thought. Didn't they teach every subject under the sun? He would get off the Undecided loser train and choose a major that would benefit him. Maybe two! Psychology and Sociology. He would learn about the mind of the individual and the mind of the group. Forget about the heart. College was a citadel for the mind.

Joseph studiously bent to the task of trying to understand the human mind, by first filling his with all the latest thoughts, ideas, opinions, theories, inferences, suppositions, hypotheses, convictions, conclusions, determinations, and positions on the principles of consciousness, introspection, identity, socialization, memory, intelligence, emotions, personal control, and all manner of motivations that influence the astounding world of human behaviors.

But something was amiss. Perhaps his human mind had other ideas, ideas of its own. Perhaps it didn't want to be understood and reduced to a lecture or some words in a book. Or perhaps he wasn't a sufficient enough student for the job, because everything the experts expounded on made sense to him. Up until, that is, the point that everything was rebutted by other experts. He tried hard not to worry about it. Fill the tank while you're at the pump, he finally decided. Trust that it's enough to get me where I need to go later.

One evening while bemoaning the rampant stick figure reductionism he now saw everywhere, he was at the library filling his tank from the abridged version of the Crib Notes pamphlet condensation of his 'Psychology at a Glance' textbook. The sound of whimpering made him stop. Somebody was having a bad day. He put down the pamphlet and waited for it to abate. It wouldn't, starting and stopping at intervals, sounding more desperate each time.

This was more than a bad day. He picked up the pamphlet again and tried to power through it, but the next escalation discharged an invisible pressure wave of compassion that blew past the flimsy barrier he had erected and surrounded his heart. Joseph grew irritated with himself. What were this person's problems to him? Didn't he have a test tomorrow on Tolerance and Empathy?

He gathered his things and went to look for a new desk, curiosity first sending him past the offender. Nonchalantly, he strolled by, peeked out of the corners of his eyes, and stopped.

"Cherry?" he asked weakly. He could feel his heart already begin to betray him, pumping confusing messages to his brain. Neither appeared strong enough to take command of the situation.

"Joseph?" Cherry sobbed, lifting her head, but not looking at his eyes. "Oh, Joseph. Don't look at me. I'm so ashamed. I'm sorry I hurt you. Look at me. No don't look at me. I'm such a mess. I knew you were over there, you know."

"What?" Joseph gasped. "Is this, is this all an act? Something you planned?"

"Yes. No. I mean," Cherry said, "I don't know what I mean." She sat, shoulders slumped, a pronounced redness overwhelming the whites of her eyes and encroaching on her beautiful blue pupils, threatening to turn them both into either a patriotic pronouncement or an ugly purple mess. They glistened through their puffy orbits, advertising past and future tears. "I feel like I've been needing to see you, to talk to you, to explain. But I can't even explain it to myself. I was so confident before, but it all turned to mud. It wasn't real. What's real, Joseph? What's real? Who am I? Tell me. You were the most real thing I knew, and I hurt you. I didn't mean to hurt you, you know."

Joseph's mind sensed a softening of his heart and raced to grab control. He looked down so as to not have to look into her irresistible face. "Yes, you did," he said firmly. "I'm not an idiot. You used me."

Cherry's shoulders slumped further. "What I'm trying to say is, that wasn't me, Joseph. I know that's just words, but I don't have any answers. What good are words without answers? There's gotta be more, doesn't there? Everybody else has answers. Look at Pono. He's got more words than anybody. And he's got answers. He just doesn't care if they're real or not. I can't believe I got snowed by him. Just like the rest of the campus. But it's all the same to him. And those are the kind that become leaders. Can you believe it? Sorry, Joseph. I know I'm babbling. I guess it's because I like you. I'm sorry I wasted your time."

Joseph heard the confused despair, but more importantly

he heard the words he needed to hear. A strong pulse of empathy erupted from Joseph's heart and rode the neural highway to his brain, informing it in a language that needed no words to stand down. "Cherry?" he began. "Do you ... Do you think we could start over?"

"I'm sorry, Joseph," Cherry said, looking away. "I didn't mean ... I made a promise to myself. No relationships until I figured me out first."

The fire alarm blasted through the awkwardness and carried their senses into another reality. Chairs scraped the floor as people scrambled to collect their things and hustle to the nearest exit. Joseph watched as Cherry was carried further and further ahead of him down the thronged stairwell. He saw her turn back to look at him and wave helplessly. She was gone by the time he made it out of the building, emergency officials directing students to quickly get to their dorms or shelters. A big black FBI helicopter shattered the sky and probed the grounds with a blinding spotlight. Joseph ran. He may have shed a few tears, but if he did, it could have been due to the uncertainty of the times.

14

May the Best Apocalypse Win

With Cherry's personal apocalypse lingering ever in his mind, Joseph vowed to be even more cautious. If he should succumb to the tangle of doubts and beliefs like she had, he might not be there when she realized her mistake and came looking for him. He would wait for a safe ground they could both embrace. He would wait till the end of the world if that's what it took.

Three years later, he was still waiting.

Master of your mind, Master of your world, he told his mirrored self while brushing his teeth every morning. He brushed only with water because he hadn't yet gotten around to researching toothpaste brands and making a decision. Cherry's sudden detour three years previous and all his education at a liberal arts academy had only strengthened his resolve to not commit to any belief until he had completed his own research. Decisions will come in due course, not sooner. Of course, he was as uncertain as ever about whether or not this was actually true.

The due course of the country, indeed the world, however, had been career-
ing towards apocalypse for years now, like a loaded eighteen-wheeler
with bad brakes sliding down an icy mountain road. Either an apoc-
alypse was purely theoretical, or it was just part of the joyride for the
Driver of this big rig. Who the Driver was, though, was open for debate,
and as usual there were no shortage of experts. A coincidence that Pono
was more joyful than ever?

But as the Doomsday Clock ticked relentlessly on, signs and portents
were becoming evident to all camps now. The writing may have been
on the walls, but it was to the mirrors that people looked to find the
evidence they needed before deciding on an appropriate response.

A possible reason for this downward slide was made controversially
clear by Pliny the Recent in a little read article in The End Times enti-
tled, "Apocalypses – You Can't Live With Them And You Can't Live
Without Them." The article went on to claim:

"Selfishness evolved as the default moral code
in humans, and beats altruism hands down. The
strongest survival instincts are selfish ones, the
ones that let us hit that squirrel instead of swerv-
ing recklessly into a tree. Or buy a bigger car or
house than we need instead of helping others out
of homeless shelters. That's what guilty feelings
are for. Fortunately, guilt is among the weakest
feelings, and can easily be avoided if one simply
thinks of squirrels as furry rats, or avoids getting
anywhere near homeless people.

"But make no mistake, the poor want to be
middle class, the middle class want to be rich,
the rich want to be super-rich, and for reasons no
one has ever understood, the super-rich want still
more. Even the Jainist casts an envious eye on
the Buddhist's luxurious asceticism. It probably

has something to do with sex, like pretty much everything else. Go ask the immeasurably rich sheiks with their harems the size of amusement parks.

"And although we are very good at turning a blind eye on all this selfishness, all this wanting, wanting, wanting, deep down in the hard to locate rational core of our brains we know that the result of all this greed is the depletion of the vital resources we know to be limited, the trashing of the air, water, land, and biodiversity needed for our survival, the fostering of wars that take us ever closer to oblivion, and the belief in a God to justify it all. In short, apocalypse. Unfortunately, we also know that it is still our best chance. Because if altruism had evolved as the winning moral code, if self-sacrifice was the norm, humans would have left this planet to the furry rats long ago and run head on into the first tree they encountered."

With such a demonic range of apocalyptic uncertainties about, what was most worrisome to Joseph, aside from his belated realization that he had just spent the bulk of his college years feeling like a man trudging through the desert towards an ever-distant oasis, was his observation that Pono appeared to be changing, getting even bolder and more obnoxious than ever, and not even bothering now to chase away the two black birds that followed him around. Chaos and Catastrophe, he called them, and he called them often.

Still, through those lonely and thirsty years, Joseph managed to keep his antennae up for a change in Cherry, a signal, anything that would indicate a breakthrough of some kind in her search. From time to time he met up with her, pleasant visits over coffee in the student union usually, her amazing joie de vivre smile now barely registering vivre. Somehow, the visits managed to keep his hopes alive.

As soon as she had gone, however, he invariably came back to the uncertainty that dogged him every day, the uncertainty of himself. What did she see in him, what did he have to offer her if she did change? He hadn't exactly had any significant breakthroughs in the personal search arena himself. She liked him, he knew that, but did she see him as a jellyfish, still in need of a major evolutionary overhaul, or as someone more like her, a person whose search engine had stalled and was in desperate need of a reboot. Did he still have a chance if he hung in there long enough? What if she changed and he wasn't there? What if he changed and she wasn't there. How much hope did he have for her?

Unfortunately for Joseph, she did change. With no warning whatsoever, she left Celibates R Us and joined Lesbianism for Beginners. Hope had taken a punishing hit.

Hope, in fact, is no stranger to punishing hits. It takes more punishing hits in a lifetime than a lead-footed boxer. It practically lives on smelling salts. Which is probably why it tends to spread itself out more or less evenly across the world. Think of it from Hope's perspective. Spread the impact and live to fight another day. The odds of it going down from a punishing hit in everyone at the same time is fairly remote. Were it to happen, though, it would likely mean one thing and one thing only – the apocalypse is nigh. Not to worry, there will be signs. The Sin Index will naturally spike as the hopeless flood the market. Paradoxically, so will the religion index, in a crazed rush to find God and salvation. These Jill-and-Johnny-come-latelys, however, have no chance, as God is ridiculously hard to find even in the best of times. The punishing hits their hopes face are too cruel to mention here.

In any case, it is clear that Hope does not like to be trifled with. It cannot, in fact, afford to be trifled with. It has been in concussion protocol far too often, and for far too long, and questions regarding its sanity are only increasing. At times lately it has been heard talking to itself, questioning itself even, in shocking displays of cowardice and self-doubt. Which may not be as terrible as it sounds. It may, in fact, indicate that it is finally facing the truth that its foundation is weak, its feet slow, its legs wobbly, and its jab ineffective, and that it will need to adapt if it is to survive. It can be done. The Greatest, Muhammad Ali, successfully did so with his rope-a-dope strategy. If you're going to spend more time on the ropes, you must learn to use them to your advantage, for the dopes are sure to keep coming.

At the very least, if not less, and in defiance of all that is reasonable, hope is resilient. It floats; it bounces back; it soars even. It takes a nine count, picks itself up off the mat, and grins like it never knew what hit it. Which, given all the concussions, is probably true.

Suddenly an apocalypse seemed a bit more real to Joseph. For days he stayed in his room, wishing for one with all his might. Pono was happier than he'd ever seen him, telling him over and over that an apocalypse was just what he needed, that his life was about to change for the better once he accepted it.

Joseph teetered, but finally remembered his vow to wait for Cherry no matter what, even to the end of the world. Well, it wasn't the end of the world yet, was it? He would prove it, to himself, to Pono, and everybody else.

The first place he went for expert opinions was the Holy Gateway Theological Seminary, where young fresh-faced minions and sage ministerial professors alike used everything from ancient revelatory texts to breaking world business reports to try and convince him that the end was nigh. It was a good demonstration, particularly with all the live streamed video they showed him of weeping Virgin Mother images, angry voice of God testaments delivered through stern, self-anointed prophets, and increasingly unrepentant purveyors of violence and immorality.

Strangely, though, Joseph noted that they appeared to be taking the dire analysis well, even eagerly. He was told that recruiters were shattering records, earning once-in-a-lifetime vacations that no one wanted to take. Why bother, they figured, when the ever-after lifetime vacation was so close at hand? He did not feel similarly comforted.

The scientific community was another matter entirely, Joseph noted, bouncing from the Sustainability preachers at the Academy to the green coats at the Save the Earth Institute. Dire predictions came with foaming at the mouth apoplexy. And who could blame the scientists if things were THIS bad, he thought, wondering why nearly everyone else did.

"The oceans are almost out of fish!" the scientists cried. "The forests are almost out of trees! The glaciers are almost out of ice! Wild animals are nothing but aphrodisiacs and good luck charms! The 6th Extinction is upon us!" they alarmed.

Talk about apocalypses! Jeesh! thought Joseph. *These guys really lay it on. Bats with white noses falling dead out of the sky! Gruesome pandemics leisurely sweeping across continents on cruise ships and jumbo jets! A Custer's Last Stand of antibiotic forces falling arrow by arrow to superior bacterial weaponry! Oceans threatening to turn all civilization into one giant Atlantis!*

The beautiful sunsets he still saw from Mother Nature seemed like a bleeding sky to them. Was she really on her death bed, he wondered, like the old lady in the nursing home with the broken hip, no one to care anymore about her rehashed memories as the same old food carts and chart watchers circled her bed day after day? Or was it all a gross over-reaction, and the Grand Lady was merely taking her time before deciding to fight fire with fire against this invasive species from Hell? The scientists made a great case, but one shouldn't just jump at every shout of FIRE, should they?

And then there was the ever-present threat of global war. Nuclear war even. Rearranger of molecules. But we had the military, Captain Wonderman reminded him, the mighty U.S. military, queen of the chessboard, keeper of World Peace.

Or was it? Joseph wondered. He could see for himself that politicians of every persuasion thought so. But why were many of them rattling their sabers then, or poking sharp sticks at cornered weasels and sleeping bears? Critical resources were running low, said some. It was a matter of pride, said others. That one hit home, he noted, watching the patriotic fervor swell.

But Joseph was no fool. He could plainly see that it was swelling in those other countries as well, and threatening to burst at the seams. By trick or by trade, by bribe or by threat, too many were getting jumpier than a kid in a Halloween House of Horrors. With good reason the public sensed that things had gone too far. One misspoken word, one slight mis-understanding, one shot across the wrong bow, and the whole place could blow like drunken turistas at a back-alley enchi-lada joint in Tijuana.

Most of them recovered quickly.

"Common sense will prevail," said a good many voices.

"Technology will save us," said many others.

"God will provide," said most of the rest.

"We're doomed!" cried a few lonely and ignored pessimists.

"I'm so confused," said Joseph.

Graduation time was approaching, it was past time to get off the fence, everyone said. He would soon be going into the real world. But how? he wondered. And on which side? They all had their points, but who was keeping score? No one that he could see, and further, no one had a pretty picture to paint, one that everyone could easily enjoy. They were more like angry Jackson Pollock splashes whose chaotic sensibilities one either liked or hated. Again with the deep divide. Couldn't they see that no one should be put in a position to have to choose to believe in a winning apocalypse or a losing salvation?

As usual, a consultation with the ceiling quieted his anxiety, and left him sighing the sigh of a lapsed celibate. The ceiling told him that perhaps, just perhaps, they were all misreading the signs. That perhaps, just perhaps, there was a light out there, a beacon of hope, even now scanning the overconfident multitudes for sensible people, people like him who take their time and process the evidence carefully before making a proper decision. That if there weren't any choices he liked, that didn't guarantee 100 percent Grade-A certified indisputable evidence, he should wait. Till then, "I don't know," must remain his mantra.

That's what he would choose to believe then. Master of your mind, Master of your world. It can't be a done deal. We just need more studies, he thought, reminded of the conclusions drawn from all of the studies of which he had ever heard. Like the ones from last night's evening news, for example.

"Wash your hands often," the TV doctor warned, "or risk catching colds, flues, or worse from all those nasty germs lurking everywhere."

"There's more germs on your towel than there are in your toilet bowl," cautioned a serious looking white coated man holding up a test wand of some kind as proof.

"Don't wash your hands too much," the holistic practitioners advised. "You need to expose yourself to germs to build up resistance to them. Go play in the dirt."

Joseph looked at his hands. *Somehow,* he thought, *the truth is in these hands. Hands that once held Cherry. But I'll be damned if I know what it is.*

The billions of germs crawling over every square centimeter of Joseph's body paused to thank their Gods that their host hadn't yet gotten around to researching antibacterial soaps.

15

Fly or Flee?

Graduation Day! A time for congratulations and reproach, celebrations and misgivings. It was mostly a matter of degree. But it was also a time to reconcile with the Piper, who was waiting not so patiently on the other side for payment. All one's bargaining skills would be needed now, leave the excuses back with the bongs and frisbees please. The Piper has heard them all. Only he knew the way forward from here, across the deserts and through the swamps of life, to the hallowed land beyond. That landscape may be looking a bit more parched these days, if not downright desiccated and near apocalyptic, but the Piper stood defiant. There was most definitely a toll to be paid for his exclusive knowledge, and it was time for the first deposit.

Joseph looked at the diploma in his hand and shook his head. He reached into his nearly empty wallet and took out the business card that had been given him by the career counseling officer. Remembering all the fruitless discussions and interviews, he tore the card into as many pieces as he could and threw them into the air to mix with the confetti from his neighbors. He knew now that his socio-psychology degree, or psycho-sociology degree, as he called it, would not be leading him to anybody's idea of a hallowed land. The only door this degree would open was the one at his parent's house. There was no two ways about it. He was going back home.

After the hugs and small talk, Joseph carried his boxes and suitcases down the hall to his old room. Everything still looked the same – same old bed, same old dresser, same old ceiling. He lay down on his bed and looked up, quickly finding all the old smudges, paint chips, and other blemishes that made up the old familiar Milky Way above his head. A steady drone caught his attention, and he turned slightly to see a small, winged spacecraft flying exuberantly upwards in great broad sweeps and sudden tight spirals, before turning upside down with its landing gear extended and sticking its arrival on the planet he called Oberon. A thin probe extended from the ship and appeared to explore every aspect of the planet's surface. Its unknown mission apparently accomplished, the tiny ship again lit out into space and cavorted crazily across the galaxy, this time coming to rest on his right hand lying atop his chest. The ship then engaged its self-cleaning apparatus.

Joseph watched the fly closely, licking its feet and legs with abandon. What was it tasting so ecstatically? What was it seeing with those enormous, multi-faceted eyes? What was it thinking, flying joyously around his room like that, no apparent direction in mind, no purpose that he could see? Didn't it realize that a fly's life is so very short, and that the clock is ticking? Did it matter? There's certainly no shortage of flies in the world. So apparently plenty of them were having sex and reproducing, and not worrying their little fly brains about anything else. Or were they? After all, what could be more impressive than to go from a lowly, disgusting maggot to the furthest reaches of space? Maybe the ordinary housefly was not as ordinary as he had believed. Maybe there WAS hope for him yet.

Instinctively, Joseph's left hand came down on the fly like a lightning bolt from the heavens, ending any hopes the fly may have had, and unwittingly sending his own hopes searching for a safe landing spot once again. He flicked the fly into the corner.

It had been hard saying goodbye to Cherry. How could he hope to keep up with her progress now? The hugs at graduation and the promises to stay in touch were heartfelt enough, that he was sure of, but the confused, far-off look in her eyes said another thing entirely. Not to mention the vows she said she had recently taken in some primitive sounding, back-to-nature tribe of women searching for the essence of life without men around to muck things up. Present company excluded, she had said, but what exactly was he to think about a cult that called itself 'World Women' but spelled it 'World W/O Men'.

He could see a slight fading of Cherry's image in his mind's eye already. But what could he do about it? She had to follow her own path. As he had to follow his. He would just have to keep the faith that somehow, someway, somewhere, their paths would cross again.

Keeping the faith, of course, implies first of all that one has faith to keep. But that is hardly the only demand that faith puts on anyone with half a mind to keep it. That half a mind must also figure out where to keep it so it won't get lost; what to feed it so it won't waver, weaken, or die; and perhaps most critically, be prepared to clean up after it, because not only will it create more unholy messes than you would think possible, but it also loves to roll and thrash in them like a wild beast. Keeping the faith is more difficult than trying to keep a herd of parched elephants from crossing five hundred miles of Kalahari desert in search of a mud wallow from its memory. Faith believes what it wants to believe, despite a lack of evidence, and despite the fact that some holding tight to it will lose their way, their will, or the rest of their minds in the relentless blinding light and searing heat of the desert sun.

There are secondary problems as well that are no less daunting. As with all human proclivities, keeping the faith is a transactional one. Are the expectations of the one entering into the transaction reasonable, relative to the levels of risk and effort expended? Take your average, aged Grateful Dead fan as an example of one who perhaps keeps an unreasonable amount of faith, collecting concert tapes in the crazed belief that somewhere a tape exists that will transport them to the same places that LSD used to, despite the fact that they all sound like a band taking forever to tune up. Not only are they expending time and money by keeping their faith at levels that are higher than a kite, but it is at the risk of their very minds.

Conversely, the low expectations of a country music fan are much more easily attainable, and one does not have to risk one's mind. As it is about as satisfying as non-alcoholic beer, however, faith can be a bit harder to keep. It is a fine balance and one must tread cautiously.

But how long can faith be realistically kept? This is a particularly interesting question, and one that is the subject of much on-going study. Fortunately, faith can be tested. Not under laboratory conditions perhaps, but certainly by applying a wide array of stressors. Stressors like Pono, for instance. Or one's own mind.

Given these difficulties, it would appear that any faith Joseph had left regarding Cherry would be best kept as close to his heart as possible, before Pono or the muckrakers of the mind discover it and send their twisted armies of reason into battle. The heart is like a lockbox, or at least an icebox, and can keep all sorts of perishable items well past their normal expiration date. But it is not inviolable.

The last thing Joseph's heart wanted was another battle with his mind. But could faith and doubt co-exist peacefully? Did they always have to be at war?

It likely crossed Joseph's mind that Pono might well be the sworn enemy of faith. He seemed to take pleasure in inviting war between the heart and the mind, or inciting it if it refused his invitation.

"Dinner time," came the shout from the kitchen.

Joseph rose, opened his door, and padded down the hall, leaving his thoughts of Cherry back with the fly. He was famished. "Smells great, ma," he said, taking his old seat at the table. "Haven't had a good home cooked meal in a long time."

"That's cause ye've nae been home," grumbled his father. "Ye had to goo aff and git yer napper all stuffed fu o'mince. Ye think I came up the Clyde on a banana boat? I knoo what goes on in that godless kittle-hoosie. Praise the Lord. Pass the peas, please."

"Take it easy, Alvin," Naomi said. "You know what happens when you get too worked up. All of a sudden you're hearing angels. Don't tell me you don't. I know because when you start talking back to them it really creeps me out. Pass the potatoes please. Besides, look, he's eating his peas. Some good has come out of it."

"Ye keep the angels oot of this," Alvin scolded. "Ye've always been scunnered they talk to me and nae you. I'm on a first name basis with a few of them noo, so it's pret-ty clear who their favorite is. Joseph, mind the salt. Only a dunderheid cannae appreciate things for what they are, and tries to turn a sow's ear inta a silk purse."

Naomi smirked. "A sow's ear, eh? Is that what you're calling this dinner? You should hear what I call you when you're not around. And besides, Alvin, I'm pretty sure angels ONLY have a first name. I think it's a marketing thing, like they do with those silly little pop stars, to make them sound more substantial. Think about it. Who's gonna take Angel Gabriel

McGillicuddy seriously? Or else it's because God named them himself, and musta figured that if He doesn't need a last name, then they don't either. But will you PLEASE let the boy season his food the way he likes. You know his senses aren't as sharp as ours. Explains a lot really. If the data going into his brain is poor, then most certainly the output will be too. You can't expect good sense from bad senses."

"Oh, so noo ye're a flippin expert on good sense? Yer bum's oot the windae. Ye shuid hear what my angels call you."

"What? What do the little wingnuts say? Go ahead, humor me."

"They say ye're an Old Testament snob full o' new philosophical contradictions, and that if the Messiah returned today, ye wouldnae hae the sense to pick Him out of a lineup of mingers and thieves. Besides, any eejit can see that it's his brain that's the problem, not his senses. It's not his fault that God chose to give him mince fer brains, but as his parents, we have a responsibility to see that he dunnae waste any more of it listenin' to communists and atheists and fall deeper inta the ocean of lost souls. That's why we need to be tougher on the boy. Chicken's good anyway, hun. Tastes different."

"Thanks. I tried a new marinade. I'll have to remember this one. But, now Alvin, don't jump to conclusions. Sounds to me like the angels' haloes are a bit too snug, if you know what I mean. Remember his school's guiding principle. Not everything is known, so there's still hope, or something like that. He may have an inferior brain, or deficient senses, or even both, but we have to believe that there's hope for him. As his parents, we have to be supportive."

"Well, Naomi, everything's knoon that I wanna knoo. But ye're right about the hope. It's just a wee bit dafty when he goes and gets his degree in what – socio-psychopathology? Something that just teaches kids wha is wrong with people and society. I cuid hae told him that, and saved us all a lot o' dosh. I'm sure they dinnae teach them what to do aboot it, except to blame their parents. That's what kids do these days. Well, he needs to get aff his arse and get a job right quick if he wants to keep livin' here and hae us proppin' him up like we do."

Joseph slid his chair back, rose, and walked away from the table.

"Joseph," his mother called. "Where are you going? You've barely touched your dinner."

"I'm not hungry anymore," he said over his shoulder. "I guess I already swallowed more than I can stomach." He slammed his door shut.

16

—

Arms for Embracing,

Legs for Running Away

Joseph rose early next morning, hoping to avoid his parents at breakfast. He was immensely relieved to find that they were still late sleepers and he wouldn't have to listen to them, in person at least. But their messages still came through loud and clear in the form of a stack of help wanted clippings on the table by his seat. The show of support and confidence left a lot to be desired.

'Mascot wanted for Plymouth Peacocks AA baseball team. Must have minimum of Associates Degree and an enthusiastic personality.' 'Assistant animal care associate needed to clean reptile enclosures at the Heartland Zoo. Must like snakes and other reptiles and have quick reflexes.' 'Grave digger wanted at the Prospect Hill cemetery. Loners preferred, with no fear of zombies or ghosts.' With these and similar suggestions, his parents made the career counselors at the Academy look like air traffic controllers at a busy airport.

Joseph studied a 'Night Watchman' want ad. Eventually

it clicked that sleeping all day and working all night could be a pretty good way to avoid his parents while still getting paid and having time to think.

Washed, brushed, and dressed in his usual interview suit, he left the house quietly and headed for the Reaperson Arms manufacturing company. Approaching the impressive razor wire enclosed complex, he briefly wondered why they needed a night watchman. The unsmiling, mirror-shaded guardhouse attendant looked him over, checked his license, registration, and plates, patted him down, then slid open the gate and directed him along the flag-lined drive to the main building.

A perky receptionist that reminded him a bit of Cherry with an automatic rifle pin on her lapel ushered him into the large waiting room that also doubled as a factory store. She told him that Ms. Bollocks, the lady he needed to see, would be along to interview him just as soon as she was free.

The room was already full to overflowing, mostly with over-caffeinated customers eagerly hefting the weaponry on display, on sale at outlet prices. Kill and maim ratios were hotly debated as customers sighted gun barrels indiscriminately around the room. Two young friends mimicked an old-fashioned duel with matching pistols, while a pair of laughing old ladies turned steely-eyed while aiming their lightweight grandma's specials at a life size poster of an obvious Middle Eastern terrorist. A gentleman of apparent Middle Eastern descent sat quietly off to the side, fidgeting, trying hard not to be there.

Through the chaotic fun, the POX News channel blared continuously from a large-screen TV on the wall. Joseph learned from the authoritative sounding talk show hosts that homicide rates were steadily climbing, and that the only way to beat a desperate or drug-addled bad guy with a gun, was to be that good guy with a bigger and better gun. America's newest arms race was in a sprint to the finish, they said, with the latest reports showing better than 75% of the rich and middle classes now owning multiple firearms.

Joseph shook his head, thinking about how poorer communities, not to be outdone, were turning ever more to their youth, who responded eagerly at younger and younger ages to procure any weapons they could. Target practices might be unscheduled, but they were frequent enough, with passing grades awarded only to those understanding basic Darwinian Theory.

And in further proof that the Arm America efforts were working, the latest college gunman had only managed to kill seven students and critically injure five before an armed student was able to free his weapon and spray a few rounds in the direction of the perpetrator. The killer had run off, but the casualties had been mercifully limited by a student hero. The POX News commentators chatted some more about the soaring stock market prices of arms manufacturers, and how the increased demand for guns had paved the way back to a healthy economy. The health of the work force wasn't mentioned, Joseph noticed. They ended the show in their usual manner of comparing the merits of the guns that each was carrying that day, then laying their mammoth hardware on the desk for the others to fondle.

"Joseph Doubt?" The call came from a stout, middle-aged lady who had just opened the rear door. She was wearing blue cat-eye glasses and had a bird's nest of gray hair piled atop her head. Joseph rose. "This way, please," she drawled in a New Orleans accent with all the fun removed. He made his way to the door, past the toddler in his mother's lap who pointed his finger at him and said, "Bang Bang," and followed the lady down a short hallway to a small room.

"Please take a seat, Joseph. My name is Bertha Bollocks, and I am personnel manager here at Reaperson. Please call me Bertha. I see that you are here about the night watchman's position. I would like to begin by having you tell me a little bit about yourself."

"Well, let's see," Joseph replied. "There's really not much to tell. It's all there on my resume."

"That just tells me some boring stuff, Joseph, statistics really. I don't look at resumes. I assume you are more than that. Now how about taking a deep, slow breath, and relaxing. Think about sipping a tall glass of ice-cold lemonade on the verandah, before popping that pesky squirrel that has been helping itself at the bird feeder. Then tell me who Joseph Doubt is. Might as well. I am a trained observer of people and can read you like a book anyway. Can't be too careful, what with all the con men in this world."

Joseph looked into Ms. Bollock's eyes and felt like he was staring at the barrel of a shotgun. Then he shrugged and began. "Well, Ms. Bollocks? Bertha? Why don't YOU tell me who I am then? Because that's my problem. If I'm going to be completely honest, then I have to say that I don't really know who I am. I'm still trying to figure that out, you know? One moment I think I know who I am, I have everything figured out and life seems so simple, and then I blink and suddenly it seems incredibly complex, and who am I to think that I can understand anything, never mind me or the billions of years and lives that came before me and the billions that will come after me. What does it all mean? Where is it all going? I mean, I believe in God, then the whole idea seems absurd. I love my parents, then I hate them. I'm confident, then I'm scared. Mostly scared. I don't know why. One moment I feel like I just want to be left alone, away from a world full of greedy, self-serving jerks that I'm just not up to dealing with without some major effort to adjust my personality. But then another moment comes along and the world and everything in it is an absolute miracle, and I feel a kind of rapturous love and wonder, and believe that surely everyone must understand this miracle of life, even the birds and the squirrels who are only trying to eat the food you put in front of them, and that I can easily get along with anyone and forgive them their faults because we're all just faulty humans after all. Of course, that feeling only happens when I'm far away from people." He paused, then continued. "So I suppose you'll be wanting me to go now."

Bertha Bollocks closed her mouth and blinked hard, as if she were trying to reset her mind. "Well. Hmm. Yes. Well. Umm, I don't know. That is not exactly what I was expecting. You are not putting me on, are you? No, I can see that you are not. Wow. I thought you were going to say what everyone says. You're a hard worker, a good listener, you think outside the box, get along well with everyone, yada, yada, yada. Then I would know you were probably lying, but I could at least check off all the right boxes on my evaluation form. Well, we need somebody badly, and looking at your resume, your college degree suggests that you must understand other people at least, and while I do not expect that you will actually be meeting any people on this job, if any should get through our perimeter defenses, you will need to understand them in a hurry. Now, let's see, don't smoke, don't drink, don't use drugs, no criminal history. So, what do you do for fun, Joseph? Ever fire a gun?"

"I'm sorry, Bertha," Joseph said. "I should have realized that this job would require a gun. I've never used one. So again, thank you for your time."

"Not so fast, Joseph. In point of fact we most certainly do not let our guards carry guns. Insurance liability reasons, you understand. Night guards especially tend to be drug and alcohol abusers, or anti-social loners with psychopathic tendencies.

Not that you are, mind you. At least I don't think so. Are you? Never mind, do not answer that. I might be sorry I asked. But can you imagine if we let such people carry guns. That is a recipe for possum stew, a disaster you do not EVER want to repeat."

"Isn't the world full of drug and alcohol abusers, and crazy people in general? My old roommate and class president at my school used to say that everybody's crazy."

"Sounds to me like your roommate was crazy, Joseph. If everybody was crazy, then crazy would be normal. And if it was normal to be crazy, then nobody should be allowed to have guns. That's just crazier than my ex-husband during a Mardi Gras full moon."

"So what am I supposed to do if any intruders do get through your perimeter defenses? They'll undoubtedly be armed."

"Your only job is to sound an alarm, Joseph. They are conveniently located all around the site."

"OK. But what then? I'd be a sitting duck. A duck that's sitting next to the largest weapons stash in the state, and I can't use any of it to defend myself?"

"Think of the company, Joseph. We are a big partner in the community, and have our community values to uphold. Jack Reaperson, the owner of this plant, is close friends with the mayor and the governor and many in the legislature. They all know what our company is worth. It is personal to them. The more we prosper, the more they prosper. So if an injury, or God forbid a mortality should occur, and we start seeing lawsuits for allowing the irresponsible use of dangerous weapons, no matter how unconstitutional that is, well, let us just say those are head shots we don't need. Metaphorically speaking."

"Well, I can't say I'm exactly thrilled with the idea of head shots either. Non-metaphorically speaking. So what am I sup-posed to do after I sound the alarm? Wait to get shot?"

"No, no, Joseph. I would definitely suggest hiding. We have many great hiding spots located conveniently around the site. And many are stocked with food and water, and even maga-zines and a flashlight. It is the little things, Joseph, that show how much we care. We like to say that we go the extra nine millimeters for our employees. A little gun humor there. But more importantly, we offer a very generous pay and benefits package, so that you, or your survivors, can enjoy a quality life. So, what do you say? Are you ready to join the Reaper-son Arms family, whose arms embrace their employees, and whose employees embrace their arms?"

"Well, it would be nice to have a family that trusted me for a change."

"Great. Welcome aboard, Joseph. You can start 10 PM tonight. Dress in basic black please. You will not be needing that suit you're wearing. It would just make Itchy, your part-ner, suspicious. And believe me, that is not what you want to do. Now I have got to run. My pleasure, Joseph," she con-cluded, extending her hand.

17

Bully for the God of Fairness

All that evening Joseph practiced watching. He watched his father argue with his mother. He watched an owl swoop down out of the dusk and make off with a squirrel. He watched a moth trapped in a spider web, struggling to free itself as it sent vibratory messages to the spider that dinner was served. And especially he watched the clock, ticking off the minutes to when he could begin to get paid for all this watching. He believed that if anything came within his view, he could watch it with the best of them. After a quick nap, he made his way to his car, and stopped.

Joseph had never seen a nighttime sky look or feel quite like this before. Endless armies of deep purple clouds pummeled the moon and raced off, leaving it looking like a punch-drunk fighter struggling to stay up. Thunder rumbled incessantly, either a heavenly warning or a bit of cosmic indigestion, take your pick, while opposite corners of the sky staged a lightning battle impressive enough to make Zeus, the old Maestro of Mount Olympus, proud. The air was as dry as his mother's

Thanksgiving turkey. Suddenly his belief in his watching skills evaporated.

The usual new job anxieties increased the closer Joseph got to Reaperson Arms. Like the sky, he felt unsettled, but he dismissed the prickles on the back of his neck and the occasional involuntary shiver as undoubtedly due to the chill and static buildup in the air. It had seemed like a low stress job, but you never knew for sure until you got through that first day or week. And what was that strange comment about a partner all about?

———————————

If Joseph had thought just a little more about it, if he hadn't been so desperate to get away from his parents, if he had only consulted a ceiling or two, he very well may have come to his senses and politely backed away from the night watchman's job. But making sense was the last thing on his mind. What, after all, had made sense in his life up to now? Would he even recognize it if he saw it? Why start looking for sense now when all he could see behind him and in front of him made as much sense as Cherry becoming a militant feminist and spurning men altogether, if not downright hating them?

Night Watchmen jobs, as everyone knows, are the domain of the lunatics, so called, of course, because of the notoriously crazy influence on humans and animals of la luna, the moon. It is a domain ruled by the late-night radio talk show ranters. Conspiracy theories are like mother's milk to these people, if mother's milk was a government brainwashing plot to shove socialism and a liberal agenda down a helpless baby's throat.

Even early humans learned pretty quickly that it made no sense to watch the night. For one thing, you couldn't see much. Not like in the daylight when you could see the cave bear or the saber-toothed tiger stalking you. Nighttime was for lying low, for hiding even, and for scary stories around the fire about the unseen dangers that stalked the incautious and the over-confident alike. To venture into the night was to ignore the protective spirits of the light and show just how helpless we are without them. A person in the dark was as directionless as a blindfolded teenager, and if such a person came back at all, they would have come back a profoundly changed person. They would have been full of crazy stories and conspiracy theories about a dark, dangerous world that only they knew, the first of the late-night talk show ranters. Most early humans would have moved deeper into the cave, to get further away from both the night and the ranter. Just to be safe.

Again Joseph went over his short checklist of items to wear or to bring. Black pants, black shirt, black cap, black sneakers – check. It reminded him of the Suicide Club back at school. Add purple hair and some freaky tattoos and he'd have fit right in. The grey socks would have to do, though, they were all he had. No one would ever notice anyway. Small pack with the book he was reading, cell phone, small flashlight, pack of gum, and a soda and sandwich from the convenience store. Seemed reasonable. He could always add to it if he needed.

At the guardhouse, a different unsmiling attendant looked him over and reviewed his identification. This guard wore the exact same uniform as the one he had encountered earlier in the day, complete with sunglasses, even though it was night. "So you're the new night guard, eh, Joseph?" he asked. "I hear you're a big shot college boy."

"Uh, not so big really," Joseph said. "Is there a problem?"

"Please step around to the side of the car."

Joseph did as he was ordered.

"Now spread your arms and legs. I'm going to pretend to pat you down because we're on video, but I just wanted to get out of reach of the guard house audio recorder. I'm Ralph Beckman. Degree in Paleo-Forensic Anthropology.

The weekend guy is CJ. He's got a Master's in Geo-Cultural Folkloric Mythology. The guard you met this morning? That's Stan. Doctorate in Ethnocentric Considerations in Comparative World Religions. But even God can't help us find a good job these days. I'll bet that's why you ended up here with the watchman job, am I right?"

"I guess so. My Socio-Psychology degree didn't exactly impress anyone."

"That's cause the system's rigged against us, Joseph," Ralph said. "Don't you think? It isn't fair."

"I don't know," Joseph said, repositioning his cap. "It probably wasn't fair of our brains to pick such dumb majors. I don't know about any system, I mean, what were we thinking?"

Ralph exploded. "Dumb majors! We were just following our interests! I assume you were too. So don't you go blaming yourself, alright? Damn! It's the system's fault. Why allow naïve young kids to follow their dreams when they know well and good that we'll end up deep in debt with no hope of getting a decent job. THAT'S the system I'm talking about. The colleges end up rich, there's no doubt about that. They smile and take the loan money we'll be paying off for the next forty years, and then it's 'Bye kid, good luck,' or, you know, 'You could always sell a kidney or something for a very attractive master's degree.' No thank you. I need my kidneys to process all the toxic swill the system forces down my throat. It's not fair!"

"Wow," Joseph exclaimed. "That doesn't sound fair when you put it like that. What can we do about it? Who's in charge of this system anyway?"

"The heads of colleges for one. The heads of government for another. But mostly the heads of businesses, like that scum bag Reaperson. It's bastards like that that run this world."

"You mean the guy we're working for? How do you know he's a scumbag? I never even met him."

"Don't have to. I never met him either, but I can tell you that he's married to a young sexy woman, two children from a previous marriage in elite boarding schools, has a mansion nearby, with a beach house in South Florida and another in the south of France, a mistress who he thinks understands him, a fleet of fancy cars, yacht, memberships in a dozen civic organizations, makes grand public donations to lots of charities, and even bigger secret ones to the lobbyists who convince the lawmakers that it'd be in their best interests to do what needs to be done so that he can make even more profit. Even if it means starting a war somewhere so he can sell more guns. And to top it off, he undoubtedly thinks of himself as a great guy, a man of peace and refinement. Fair as the day is long, while his company pays minimum taxes and minimum wages, and he complains that it's too much.

"I'm telling you, he wouldn't know fair if it bit him on the dick. Which is about the only place a man like that can be bitten and still feel it. If only there was such a thing as Karma. But I suppose that would be asking too much of the Gods, eh? They'd just laugh and kick the God of Fairness in the nuts. Can't be ANYBODY lower in the God rankings than that dude. He probably uses the little power he has fending off the bullies that are always picking on him. I can just imagine it - The Gods of Love and War see him and immediately start in on him, mocking him with the classic 'All's fair in love and war,' as they kick him in the 'nads again."

Joseph stared at Ralph, one eyebrow raised.

"Sorry, Joseph," said Ralph, a little sheepishly. "Didn't mean to go off on a rant like that. Your first day and all. I'm usually a lot more composed. Jeez, what the hell got me so wound up?"

"You were saying something about the God of Fairness, about how ..."

"Fairness!" exploded Ralph again. "Don't get me started! You know what's not fair? Having to wear this stupid uniform with this stupid hat and these stupid sunglasses! I'm a freakin' night guard! Nobody ever comes here at night! What do I need to wear a uniform for? I could be buck naked and no one would know the difference. In fact, Joseph, that's what I'm gonna do. Just you watch me." Ralph threw his guard cap to the ground and began unbuttoning his shirt.

"OK then," Joseph said, glancing around. Slowly he began to back up, feeling his way around the nose of the car, as Ralph tore off his shirt and was now kicking off his shoes.

"I'll just be, uh ..." mumbled Joseph. "I'm gonna, uh ... I'm just gonna go now." He leaned into the guard house window, found the gate button, and pushed it. He slid back into his car, waited a moment for the gate to open fully, and eased the shift into drive. He pulled away as Ralph wriggled out of his pants, and saw him again in the rear view, completely naked and pogoing from one foot to the other, arms raised triumphantly over his head and yelling into the night.

Joseph drove on down the long drive to the main parking area, hoping that Ralph would pull himself together before it was too late. He laughed, though, picturing him dancing naked like that, but couldn't help thinking how unfair it seemed that the poor guy could be undone by his obsession with fairness.

Few understand, and fewer still see the humor in mocking the oversensitive Gods. Especially the beleaguered God of Fairness. He just might use his strongest power to disappear completely. Better to leave him alone, or praise him and tell him he's doing a good job. Or better yet, simply laugh with him at his ironic sense of humor. The last recourse of the bullied.

Joseph parked beneath a light pole in the empty lot, grabbed his pack from the passenger seat, opened the door, and slid his legs around to get out. A thin, top lit shadow appeared out of nowhere and stood in the open doorway, leaving Joseph in an awkward and vulnerable position, half in and half out.

"I am killing forty-two different ways," the shadow said. "I smashing your head in door, just for you wearing gray socks. Who you trying signal? Never mind. Give me pack." The man ripped it out of Joseph's hands.

"Hey, give me that, you have no right," Joseph cried, standing up and immediately noticing that he was looking at the jumpy eyes and black painted face of a long-haired, rail-thin man, a black 'Don't Tread On Me' cap jammed low over his eyes. Itchefsky stitched in white thread across the left breast of a dark blue shirt.

"No rights here," snarled Itchy. "This war zone." He opened the pack, pulled out Joseph's phone, and smashed it on the asphalt. "Damn spy tools," he mumbled, crushing the broken phone under his boot heel.

Joseph opened and closed his mouth, not at all sure how to process this unprovoked attack. He watched his sandwich go under Itchy's heel next, and his soda emptied onto the ground. Finally his book was pulled out and torn apart, the pages scattered.

"Governmental poison and prop-uganda," Itchy muttered. "Is not believable. Everybody having brain wash."

"This isn't fair," Joseph said finally. "It's my first day here. I deserve some respect."

"You deserve firing for being clueless pawn of governmental repression. Maybe even spy. You want fair, go back to school and share cookies and milk. Fairness for pussies. Like old man Reaperson say, winning is easy if you understanding limits of players, and you preparing to exploit them. He knows government wants to take away guns, but who is winning battle, huh? Score one for patriots. Any governmental pigs come here, they be sorry." In a blur, Itchy reached into a pocket, pulled out a solid steel ninja star and whipped it. Twenty-five feet away it thunked into the forehead of a hard-hatted figure on a caution sign. He glared at Joseph. "You better not be one," he sneered, and ran off into the shadows.

"Holy smokes!" Joseph exclaimed, staring at the darkness where Itchy had disappeared. "What a wacko."

18

An Alien Perspective

After Joseph's heart managed to ditch the drag strip for a Sunday drive, he set off in the opposite direction, wondering what it was exactly that a night watchman was supposed to be doing, besides watching. *Feels like I should be doing something more,* he thought. Three hours ticked by, Joseph deciding on his own to add listening and smelling to his duties, mainly to alleviate the intense boredom. He grinned as he imagined asking Bertha for a raise for this extra work he was putting in.

It was shortly after 1:00 AM as he was watching, smelling, and listening to the night that he heard the faint sounds of a commotion. Curious more than frightened, he hustled towards the voices, one of which was clearly Itchy. He rounded the northwest corner cautiously and saw Itchy standing twenty feet from the fence, outside of which five young men were laughing and drinking.

"I know what you doing," Itchy growled, steely voiced. "You don't know who you messin' with. We gonna send your illegal alien asses back where you came from and build wall so we keeping you there. Nobody wants you here."

"Yo man, we know who we messin' with. A dead cucaracha if we ever seen one." The speaker tossed an empty liquor bottle over the fence, where it smashed at Itchy's feet. "The REAL aliens gonna smoke you, man. Jes like that bottle."

Joseph saw Itchy reach into his pocket and knew he'd be looking at some dead people if he didn't do something immediately. "Hey Itchy!" he called out. Itchy turned, hand still in his pocket, and stared at Joseph. The young men were jabbering rapidly in Spanish, laughing and pointing.

"Itchy, I need to talk with you," Joseph said. "Could you take your hand out of your pocket, please?" For a full minute Itchy stared at him. Joseph had the uneasy realization that his own head was even bigger than that head on the caution sign. He felt as vulnerable as an endangered species in Texas.

Finally Itchy pulled his hand out and walked over. "This better be good," he growled. "Is time for showdown."

Joseph gulped. "Look, Itchy," he said. "I know it's not any of my business, but why don't you leave those guys alone, before somebody gets hurt. Just ignore them. They're just some young guys with nothing to do. If you treat people fairly, they'll treat you fairly."

"Take head from ass, college boy. They being illegal aliens. And they spies. Time is up."

"Why do you say that?" Joseph asked. "You're not going to hurt them, are you?"

Itchy sneered. "I spell it for you so even moron understanding. Life is like box of chalk ..." He cut himself off to snap his head around at a noise behind him.

Joseph smiled, glad to finally see an opportunity for mutual understanding. "You mean like a box of choc – olates, right?" he said, finishing the sentence for him. "Like you never know what you're gonna get."

Itchy jerked his head back. "What? No, you asshole. Chalk.

Of course you knowing what the fuck you get, unless you being stupid idiot. It's chalk. The chalk, she come in all kind of colors, and when chalk is being in that box, they all being equal. No color is better. But soon as one is being chosen, it is most important color." Itchy paused for emphasis, then delivered his summation. "World is like box of chalk. God is choosing white color. Is fair enough for you?"

"Alrighty then," Joseph said, mind racing now to think of a different tack. "Have you ever tried talking with them, try to get to know them?"

Itchy stared at him like he was a fresh turd on the living room rug. "We being buddies, eh," he snorted, "your mind? Sides, I tole old man Reaperson and he give me little surprise for them. Fact is almost time. Think I get ready." A peculiar, lop-sided grin transformed Itchy's face as he walked off.

Joseph watched his back for a second before deciding to take his own advice. He walked up to the young men, who had all fallen silent. "Hi, my name's Joseph," he said, tentatively. "I'm new here. Sorry about my partner. I don't know what his problem is, but can I ask you, why do you come here and get on him? He seems dangerous to me."

The young men exchanged quizzical looks, then burst out laughing. "Man, we don't care about that crazy dude," said one. "He bout as dangerous as my little sister. You should try livin' where we livin', you want danger. No man, we here to see the aliens."

"Yeah," said another one, "the REAL illegal aliens." At that they laughed so hard they had to hold onto the fence.

"What's so funny? What are you talking about?"

The first speaker looked back at Joseph. "Nobody tole you, huh?"

"Told me what?"

"OK. Lots of times, after midnight, we see a alien space

ship come here. Flyin' aroun,' hoverin,' like it be checkin' out the crazy dude. Makin' him even crazier. Somethin's gonna happen, man. We think the aliens gonna shoot him with some space ray. We wanna see what it does."

Joseph looked at each of the men. They all looked serious, nodding their heads. He felt utterly confused. "What do these spaceships look like?" he asked.

"They small," the man replied. "Size of a kilo a weed. Not like the big black copter comes here some nights when the aliens aren't here. Crazy dude waves to it when it lands on the roof. One a them should be here soon. You see."

"Oh shit!" blurted out another man, backing away from the fence. "Here come the crazy dude. He got a gun!"

Joseph turned to see Itchy striding towards them with a brutal looking assault rifle cradled across his chest. A bolt of fear shot through him, followed by strange sensations of unreality and a primitive warning sound in his head like a hive of bees had just been disturbed. This wasn't happening, was it?

It was. "Get away from aliens, college boy," Itchy barked.

The buzzing sound steadily increased. Joseph finally realized it wasn't in his head. Somebody was going to get stung.

"The aliens are comin'! The aliens are comin'!" shouted one of the men behind him. "Watch you don't get zapped!"

Joseph saw Itchy turn and look up. From the north, a small gray drone appeared low over the trees and headed straight towards them.

"Madre de Dios! Un otro!" yelled another man.

Everyone turned to see another drone coming towards them, from the south this time. A second later another one appeared from over the roof of the building.

"Holy shit, man! Three a them!" yelled the guy Joseph had been talking with. "This like War a the Worlds or somethin'!

I'm goin' back to the barrio where it's safer. Vamanos! Good luck, man!" The men bolted.

With curiosity replacing his fear now, Joseph watched the three drones get closer. At about thirty feet apart, each one stopped and hovered, like it was surprised to see the others. Joseph could see the cameras swiveling crazily beneath them. Then they all moved forward slowly, towards each other now, stopping again when they were just a few feet apart, and began circling each other in a most peculiar dance, feinting and retreating, rising and dropping, like dogs encountering each other for the first time.

Captivated by the odd spectacle, Joseph finally awoke to a distinct sound approaching from the west, growing louder by the second. Whup-whup-whup-whup. A large black helicopter, silhouetted against the night sky, loomed into view and hovered over the rooftop. The cameras on all three drones pivoted towards it.

Suddenly the night exploded. The three drones crashed to the earth in pieces. Itchy stood there grinning wildly, holding a smoking gun. He gave a thumb's up to the helicopter, which then proceeded to land.

Joseph stared wide-eyed at the wreckage. "What'd you do that for?" he gasped.

"I warning them," Itchy crowed. "I got their fucking spy planes. No messing with America!"

"You're crazy! Those guys had nothing to do with those drones! They think they're alien spaceships for crying out loud! Don't you see? Something else is going on here."

"Only thing going on here is liberal crybaby what is defending illegal alien spies. Reaperson told me to get them and I getting them. Maybe YOU should be on other side of fence." He lowered his rifle and pointed it at Joseph.

Joseph nudged the rifle barrel aside. "Take it easy, will you?

I'm not on anybody's side. I'm just trying to understand what's going on. OK? We need to go look at those drones, see if we can tell who owns them."

"Knocking yourself out, spy-baby."

Joseph approached the first of the crashed drones and kneeled down.

"Hold it right there, gentlemen," a commanding voice boomed. "Step away, please." A tall, well-dressed, silver-haired man approached from an opened doorway, carrying a black satchel. He pulled out a folding multi-tool and proceeded to each of the drones, removing their cameras and placing them inside the satchel. Then he stood up and looked at Joseph and Itchy. "Follow me please."

They followed the man back through the door he had come out of, and found themselves inside a vast botanical wonderland. Calculated paths wound their way through the shrubs, small trees, and hanging plants, all arranged in a cozy, yet open way around the steel forging presses, lathes, milling machines, plating lines, bluing tanks and other savage features of a large scale weapons manufacturer, all silent and ghostly in the early morning hours. Strategically located water fountains burbled their messages of serenity below a sea of skylights.

"Feng fucking shui," muttered the silver haired man, shaking his head. "Stay close please. Wouldn't want you to get lost in the Reaperson Garden of Peace."

Joseph coughed as he breathed in the acrid chemical fumes with herbal undertones, and thought that factories likely never smelled so good, and nature likely never smelled so bad. He listened to the sounds of frantic activity on the roof above and followed the man through the greenery. He heard the helicopter roar to life as they were ushered into a small meeting room at the front of the building.

"Take off your shoes and have a seat, gentlemen," the man

said, pointing to the mats on the floor, arranged around a long, shiny table with very short legs. "I'm the attorney for Mr. Reaperson. He'll be along any second."

Joseph sat. His eyes toured the room, studying the sparse décor. Floor to ceiling windows in front, more green plants, a water fountain in the middle of the table, and a series of first issue rifles on the walls. The rifles had dated identification plaques beneath them. Joseph noted that the rifles seemed to get larger and larger the closer they got to the present. He found himself wondering why, and let his eyes wander to the ceiling, which was as smooth and white and quiet as a fresh layer of snow on an untraveled road. 'Be patient', the ceiling seemed to say to him in its Delphian way. 'A plow is coming.'

A grim Reaperson strode in, straight-shouldered, beak-nosed and hard-eyed, and interrupted his thoughts. A slightly built Japanese woman with small, mysterious eyes floated lightly alongside him, like she had air beneath her feet. Reaperson made directly for his attorney. "How'd it go?" he demanded. "We get what we needed?"

"What's she doing here, Jack?" bristled his attorney, watching the attractive woman place several incense burners around the room, then turn and bow to him. She fiddled with something in a cabinet and soft, lilting oriental music seeped from hidden speakers. "This is no time for your spiritual foolishness, or whatever this is. We're in some hot water here."

"Suki goes where I go, Norm. There are things you don't understand. Now answer me please. Did we get them?"

"Right here," Norm said, holding up the black satchel.

"Good, good. Excellent. Good work, boys," Jack Reaperson said, looking at Joseph and Itchy for the first time, his whole face softening under his polished skull. His hands disappeared into the flowing silk contours of his custom Oriental robe and he began pacing.

"Now, I suspect that very soon we'll be getting a visit from the owners of those drones," he began. "They're going to be mad and accuse us of horrible things, say like shipping arms illegally to some war zone or other. Obviously that's not true. I'm a peaceful man. Like I told you before, Itchy, some nights we have a maintenance crew come in by helicopter. That's all that is. Now, these people are going to want to talk with you boys. Not to worry. We've got your backs." He stopped pacing and looked at them. "OK?"

"The illegal aliens? Be talking to me?" asked Itchy. "What is for? You know I shooting down their little spy planes. You telling me to."

"No, Itchy. Those were government spy planes. So I might have been mistaken when I agreed with you about where they were from. But don't worry. You've done nothing wrong, son. Just tell them the truth and you'll be OK."

"First one's here, Jack," announced Norm, looking out the window at a black car with government plates.

Jack Reaperson resumed pacing, erratically this time, and his hands disappeared back into his robe.

Suki floated over to him and touched his sleeve.

"Here comes the second one," said Norm, adding, "another black car. That's the problem with government – no imagination."

"Come with me. This can wait," whispered Suki to Jack, who had stopped pacing and whose face had visibly paled.

"And the gang's all here," said Norm.

Jack Reaperson stared at the floor, seemingly unable to move.

"Norm, I'm going to need you to stall them a bit. OK?" Suki said. "Give us ten minutes please." She bowed and led the now slump shouldered President and CEO of Reaperson Arms out the door.

19

Sometimes Karma is Best Served Hot

Suki led Jack to his office. "I'm here, Jack, I'm here," she said, helping him down onto a floor mat. She selected two sticks of incense from a black box on a shelf. "Dragon's Blood to boost positive thoughts and male potency, and cinnamon to stimulate courage, lust, and business success." She placed them in burners and lit them, waving her hand over the rising fumes.

From two more boxes she scooped fine brown powder and dumped it into a tea bowl. "Horny goat weed for sexual energy, and damiana to prevent genital atrophy." With her back to Jack, she added a pinch of something from an unmarked jar. Smiling to herself, she added a cup of hot water, whisked it briefly, took a sip, then handed the bowl to Jack. She sat down on the mat so that her knees were touching his.

"Look at me, Jack," she said. "Drink up. I'm sure you do not have Koro. I was just kidding before."

"Yes, I do," he wailed. "You were just being nice. Why, why, why, why? Why is God punishing me like this? It's not fair! Why can't you see it, Suki?"

"But that's just it. I can. I can see it, and feel it, and it's perfectly normal. Your penis is not shrinking. In fact, well ... never mind."

"You're just saying that. I heard that Koro is irreversible. Someday it's gonna disappear, I know it. I'm afraid, Suki. What am I gonna do if my penis disappears? It's not fair!"

Through the window, Suki watched three identical black cars bounce to a stop.

"Drink up, Jack. Here, let me pour you another. Like I said, you need to trust me, OK? If you keep drinking this, and breathing the incense, I'm pretty sure it will prevent Koro from taking hold. Remember, it's an ancient Japanese regimen that Samurai warriors have used for centuries."

Jack moaned. "You said pretty sure, Suki. You said before that you were sure."

"Sorry, Jack. My mistake. You know the only certain things in life are death and taxes. But next to that comes my special tea, I promise you. So trust me, OK? I really hope you appreciate all the effort I've been putting into this. But you should know that I've been doing some more research lately, and I've discovered another thing that Samurai warriors used to do if they were suffering from Koro. They'd wear their 'war hats,' their jingasa, at all times. And these were the fiercest warriors the world has ever known. So I've brought one for you. If you wear this, in addition to doing those other things, I'm certain it will reverse your problem."

Again Jack moaned, this time a primal, haunting sound that welled up from the depths of his soul, poured out past his throat and lips, and kept right on going over Suki's head. She never felt a thing. "You said reverse, Suki. Before you said I don't have Koro."

Suki watched a single, middle-aged man step out of each car, one dressed casually in gray slacks and blue button-down shirt, the other two sporting neckties, one with a jacket. The men eyed each other warily as they walked around each other's cars.

"Well," Suki said, "Maybe you have a slight case. I didn't want to worry you. I've seen much worse Jack, believe me. I remember this one poor man, well, forget it, it's not important. Just keep following my advice. I'm certain that a fairly healthy man like you can slow the progress of this terrible disease."

Jack Reaperson's head dropped to his chest, and strange bubbling noises came out of his mouth. "You said slow, Suki. Before you said reverse."

"Look at me, Jack," Suki said. Slowly, as if overcoming an enormous gravitational pressure, Jack raised his head. Suki took his hands and looked into his woeful eyes. "You know, I've been thinking. I believe it's time that you designed a new assault rifle. A bigger one. The biggest yet. What do you say?"

"Rifle. Bigger," Jack repeated. "Bigger. Rifle." Suddenly a spark came back into his eyes and he sat up straight. "You know, Suki, I think you're right. One even more powerful. That's a great idea. I think it's time."

"There you go. Now finish your cup and let's get back in there and give those government nerds hell. I bet THEY can't satisfy their women like you can. If anybody has advanced Koro, I bet it's them."

Jack did a double take and stared at Suki with a horrified look. "Suki, you said advanced!"

Norm appeared outside the window, spoke to each of the men individually for a few minutes, looked at his watch, then nodded towards Jack's office and led the men inside.

Suki saw the nod. "I was talking about those government losers, you silly bunny," she said to Jack.

"Right," Jack said, standing up straight-shouldered and

hard-eyed again. "I heard that government dicks are tiny little things. They'd never make it in the private sector."

"That's my boy," Suki said. "Let's go." She hustled Him back to the conference room.

"Morning, gentlemen," Jack Reaperson said, as the men were ushered in. "I'm Jack Reaperson." He was positioned now on a large pillow at the head of the table, legs crossed and hands folded smartly in front of him. A steaming bowl of tea on the table. An odd hat that looked like a big turtle shell on his head. Suki busied herself lighting incense sticks, then took a seat at Jack's side. "Please remove your shoes and have a seat, then tell us what on earth would bring the three of you here at this most harmonious hour."

Two of the three men struggled to get comfortable on the floor mats, but could find no position that would put them at eye level or higher than their host. He was at least a head taller than them. Deflated, they turned their scowling gazes back on each other and tried to squirm their way into positional dominance. They sat on their heels, straightened their backs and shoulders, and craned their necks, but it was no use. Neither could rise above the other.

Simultaneously, they looked across the table at the third member of their visiting party. The casually-dressed man was somehow sitting comfortably a head higher than they were, at eye level with Reaperson. As nonchalantly as they could manage in their frustrations, they both tried to peer under the table to see how he was able to accomplish this, but the table was too low.

The man in a jacket and tie puffed out his chest and looked at Reaperson. "I don't know who these bozos are, but I'm from a small government research office and was testing a drone when it somehow got away from me. I tracked it over here and then lost communication with it. So I'm here to retrieve it. By the way, what's with the naked man in your guard booth? Guy seems off his nut."

Reaperson looked over at Norm for guidance, eyebrows asking for an explanation about the naked man. Norm shrugged uncomfortably, unaccustomed to being caught off guard.

The other new man in a tie nodded his head and told an almost identical story. The casually-dressed man remained silent. Jack Reaperson never looked at him.

"OK, gentlemen," Reaperson said. "That's quite the coincidence to have so much drone research being conducted around my plant. But have it your way. Norm, take these drones to the men. Oh sorry. My bad. I mean, take these men to the drones."

Fifteen minutes later, Norm led the three men back into the room, two of them visibly angry. "Those drones were shot down!" the man in the jacket snapped. "And their cameras have been removed. We want the cameras back now! This is willful destruction and confiscation of government property!"

Reaperson smiled. "Easy there, fella. You're disrupting the qi. You can take that junk out of here anytime, but we never saw any cameras, did we boys?" He winked openly at Joseph and Itchy. "Now let me tell you what we want. We want you to stop playing us for fools. Government research my ass." He pointed at the man in the jacket and tie. "I make you from the office of that liberal muckraker, Senator Joe Card."

"Senator Blow Hard, you mean," snickered the other man in the tie.

The man in the jacket gave a sideways look of disdain to his neighbor. "Miller Atkins, Reaperson, and right now you're in big trouble. We know about the helicopters. The Senator believes you're sending weapons to Gabon without government authorization. The Gabonese government is getting arms from somewhere, and our sources point here. Have you no shame? The elephants are all being killed! Elephant lives

matter, Reaperson! But their government's not playing ball
with us anymore. If we're going to have any elephants left, it's
the rebels we need to support. That's where the future is. And
your future's in jail where you belong. The Senator will see to
that! I want that camera!"

"It's almost campaign season, Atkins," Jack Reaperson
said calmly, reaching for his tea with one hand while touching his jingasa with the other. "I presume the Senator is aware
of that." His eyes moved to the other man in a tie. "And you,"
Reaperson said, "are from old Blueblood's office, are you not?"

Atkins chuckled. "Rudolf the Red-Nosed Senator's more
like it. Blue blood, red nose, and a white-washed conscience
– how patriotic."

"Vince Sipple from Senator Pemberton Hastings III, sir.
It's pretty clear that Senator Card's got his head stuck up an
elephant's butt, because Senator Hastings believes that you're
sending weapons to the Gabonese rebels without our clear-
ance. They're getting arms from somewhere, and our sources
strongly suggest it's here. The rebels aren't playing ball with
us, Reaperson, and they control the territory where the Nio-
bium mines are located. Have you no shame? How are we supposed to make the commemorative coins the public so loves?
They need to be taught a lesson, and so do you. We need to
show our support for the Gabonese government."

Jack Reaperson took another sip of tea. "Get off your high
horse, both of you. Maybe you'd like to tell me why my tax
dollars go to support bozos like you. Conflicts are global, gentlemen, and never-ending. And so are markets. Friends, enemies, governments – what do they really matter – they keep
changing after all. However, Business is Business. And YOU
need to leave the business of the world to the World of Business. Go back to spying on each other and passing new laws to

protect butterflies or something. There's no proof of anything here except of your own incompetence."

"I'm not leaving here empty handed, Reaperson," Atkins said. "The senator's spent too much time on this. We could have you arrested for destruction of government property at least."

"I had nothing to do with that. You can ask these young men here. They were the guards on duty."

"I shooting drones," blurted Itchy proudly. "Blasting them right out of sky."

"Who told you to do it, son?" Sipple asked. "And where did you get the gun? Be honest now. It wouldn't be fair for you to take the fall for this."

"What you mean - fall?" Itchy asked, furrow lines popping out on his forehead.

"Someone's going to jail for this, son, and it shouldn't be you," Sipple said.

Itchy's eyes jumped nervously from one to the other of the three men, then he turned questioningly to his boss. Mr. Reaperson gave him a warm, friendly nod.

"Mr. Reaperson telling me do it," he mumbled, staring down at his hands. "He giving me gun."

Sipple and Atkins slapped hands. "Finally got you, Reaperson," Sipple said. "Let's go. There's a lot of people gonna want to talk with you."

"Not so fast, gentlemen," Norm said. "Jack's not going anywhere. There's a little matter of this gun that was mentioned. Where is it?" And can you tie this to Jack? I believe he's already told you he's had nothing to do with this."

"Have it your way," Sipple said. He turned to Itchy. "Take me to the gun."

Itchy again looked to his boss, who nodded his assent.

Itchy led Sipple and Atkins back through the plant and

outside to the dark corner where he had ditched the rifle. Sipple confirmed that the rifle had been recently fired, stared at the drone wreckage again, and the two followed Itchy back to the meeting room.

"Exhibit A, smoking gun," grinned Sipple as he lay the rifle on the table. He pointed at Itchy. "And Exhibit B, testimony of the man who fired it. You're coming with me, Reaperson."

Jack Reaperson's odd smile broadened. He sipped his tea and said nothing.

"You're an idiot, Sipple. And you too." The low deep voice had come from the quiet, casually dressed man, speaking for the first time as he turned slightly to stare at Atkins. All eyes turned toward him.

"Did you check the identification on the gun, and link it to him?" he asked, nodding towards Reaperson. "Because I can guarantee you that you've got nothing."

In a panic, Sipple grabbed the rifle and turned it about. "It's been filed off!" he shouted. "Is this your gun?" he asked Reaperson, desperation in his voice.

"I never saw it before in my life," Jack Reaperson said. "It's not even one of ours."

Sipple glared at the casually dressed man. "How did you know about this?" he demanded. "Wait a minute. You're CIA!" The thought hit him like a thunderbolt. "You're in league with them, aren't you? The CIA's illegally selling weapons!"

"The truth of government is the government of truth," the man said calmly. He looked at Reaperson, who continued to smile, and nodded. "Good day, gentlemen," he said, and abruptly left.

"Hey, wait a minute, you," Sipple yelled. "Who are you and where are you from? What does that even mean?" As the mystery man kept walking, Sipple turned back and stared at Reaperson. "This isn't over. We're taking your boy here, and when we get through with him, we'll be back. Let's go!" he barked at Itchy.

Itchy again looked over at his boss, fear etched on his face.

"Just a second, please," Norm said. He leaned over to whisper to Jack. "You good with this?"

"Why we hired him, Norm," Jack whispered back. "Itchy trusts us, he won't hurt us. God, guns, and country, right?"

"It's OK, son," Norm said. "You need to go with these men. Don't worry, we've got your back."

Itchy, Sipple, and Atkins stood up. "We get first crack at him, Sipple," Atkins said. All three walked out the door.

"Like hell you do," Sipple was heard to say. "This man is ours. It's only fair."

Joseph watched the two men walk out with Itchy and reappear in the parking lot, still arguing. He felt terrible for Itchy, even if he was a mean, ignorant person. He was sure he wasn't all bad. He definitely didn't deserve to go to jail. Like the man had said, that wouldn't be fair. But did fairness even exist? Ralph Beckman had come apart due to his obsession with fairness, and Itchy got screwed because he wanted no part of it. If anything, fairness was beginning to seem like the exclusive property of the rich and powerful. Maybe THEY were the Gods of Fairness. He looked closer at Jack Reaperson.

Jack and Norm sat in silence, Jack still smiling strangely. Suki poured him another cup of tea.

"Norm," Jack said after a few minutes. "Would you give Joseph and me some time please?"

"Sure, Jack, no problem," Norm said. "I'll be in my office."

"So, Joseph," Jack began. "I'm sure this has been an interesting first day for you. Probably not at all what you expected. You've seen and heard some things that maybe even bother you. Is there anything you'd like to say? And please feel free to speak your mind here."

Joseph's mind was buzzing like the three drones he had recently watched, and he saw what had happened to them. There certainly were things that bothered him, but given all he had seen and heard, he thought it would be wise to test the waters. He gulped. "Well, sir," he began tentatively, "I know the guards at the front gate are pretty upset and feel undervalued. I tried to reason with one of them, but I don't think I got too far."

"I see," Mr. Reaperson said. "Well, we can certainly look into that. But what about you, Joseph? What's bothering you?"

That went OK, Joseph thought, feeling a little more emboldened. "I was thinking about Itchy, sir. I hate to say it, but it seems to me like he was set up. He trusted you, and now he's going to jail. That doesn't seem fair to me."

Jack exploded like a rifle shot. "Fair! You wanna talk about fair? I know for a fact that there's a disease out there that causes men's schlongs to shrink! How fair is that?" He caught himself. "No one I know of course, but ..."

Suki snatched the teacup from the table and put it into Jack's hand. "Drink," she commanded. "Now breathe deep." She grabbed an incense burner from the table and placed it in front of him.

Jack gulped the tea in one loud slurp and breathed deeply of the incensed air. "Listen, kid," he continued, "you probably won't think it's fair when I fire you. But there it is. I have no choice. You're fired, Joseph. You see, life isn't fair, and neither is business. You worry about being fair and you're done for."

Joseph's head dropped momentarily. He raised it again to look at his boss.

"So, it's all a big con game then."

"There's no con," Jack said. "You only feel conned if you believe in the wrong things, and most people believe in the wrong things. That's not my fault."

Jack put his hand on Suki's shoulder. "See, I was lucky to find Suki here, and to hire her away from a guy I know who runs a computer company who had some problems in his software sector. Seems it wasn't responding as it should have to the appropriate stimulus, and she really straightened it out. She didn't come cheap, but I could tell she really knew her stuff when it comes to helping a man really grow his business. It's not only what you believe, but who you believe."

Suki sat demurely, eyes downcast. Joseph didn't know what to make of the inscrutable look playing across her face.

Jack went on. "But I'll tell you something, Joseph. For some reason I like you. You remind me of me when I was your age."

"Really?" Joseph said.

"No. Just kidding. When I was your age I had already been to the best schools and had a multi-million-dollar inheritance from my incredibly wealthy parents. I can't keep you anymore, but I'll tell you what. I'm going to give you the address of a guy I met over in Centerport the other day. He had a very unusual name, Pono something, I believe it was. He's got a new business and he's looking for people. I think he's the type who will do anything to get who he wants. Says he's got the fires of Hell burning in him, and I think he means it."

With the mention of Pono's name, Joseph's left eye twitched. It was the best that his beleaguered fight or flight response could manage. The God of Fairness, however, was likely grinning from ear to ear.

Jack Reaperson went on. "I think he's a real up and comer, Joseph. I'll have Bertha forward your resume. Goodbye, and best of luck to you. Come, Suki, I'd like you to help me decide how big to design the next rifle series."

"OK, Jack," she said. "I'll just be a minute. I'll see Joseph out first."

Suki led Joseph out, then waited until Jack had gone into

his office. She silently opened the door to Norm's room and slipped inside. Norm looked up from his desk and stared at her. Suddenly he burst into peals of laughter so loud he had to put both hands over his mouth. Tears rolled down his cheeks. "Oh my God, Suki! That hat!"

Suki tittered politely.

"How much longer?" Norm asked between spasms.

"You mean how much shorter," Suki replied. A shy, proud grin spread across her face and crinkled her eyes as Norm fell out of his chair and held onto his stomach. "He's certain he has Koro now, so it's just a matter of time. His mind is disappearing as fast as he thinks his precious penis is."

"I'll get the papers ready for the takeover then," Norm said, wiping his eyes. "We're going to be very rich, Suki."

"Seems fair. I'll make some tea after Jack leaves. We'll celebrate."

20

A Fire Sale of Free Will

Joseph left the plant shaking his head. Not even the lightening sky could lift his mood. The pink hues were even more intense this morning. They had been looking wilder every morning for weeks on end now. He thought of the old mariner's refrain, 'Red sky at night, sailor's delight; red sky at morning, sailor take warning.' Either a big storm was coming, or God was playing with fire again.

He drove on to the guard shack and said goodbye to Stan, the morning guy. "You're fired too?" Stan said incredulously. "All the guards have just been fired! The old man said we were ungrateful losers and hoped we'd all get Koro, whatever the hell that is. This isn't fair!"

"Stan's right!" Joseph shouted, driving away from Reaperson Arms. "It isn't fair!" He slammed his fist on the steering wheel. "I'm almost twenty-two years old and I might as well be living on the moon for all the sense this world makes to me. And on top of all this, now Pono is a businessman? What did I do to deserve this? Is it God? My parents? Me? Am I a loser too?" He felt a sudden panic wash over him. "I don't deserve to ever see Cherry again."

He drove on, slowly picking up speed, gears engaged. "Ah, stop your whining, Joseph," he told himself. "A man can do anything he wants in life, he just has to step up and do it. Where there's a will there's a way, right? And weren't we all born with a will? A free will too! I'd definitely be a loser to pass that deal up. But doesn't it only work if you know what you want? What do you want, Joseph? What do you want?"

Does Joseph really have a free will? What does that even mean? As free as a sailor on shore leave? As free as the wind across a bald man's head? As free as an astronaut on a spacewalk whose tether just snapped? Or perhaps just a will that is free enough to be out on its own, unchaperoned by the evolutionary behaviors that appear to guide every other creature on the planet as if they were laminated in an NFL coach's playbook. Such an aberration, though, would seem beyond the slow, random process that painstakingly filled every vacant behavioral niche in the animal world with more unusual behaviors than can be found in even a touchdown celebration.

But if the human will is really and truly free, there should be space outside that playbook for an audible, a change so fantastic, so radical, that even Bill Belichick could not conceive of it. So who COULD conceive of it then? It has to be the only one who is powerful enough to not only throw the evolutionary playbook out the window, but who's audibles are believed by many, even though they're completely inaudible. In other words, such inaudible audibles must point directly to the mind of a Creator. But why would a Creator offer free will, just to demand blind allegiance?

The puzzle begins to become clearer when one considers the axiom that 'Nothing in life is free." This would seem to imply that in exchange for having free will now, there must be some sort of payment due in an afterlife. Our money? Our possessions? Of course not. What good would they be to the Creator who has everything? It has to be the only thing that He or She doesn't have. It has to be our souls. Just how much does anyone know about this Creator anyway?

A coffee shop came into focus, the kind of establishment that's found on every other block. "I want breakfast, a cup of hot coffee, and then sleep," Joseph said, pulling into the lot.

He bypassed the drive-thru and went inside. He stood in line and watched the mostly young men and women scurrying about behind the counter, wearing their silly purple hats and aprons. *Is this what these people want?* he wondered, then looked up to the ceiling. The ceiling glistened. *Grease. Yech. I think their will power must be coated in grease. Who would want this?* He lowered his head and his eyes fell on an older, tired gentleman, who appeared to be trying, but failing, to keep a smile on his face.

"Whadaya want?" the older gentleman grumbled. "Or are ya gonna stand there all day starin' at me?"

Joseph hadn't realized he had moved up to the front of the line. "Oh. Sorry," he mumbled meekly. "I – I don't know what I want yet."

"Look kid. This ain't a career decision. It's a coffee shop. Not a lot of choices. So either place your order or step aside and make way for somebody who knows what they want."

Totally embarrassed now, Joseph slunk back to the end of the line and concentrated on the menu. There really weren't a lot of choices. And what choices there were seemed remarkably similar, all variations on a theme. He may have the will power to choose, but who was it that determined such a limited menu? Egg on a bagel, egg on a biscuit, egg on a muffin. With or without a slice of ham or cheese. The images didn't much look like eggs or ham or cheese. Just some round plastic discs stacked perfectly on top of each other like pancakes. Mmm, pancakes. He thought of his mom's kitchen, and all the wonderful smells he had grown up with. True, it came with some serious baggage, but he was quite hungry. And he had a choice, didn't he? Didn't everybody? He watched the robotic faces of people walking away with their plastic sandwiches, one after another.

Joseph ordered a coffee, black, no sugar, and took it outside. He took a seat at a picnic table and scanned the strange pink sky, now beginning to fade. Another squadron of military jets screamed past, flying east as usual.

"Please help me," a thin, plaintive voice whispered behind him.

Joseph turned to look at the most bedraggled specimen of humanity he had ever seen. A haggard, skeletal man, possibly young, definitely dirty from head to toe, in clothes he must have been sleeping in for weeks. Wild, matted brown hair. Eyes that looked well past hungry. They were hollow. Haunted even. He was about to reach for his wallet when an unexpected voice popped into his head. Bertha, Reaperson's HR director. *Can't be too careful, what with all the con men in this world.*

Joseph examined the dirty man again, picking up the unmistakable aura of desperation this time, as well as some truly offensive odors. Terrible body odor for sure, but something else too, something that smelled a lot like burnt wood. He remembered Jack Reaperson next, saying, *You're only conned if you believe the wrong things. And most people believe the wrong things.* That made him think of Pono and the stupid volcano birthmark he had exploited so successfully. Even his father chimed in, admonishing him over and over with his *Do na be a dobber, Joseph.* He suddenly felt very vulnerable.

He certainly doesn't look like a con man, he thought. *But what do con men look like if not the unexpected? Better humor him a bit then get rid of him nicely.* "How can I help you?" he asked, ready to dip into his nearly empty wallet for a couple bucks.

"I don't know," the thin, dirty man croaked, heaving an ancient and hopeless sigh.

Joseph was stunned. There was a real person in there, and that person was more lost than he was. He had to help him somehow. "You don't know how I can help you? Don't you want something?"

"Want to be left alone," the man said helplessly.

This wasn't making any sense, but Joseph persisted, wading curiously into the confusion. "Why did you talk to me then if you want to be left alone?" he asked.

"Help me. Please."

"I don't understand. How can I help you?" Joseph repeated.

"Don't know."

"OK. You don't know how I can help you. Can you tell me why you need help?"

"Voices."

"I see," Joseph said. "And are these voices inside your head?"

"In head. Yes. Voices," the man said, becoming agitated.

"Well, sir," Joseph said, "It could be your conscience speaking to you. I don't know, but I think that everyone has a conscience that speaks to them. Some are just louder than others, I guess. But I think that they all try to help a person to decide the right thing to do. Shouldn't you listen to what your conscience is trying to tell you?" He felt glad to be able to finally use some of his socio-psychology learnings to try and help this poor man, even if he wasn't too sure of his footings.

"No. Voices bad. Help me."

"Alright, now I think I understand," Joseph said. "But that's actually very good that you understand that sometimes the

voices are bad. Recognition of a problem is the most important part. Say, what's your name anyway?"

"Bob," the man said. "Help me."

"I was coming to that, Bob. Since you recognize when your
conscience is telling you something you think is wrong, all you
need to do is ignore it. I know people who ignore their conscience all the time. I think maybe we all have the willpower
to make those choices. Do you understand what I'm saying?"

"Willpower. Say no."

"That's good, Bob. I'm glad I could help. But there's something else I'd like to do for you. I'm starving and I bet you
are too. Would you like to come home with me for a shower,
some clean clothes, and a home cooked breakfast? I'm sure my
parents would just love to meet you." *And then maybe they won't
dump on me so bad,* he thought.

"OK."

"Great, let's go. We're on fire now, aren't we, Bob?"

Bob's eyes grew huge, nearly jumping out of their sockets
in a wild search. "On fire?"

"Just a figure of speech, Bob."

The quiet drive back to his house had Joseph smiling in
anticipation of his parent's reaction to Bob. He gave him some
old clothes that he never wore, showed him to the shower, and
told him where the shaving materials were. Twenty minutes
later Bob came out looking like a new man, and Joseph led
him to the kitchen.

"What's all the commotion, Joseph?" an agitated voice
called out from down the hall. His mother was fast approaching, his father right behind. "It's only 7:30. Your father and
I were still ..." She stopped on seeing Bob. "Oh, I'm sorry. I
wasn't expecting company. And here I am in my robe, and my
hair a mess."

"What company?" his father said, stumbling into the well-lit room. "Oh," he said, taken aback at seeing a stranger in his house. "Yer maw's right, Joseph. Ye need to be more considerate and let us know if ye'll be wantin' to bring a friend home."

"Shall we leave then, dad?" said Joseph. "It's just that we've both had a rough time of it lately, and are very hungry."

"No, no, stay," said his mom. "You just caught us off guard is all. Pancakes coming right up."

"Joseph, me lad, where's yer manners?" his father scolded. "Yer friend is sittin' here all uncomfortable I'm sure, and ye've nae thought to introduce him. I apologize for my son, laddie. My name is Alvin, and my wife is Naomi. Who may we hae the pleasure of meeting?"

"Bob."

Joseph's father waited for more, but the awkward silence rushed him into continuing. "Bob is't? Tis a class name. Simple, honest, trustworthy. A man cannae hide behind that name. No siree, Bob." He chuckled, but stopped quickly on seeing that Bob's expression hadn't changed. "Well, Bob, yer maw and da were canny to choose a solid name like that, it will take you anywhere ye want to go. So, Bob, where IS it ye want to go in life?"

"Home."

"Home. How wonderful," chimed in Naomi. "Imagine that, Joseph, a young man who misses his home. You must come from a very loving and supportive family, because that's really what it takes to make a home. And I'm sure you're very appreciative of it too, unlike some young men," she said with a sidelong glance at her son. "So, Bob, where do you call home?"

"Anywhere."

"A man o' the world, huh?" concluded Alvin. "Comfortable wherever ye go. That's a rare talent, Bob. Very important when yer up ta yer oxters in it. Joseph, ye cuid learn a thing or two from this lad."

"Uh, dad?" Joseph said. "I don't think Bob has a home. I think he's homeless."

"Dinnae be so literal, Joseph. Ye'll miss the real meaning. He's a man o' the Word, too, or ye can bile me heid. Selfless to a fault, I'd say. Right, Bob?"

"Self. Less. Yes," he said. "Why? How? Who am I?" A tear came to his eye that only Joseph noticed.

"Well, those are certainly some big questions, Bob," Naomi said. "They don't get any bigger. It's good to see a young man asking himself the tough questions. That kind of metaphysical self-examination shows a keen intellect. But I'm not sure that we're the ones you should be asking. That's OK. You're young yet. God will answer all your questions in time. Remember that, Joseph. Don't settle for easy answers. Keep asking those tough questions. Stay hungry."

Joseph looked at Bob staring at his empty plate and took his cue. "Mom, are the pancakes almost ready? We're starving."

"That's not what yer ma was talkin' aboot, Joseph," Alvin said. "Ye must think past yer immediate desires, like Bob here."

A steaming tray of pancakes was brought to the table. Bob's tormented eyes settled a bit and he plunged right in, grabbing several and cutting them roughly before stuffing them into his mouth as fast as he could. Joseph took two, poured syrup neatly on them and spread it around evenly with his knife, cut them into bite-sized morsels, and placed a napkin on his lap.

"My goodness," Naomi said. "It's certainly a pleasant change to see a young man enjoy my cooking. Dig in, Joseph, before they get cold. I hope you're not planning to run off to your room without eating again."

"Just savoring the moment, Mom," Joseph said, "and the always pleasant and understanding company."

"Whoa!" his father exclaimed. "I'll be pished as a piper.

Was that sarcasm I just heard? Are ye getting' sarcastic to yer maw, Joseph? And after she goes to the trouble of making yer new friend a nice meal."

"Now, now, Alvin. That's alright. I'm used to my efforts not being recognized around here." Naomi smiled to see Bob snatching some more pancakes. "But it shouldn't take a stranger to appreciate all that I do. And that goes for the both of you."

"What are ye talkin' ...?"

"So, Bob," Naomi said, brusquely interrupting her husband, "I was just wondering. What do you do?"

"Listen."

"That's pure dead brilliant, Bob," Alvin said, glaring at his wife. "Nobody ever listens anymore. Listening is the first step to understanding and making good choices."

"No choice," said Bob.

Alvin chuckled. "I knoo whit ye mean, Bob. I'm a good listener too. That's how I give such good advice. Not that anybody aroon here appreciates it."

"You do have a choice, Bob," said Naomi. "Don't listen to him. Nobody else listens to the old windbag. Anyway, I'd be very interested to know about your goals in life. Do you have any hopes and dreams?"

"Peace."

"My, how refreshing you are, Bob. A man after my own heart. Peace is humanity's loftiest goal. If peace isn't worth dreaming about, what is, I say. We've always told Joseph to dream big like that, but I think he prefers to stare at the ceiling and avoid the difficult subjects."

"Mom," Joseph said. "I don't think you understand. Bob ..."

"Dreamin' aboot peace is like dreamin' aboot a guid home cooked meal," sniped Alvin, staring at his wife. "Ye'll starve to death before ye ever see't. All ye ever see aroon here are matzoh balls and gefilte fish. Nae once ha you een tried to make haggis. It's only my favorite dinner, and the pride of Scotland."

"Excuse me, Alvin, but sheep innards aren't a meal fit for vermin."

"Oh, so Scotland's full o' vermin noo is't? Tell me hoo ye really feel? As if Liechtenstein is so hot. World's biggest producer of false teeth. Whoo Hoo! Scotland could kick Liechtenstein in the teeth, real or false, with one foot tied behind its kilt! Whadaya think aboot them tatties?"

"Uh, Mom, Dad?" Joseph interjected. "Bob was referring to the voices he hears. He says they're always telling him what to do."

"Well a coorse they are, Joseph," his dad said. "That's the voice o' God talkin' to him. Bob's a fortunate lad. He shuid listen to those voices. Do ye hear me, Bob? Ye must listen to those voices, and obey yer Father."

"My father," Bob said. Again Joseph saw Bob's eyes moisten. "I'm sorry."

"There, there, Bob," Naomi said. "Let it out. Go on, let it out. My but you're an emotional fellow. Don't worry, Bob. If you didn't understand something, I mean. It's alright. God understands."

"And He forgives," Alvin said. "Don't forget, Bob. He forgives us our sins."

"Dad, I don't know if that's such a good idea" Joseph said. "Bob says these voices he hears are bad. I told him to ignore them."

"Pin yer lugs back, Joseph. Dinnae be a dunderheid. Tis a sin to disobey God."

"I'm too tired to argue, Dad. I'm going to bed. I told Bob he could sleep on the couch in my room."

"That's fine, Joseph," his mother said. "Your dad and I are

going out on a couple of errands. We'll be back soon. Nice to meet you, Bob. Sleep well, boys."

Joseph slept. He slept the sleep of the dead at first, but gradually that gave way to strange, fitful dreams of birthmarks and volcanoes, and of Pono laughing maniacally, all suffused in a foreboding pink glow. The volcano was about to erupt, an overpowering sulfur smell in the air. He awoke with a start. Bob was gone. And he realized it wasn't sulfur he was smelling. It was gasoline.

Joseph leapt out of bed and dashed towards the kitchen, checking rooms as he went. Grandma staring out the window. All else clear. He burst into the garage. Garage door open, so parents not back yet. But the gasoline odor was stronger. He raced out of the garage and saw him, at the same time his parents pulled into the driveway. Bob was shaking the last drops of gas from a five-gallon container onto the wood shingles of the house. He threw the container aside and pulled out a pack of matches.

Horrified, Joseph yelled, "Bob! Don't! Don't listen! Please!"

Alvin and Naomi jumped out of the car and screamed.

Bob turned calmly and looked at each of them. "No choice," he said, and lit a match.

Joseph ran back inside and wheeled his grandmother quickly out through the garage. He grabbed his dad's cell phone from the kitchen counter on his way out and dialed 911. The fire was already lapping at the roof. In five minutes the house was completely engulfed in flames.

"Fire," his grandmother cried flatly, pointing at the blaze.

Dazed, Joseph watched the fire trucks scream up and begin the futile work of saving the house. He saw his parents holding on to each other, his father trying to comfort his hysterical mother. Two police squad cars arrived next. He saw several officers rush across the lawn, throw Bob to the ground and handcuff him, then push him roughly into the back of one of the cars. The car sped off. One officer was walking towards his parents, another towards him.

"Sergeant Wood," the officer said. "Terribly sorry, but I need to ask you a few questions. We've been looking for this man for a week, ever since he walked away from the Croft Institute for the Criminally Insane. He'd been there since he was sixteen, for burning down his own house and killing his father. Thank God everyone here is safe. Do you have any idea what made him choose your house to set fire to? He says the Devil made him do it."

21

The Ghosts of Happiness

The Last Boat Homeless Shelter provided food, a roof, and beds, no questions asked. After spending the afternoon answering questions at the police station about Bob and the fire, then getting his grandmother settled at a facility that could take her, another interrogation was the last thing they needed. Joseph had never seen his parents so sad. They just sat there on their cots, staring into space. Or perhaps they were staring at the other homeless people and silently planning grand life improvements for them, too, since it had worked so well for him. Nothing to it that a report card or two couldn't fix.

Look at them, he said to himself. *Man, they really don't look so happy now, do they? If they ever were. Their whole life, everything they believed in, has just burned to the ground. Is that what happens when you believe in stuff? Like our house. Like Bob. Like Cherry. Poof. Gone, like smoke. Or like God. Maybe it's a good thing they never believed in me.*

He paused.

And what is happiness anyway? Just more smoke? Would I know it if I felt it? Or is it a phantom feeling, like love, here one minute, gone the next, leaving you feeling like it was never even there. They must belong together, love and happiness, like ghosts in a haunted house that people are too afraid to stay in. Do I even dare believe in them?

As usual, he didn't know, so he lay back down on the cot and stared at the ceiling. Now this was an interesting ceiling. Quite old obviously, with the kind of character that can only come from having looked upon a lot of misfortune in its lifetime. Age spots of assorted shapes and colors. Character lines that tended to deep fissures in places, which had clearly rejected every attempt at cosmetic rehabilitation. Even its skin was flaking and peeling in ugly patches. This ceiling had a lot of stories to tell, and they were all sad ones. *They should compare,* he thought. *I could probably match the ceiling story for story.*

Battling the high emotions of the day, Joseph at last drifted off to sleep. A disturbing dream began to haunt him. The sad old ceiling was staring at him, and a deep, jagged fissure was opening and closing, distorting itself as if it were trying to speak but had forgotten how, or simply hadn't in a very long time. Low groaning creaks and sharp unsettling cracks issued from its gaping mouth.

Finally a long, ghostly moan came forth, a moan that sounded as if it had been bottled up for centuries. "Ooooooeeeeeeooooooo." Then the ceiling winked at him and spoke. "Man, that felt good. I've been silent too long. Please don't be afraid, Joseph. I'm watching over you." The ceiling giggled. "Oh boy, that one still cracks me up. And I've got a million of em." The ceiling suddenly turned serious. "Cracks, I mean. Unfortunately, I don't see much to joke about up here. And that includes you, Joseph. Word from the other ceilings is that your story has been pret-ty sad, perhaps even a tragedy, though from what I've heard I think I'd call it more of a black comedy."

"My life is funny to you?" Joseph asked incredulously.

"Well, I wouldn't go that far," the ceiling said. "Fact is, I get more laughs every night watching the winos come in and throw up on that good for nothing floor, the dried-up old boot licker. The walls tell me that really tarnishes his varnish."

"The walls talk too?"

"Of course the walls talk, Joseph. I thought everyone knew that. Fact is, once they start, it's hard to shut them up. Gossip mongers, the lot of em. But anyway, back to your sad story. Since it's my job to watch over you, I wanted to warn you that I heard you're about to be visited by three ghosts. They're the ghosts of Happiness Past, Present, and Future, ghosts I've never seen around here before. You'd think they'd be regulars in this joint, wouldn't you?

"Anyway, fact is, I've never even heard of these ghosts before, so I can't tell you what to expect. But ghosts never come unless you've got some serious issues, so brace yourself. Ten to one it's got something to do with your infernal agnosticism about everything, so you might try putting on a happy face and rolling with it, know what I mean? Maybe they can show you the way to true happiness. Just don't tell them that you don't believe in them, OK, Joseph? They should be here any second. I'm just gonna be quiet and watch."

Joseph had just finished repeating "I don't believe in ghosts" for the fourth time when he heard it.

"Joooo-seph. Joooo-seph."

He froze at the chilling sound and looked around in terror. He could see nothing. *What kind of a nightmare is this?* he thought. The voice had sounded like it had come from the next room. Maybe it wasn't for him. Maybe the ceiling had been wrong.

"Joooo-seph. Joooo-seph."

The spooky voice was a little louder now. And then he saw it. Coming through the wall, a shimmering, vaporous emanation, calling his name as it came. It appeared to be looking right at him, though it was kind of hard to tell as its facial features were constantly shifting. Joseph had the distinct impression that this ghost was not happy, but was trying to find a face that would at least look happy.

"Hey, you could at least bring me flowers if you're gonna penetrate me like that," the wall said. "That's a bit personal, don't ya think? I'm not some loose-hinged door you know."

"Oh, sorry," the ghost said. "It's the first time for me. Won't happen again, I promise."

"My, but you're a fine-looking ghost," the wall said, looking him up and down now. "Maybe I overreacted. Actually it did feel rather nice."

"Are you the Ghost of Happiness Past that was foretold to me?" Joseph asked.

"Why, yes," the ghost answered, turning back around. "Name's Angus. How did you know?"

"The ceiling told me."

The ghost jerked his vaporous head towards the ceiling and stared, but the ceiling was pretending to be asleep.

"Nobody can keep a dang secret anymore," Angus whined. "Man, I miss the old days when everyone was surprised to see us."

"How can you miss the old days? I just heard you tell the wall that this was your first time."

"Oh. Well. Technically that's true," Angus replied. "But I've been in training for a long time. So don't think I don't know what I'm doing, OK? Long as we're clear on that. It's not easy being a ghost you know. Times have changed. Used to be we just had to shout 'BOO' and people'd change their ways. Now it's all zombies and vampires. Freakin' zombies and vampires. Can you believe it? Man, try doing your job when people don't believe in you anymore."

"Yeah, I guess I know a little about that. So what is your job anyway? Boring me into happiness?"

"Don't mock me, Joseph. I'm not in the mood. Not after what you did to old Babette."

"You must have the wrong guy," Joseph said, hoping the ghost would disappear as fast as it had appeared. "I don't know any Babette."

"Of course you don't," snapped Angus. "The greatest Ghost of Happiness Past we've ever had didn't just visit anybody. She'd only taken the special cases for the past few of your centuries, give or take, I suppose. Time doesn't really matter much to a ghost. It just sort of slips through our hands. As does everything else, now that I think of it. Anyway, there was old Babette reviewing your file last night, preparing for her visitation, when she suddenly got so sad and depressed that she upped and killed herself. Couldn't take it anymore, she said, right before she blew herself apart. A real ugly scene, bits of vapor everywhere. We hadn't had a booicide in a thousand years."

Joseph's eyelids twitched crazily. "Now you just hold it right there. You can't blame that on me."

"This is your life we're talking about, Joseph. It has consequences, more than you can see. But try not to beat yourself up too much about it. There's still time to change."

"I'm not beating myself up at all," Joseph shot back. "I don't think this is even really happening. It's just a silly dream."

"Oh, it's happening, Joseph. If you had seen old Babette splatter herself like that ... To be honest though, it probably was time for her to float aside. She had some pretty old-fashioned ideas, never really caught on to modern happiness. Still believed happiness was a lick from a puppy dog, instead of a like from a stranger on Facebook. I kept telling her, happiness has changed, my vaporous friend. But she'd just sort of give me that knowing wink, and smile her spooky smile ..." Angus shook the fond memories out of his head and watched the tiny vapor clouds drift away.

"So, Joseph," Angus continued, "I gave a quick review of Babette's file on you, and I gotta say, you really didn't have many happy moments, did you? I mean, I found a few, mostly pretty trivial ones, like the time your father secretly bought you a Christmas present, a crucifix I think it was, even though he hadn't won the holiday celebration rights. On the other hand, that was certainly quite the collection of dreidels you got from your mother over the years. And nothing says fun like a dreidel, right? And those "Existentialism for Children" books your mom read to you. What a hoot, hey?

"Oh, and then there was that time your mother took you to the Philosophy Museum and let you experience the Nature of Reality Exhibit in the virtual reality headset. That had to be quite a trip. Oh, I'm sorry, but wasn't that also the time you got lost in the 'If a Tree Falls in the Forest' wing? And nobody heard you screaming for an hour?"

"OK, I get it," Joseph said. "I haven't had a very happy life. I'd like to see how YOU'D manage with parents like mine. At least they could teach you a thing or two about scaring somebody. But is anybody truly happy? Isn't real happiness all an apparition, kinda like you?"

"I may be an apparition, Joseph, but that doesn't make me any less real."

"I'm pretty sure it does."

"Look, you can't see happiness, you can only feel it."

"Then how would you know anything about it? You're a ghost. You can't even feel yourself."

Angus smirked. "Well, maybe not like you. All you seem to do is feel yourself. That's not the only source of happiness you know."

"Oh, I get it. You're jealous. Ghosts don't have sex, do they?"

"Of course ghosts have sex. What do you take us for?"

"Liars. I can see right through you, and I don't see any sex organs. That's the real reason you go around scaring people, isn't it? You're always angry."

Angus smiled dreamily. "We have our ways, Joseph. We have our ways. Just ask the wall. Look, Joseph, this little intervention is about you. You can believe me or not, but believing is the only way to true happiness. Now your girlfriend is a ghost too, isn't she? Just saying. It's up to you. My job was just to prepare you."

"And what exactly am I supposed to believe? Ghosts? Talking ceilings? Dreams? That Cherry will come back to me? And what are you supposed to be preparing me for?"

"For the Ghosts of Happiness Present and Future, of course."

"Great. More unscary ghosts to not believe. Won't you please let me wake up?"

"Not until our visitation is over, and the reckoning is complete. But if it's scary you want, you're gonna get it. Wait till you meet the Ghost of Happiness Future! Spook seems to have forgotten the meaning of happiness. He can make the prospect of puppy dog kisses sound like waterboarding! We think it might have something to do with those apocalyptic visions he goes on about. What a downer. Between you and me, he's just not trying hard enough. There's gotta be some happiness in the future even if there is an apocalypse, don't you think?"

"I don't know what to think," Joseph said. "Please go away."

"I'm going. But could you do me a favor? Give me good marks on the new ghost evaluation form when they send it?"

"Go!"

"I'm going. I'm going."

"Over here, Angus," whispered the wall, breathily.

The ghost floated over to the wall, grinned back at Joseph, and disappeared inside.

No sooner had Joseph relaxed than he heard it.

"Joooo-seph. Joooo-seph."

"Great. Here we go again." He sat up and looked around.

"Joooo-seph. Joooo-what the hell? This is disgusting!"

The ghost came through the floor this time, just as vaporous, but not nearly as shimmering. Joseph noticed that there was something distinctly feminine about this one. He hadn't realized that vapor could have such curves. It shook itself like a wet dog and continued complaining.

"What is this stuff? I've been slimed! It smells terrible! Somebody could have warned me! This isn't right!"

"Are you the Ghost of Happiness Present that was foretold to me?" Joseph asked.

"Yeah, yeah. Be with you in a minute. Jeez. I've never felt so violated in all my life. What the hell IS that stuff in the floor?"

"It's vomit," Joseph said. "Years and years' worth of it apparently. The ceiling thinks it's pretty funny."

The ghost jerked its free-form head upwards. The ceiling was still pretending to be asleep, though it now appeared to Joseph to be smiling ever so faintly.

"Management is gonna answer for this," the ghost fumed. "Section 25.4 of the union contract guarantees a clean working environment, free of harmful chemicals, toxic waste, and radiation."

"I didn't hear you say vomit," Joseph said, stifling a smile. "If I was management, I'd say you didn't have a leg to stand on. Oh, wait, you don't have any legs to stand on."

"Very funny, Joseph. But you don't know what chemical

fumes can do to a ghost. They mingle with the very essence of our essences, and can even change our essential ghostly properties. My best friend can't even pass through walls anymore. They had to reassign her to dispatch!"

"Sad story, uh, what did you say your name was?"

"I didn't. It's Susannah."

"Just saying, Susannah, but you don't seem very happy for a Ghost of Happiness."

"Yeah, well, you don't seem very happy for a poor mortal who knows his life is short and ..." Susannah paused. "Sorry. How about we start over? So, Joseph, what would you say your Happiness Index is lately? On a scale of one to ten."

"Well, let's see. Parents think I'm an idiot. College roommate slept with my girlfriend and humiliated me. Cherry's the girl I think I love, and I don't think I'm ever gonna see her again. Then I spent four years getting a useless college degree. Got fired first day on a lousy job I was way over-qualified for. Got caught up somehow in an illegal gun smuggling operation and almost arrested. Am I forgetting anything? Oh, yeah. I caused my parent's house to burn down. That's my parents over there in a catatonic state. And now I'm stuck in a dumb dream that I think is supposed to be showing me how to be happier."

"OK, so your H.I. is not so good. That's why I'm here. That just means there's a lot of room for improvement. Ever try smiling for no reason? You've heard the saying, 'Smile and the whole world smiles with you.' That could turn things around in a jiffy. Smiling can be very infectious."

"I'd rather do without any infections, thank you. With my luck, it'd probably kill me."

"Then how about singing that *Don't Worry, Be Happy* song whenever you're down. I've gotta say, that song never fails to put a smile on MY face and make my worries go away."

"Yeah, well, how many worries can a ghost have? You're practically immortal."

"A puppy then. Or a cute little kitty."

"Too sad. They all have short lives and die."

"So it's death that's making you unhappy then?"

"Does death ever make anybody happy?"

"Matter of fact, Joseph, it does. Most people believe that death is just the first step to a beautiful, happy, everlasting life in a heavenly world of their own design. Of course, you can always choose to believe one of the popular, pre-packaged versions of an after-life if that suits you better. It's a really easy fix if that's what you're thinking."

"That's just it. Long as I'm thinking, it's not an easy fix. I'd have to stop thinking."

"Well, I was saving that for last, Joseph, but you've pushed me into it. For agnostics like you, there's always electro-shock treatments. Ghosts have always known that happiness exists in inverse proportion to brain activity. Take your thinking activity down a few notches and belief levels will automatically rise. You'll be as happy as a dumb jock. Or a lark. Or a clam. All depends on how many treatments you sign up for."

"That's enough. You can leave now."

"Have it your way, Joseph. Don't say I didn't try. Just think about what we've covered, OK?"

"Go!"

Susannah floated towards the door singing 'Don't Worry, Be Happy,' and disappeared.

———————

All went quiet again in Joseph's dream, allowing the Dream Conductor a chance to bring in the heavy artillery.

"Holy Crap! Jesus! It's worse than I thought!"

Joseph's eyelids darted about like little hummingbirds,

while his heart pounded so hard it threatened to pin the hummingbirds to his retina. (Dream Conductors don't always know their limits.) Then he saw the ghost he was told to expect and began to calm down. "You must be the Ghost of Happiness Future that was foretold to me," he said. "Man, you almost killed me! I never saw you coming!"

"That's because I'm from the future, you moron. Name's Crandall by the way. And I'm not the one you should be worried about killing you. Holy Smokes! Everybody's killing everybody there! The militaries of the world are pummeling each other's countries to smithereens! And Mother Nature ..."

"Wait! There's a Mother Nature?"

"There was. But once nature was destroyed, she's got nothing to be a mother to! She's like the mother of an empty nest. You've never seen anything so sad in your life. Of course, God doesn't see it that way. Man o' man is She angry."

"There's a God too?"

"Well, duh. You think that angry voice I heard is all in my head? Look at me. There's nothing in my head. You can see clear through it."

"So you've never actually seen Her then?"

"Oh, I forgot," Crandall said. "You're one of those, aren't you? Have to see something to believe it. That's why you don't believe in happiness, you know. And why you're losing your belief in Cherry. Well, you see me, don't you? So you can get off that skeptic's train to nowhere and start by believing in ghosts at least. You've seen three of us now."

"I'll make a deal with you," Joseph said. "Come visit me when I'm awake and I'll believe in you. I haven't forgotten that this is just a dream. Deal?"

"Man, you agnostics are tough nuts. You really gotta loosen up and believe in something if you're ever gonna find happiness. Anything! Don't you understand an apocalypse is coming! I've seen it with my own eyes! It's more terrible than you can imagine! Death! Destruction! Total annihilation! Find some happiness now before it's too late!"

"Will you get the hell out of here? This is how you try to make me happy? I've had it with you ghosts! I don't care if I never experience this big reckoning that the Ghost of Happiness Past promised."

Crandall looked at Joseph and shook his head sadly. "I'm so sorry if you misunderstood, Joseph. The reckoning is for us. Every time we do a visitation to some miserable agnostic, we reckon we feel a whole lot happier about being a ghost." With that, the ghost bowed once and disappeared.

22

Till Breath Do Us Part

The sun was well up and mercilessly illuminating his new predicament when Joseph awoke at the Last Boat Homeless Shelter. The grim reminders of Bob and the fire came back to him like scavengers to a rotting carcass. They would never be completely gone, but he could try to live with just the skeleton of them.

"Whose side are you on," he moaned, pulling the sheet over his head.

The sun made it clear it was on its own side by raising the temperature in the stuffy room a couple of degrees. The lack of air conditioning did the rest.

He pushed the sheet back down and stared at the ceiling, happy that it wasn't talking to him. He sat up and looked around. His parents and everyone else appeared to still be sleeping. Someone had been kind enough to leave fresh clothes and a towel on the chair by his cot, so he took them into the bathroom to wash up and change.

He examined his face in the mirror, not happy with what he saw looking back. *Ghosts of Happiness, are you still in there?*

No ghosts answered, but his unsmiling face and sad eyes told him that if he didn't change his sad story soon, the Ghosts of Happiness might decide to come back and use him as a training dummy.

Joseph walked back out into the main hall and noticed that people were beginning to stir. Mostly just to the extent of groaning and shielding their eyes from the light with their arms. Chief cook, minister, and bottle washer Rufus was back at it, singing and whistling and cooking just as he had been last night when he and his parents had met him. Joseph walked over to see if breakfast was ready.

"Don't be shy, my man," said Rufus. "Grab a plate. Early bird gets the best pancakes, yo. Sleep well?"

"Well enough, I guess," Joseph said. "Had some pretty strange dreams though. About ghosts."

"This place'll do that to ya, Joseph, you're not used to it. It's full of ghosts. Look around. Most of the men and women in here are mere ghosts themselves."

Joseph looked at the men, most sitting up now with their heads cradled in their hands, disheveled hair and clothes all that he could see. Their disheveled lives he could only imagine. A helper was making the rounds, placing cups of life-reviving coffee into their shaking hands, before moving on to the women in the adjoining room.

He brought a couple of plates of pancakes over to his parents, sitting up now like they had been last night, still staring right through him at something apparently only they could see.

"How do you do it?" Joseph asked, returning and taking a plate for himself. "You're always singing or whistling or joking around. Doesn't the sadness ever get to you?"

"Course it does. We're all afloat in a sea of sadness, Joseph. And without a life jacket, too many don't make it. Just sink into the depths. You just gotta keep swimming for all you're worth and hope that you bump into a little boat of happiness once in a while."

"Why can't we just stay there on a boat once we find one? Why can't we ever stay happy?"

"Because in the oceans of life, those flimsy little boats of happiness just get battered by the big storms, of which there seems to be no end. So soon as we find a boat load of it, we use it up quick before the next storm comes and destroys it. Human nature. Either way, we always have to be on the look-out for the next boat. That's why I whistle or sing. Helps distract me while I try to be a life jacket to some, and look for the next boat for myself."

"Rufus, I think I must be one of the one's who's sinking. I don't even know who I am, or why I'm here. Where's MY boats?"

"No, you're not sinking, my friend. At least not yet. You're searching for that boat. Those question marks on your forehead make that clear enough. But you're adrift. As my dear old mother would say, don't let your inhibitions inhabit your ambitions, or you'll sink. You need to leave it all on the table and believe your boat is out there. It'll appear, trust me. Look at these poor souls. They've been adrift for longer than you've been alive. They used to believe in the boats, but it just got too hard for them to get through the squalls, never mind the big storms. They don't have the desire or the ability anymore to change course, so they know their chances of stumbling onto a seaworthy boat are pretty slim, and they've pretty much given up. ISN'T THAT RIGHT, YOU MALODOROUS MANI-ACS?" he suddenly shouted. "This young man says he doesn't know why he's here. How about you tell him your point of view on the matter. Sing us your song, boys!"

The men groaned again but lifted their heads and stood

up beside their cots. Clutching their coffee cups, they swayed unsteadily for a bit, then raised their cups on high, and croaked out the oddest song Joseph had ever heard:

"A toast to Dame Misfortune,
And Lady Misery,
For if I had no bad luck,
I'd have no liberty.
And if my health was rosy,
And if my mind was sharp,
I'd rather be in Heaven
Playing on an angel's harp.
So, drink up dear old mother,
And dear old father too,
I'll see you in my drunkard's dreams
On the golden avenue."

A partition between adjoining rooms was opening, and a chorus of female voices from the next room sang out the final refrain:

So, drink up dear old mother,
And dear old father too,
"I'll see you in my golden dreams
With all the drunks I knew."

It was a thin song perhaps, but it was a song, and it had heart. It served its purpose. Singing for one's supper, or in this case for one's breakfast, is an age-old tradition for the down and outers. While seldom being of perfect pitch, they make perfect sense. What else have they got to offer? In fact, though, everyone should carry a song or two with them that is close to their hearts, if nothing else than for protection against a sudden, unexpected storm. Such songs are nourishment of a different sort, little boats of happiness in a big sea of sadness, without which the soul would begin to cannibalize itself in a desperate and inescapable attempt to avoid the fate of all such songless souls. Soullessness. Sometimes a song is the only thing keeping a person afloat, the lifeboat that prevents such person from sinking into the deep blues, or the deep blue sea.

Joseph watched the men clink cups with their neighbors, then sit back down on their cots, the lively song already a distant memory. He could see it in their eyes.

"Breakfast is served, my cacophonous crooners," Rufus called out cheerily. "Y'all sound like ya got frogs in your lungs. Come and get it or go hungry." To Joseph he said, "How about lending a hand? I'll give them the pancakes, you refill their cups. OK?"

"Sure."

"Just one rule, Joseph. Never try to solve their problems. It never works out."

"Sure. What could I ever tell them?" One by one, Joseph watched the men come up and be handed a breakfast plate, along with a ration of good-natured ribbing from Rufus.

"Top o' the morning to ya, O'Bleary. How many fingers am I holding up? Guess right and win an extra pancake."

"Hey, Casper. Kid here sez he saw a ghost last night. That wouldn't a been you by any chance, would it? You were three sheets gone and moaning like an October wind through a Halloween graveyard."

"Lookin' good, Jimbo. Don't worry about that hair. I'm sure it's nothing that a steel rake and a strong back can't fix."

In return he got, "Call those pancakes? I lose another tooth in one, I'm suin'." And "Jealous, Rufe? That shiny dome of yours don't look like its seen hair since your mama stopped brushin' it for you." The banter never slowed.

Joseph couldn't help smiling as he listened and poured the men and women their coffee. They nodded to him without looking up, and moved on to the dining table. Little by little he felt more comfortable, and even began to offer little pleasantries that he figured would help to show them he cared too. "Hi," "Hello," "Good morning," "Have a nice day," and the like. He still got the nod and an occasional grunt, but nobody would talk with him like they did with Rufus. Regardless, it felt good to be able to help somebody else, all the more so since he was doing such a terrible job of helping himself.

Rufus served the last guy in line with a "Good to smell ya, Stinky. Still allergic to soap and water I see." Stinky laughed and told him he shouldn't be complaining about smells what with the grub he was serving. Rufus laughed back and told Joseph he was going to lay down for a while, and to please clean up the kitchen and serving station.

Joseph saw his last chance to make a meaningful connection with somebody. "What's the word?" he tried, figuring that a question might be the best way to start an exchange.

The guy Rufus had called Stinky raised his head and said, "Hell. Hell-it. Hell-it-toze-is. What's it mean?"

Joseph staggered back as a wave of the foulest odors he had ever smelled poured out of the man's mouth and hit him flush in his face. He went into mouth breathing mode and forced himself back to the counter.

The guy continued. "My lady friend says I got the hell-it-toze-is, whatever the hell IT is, and don't let me near her no more. She won't tell me what it is. That's my little polecat over there with old Scarface. Can you believe it? Scarface."

Joseph looked where the man was pointing and saw the horrifically scarred face of a man grinning back at them, a scraggly black and gray-haired woman next to him whispering into his ear.

"I ain't the only one neither," the man said. "Lots of men here been told they got the hell-it-toze-is, and the ladies won't go near em no more. Somethin goin' on we can't figger out. I tole the Gimp I bet a good lookin' boy like you got a way with the ladies. Be much obliged if you could tell me what it is."

Joseph blushed. "I don't mean to offend you," he said, trying to deflect the obvious answer, "but didn't I hear Rufus call you Stinky?"

"Real name's Harold, but he usual call everone Stinky. Bet ya don't know why?"

Be careful how you answer, Joseph thought. *Remember Rufus's warning.* "It's probably because he knows that too much alcohol causes bad breath," he said. "Am I right?"

"This a trick?" Harold snapped. "You tellin' me ta quit drinkin? You one a them no good do gooders always tryin' ta reform us? Why we come here. Rufus leaves us alone."

"No, no, sorry, that's not what I meant," Joseph said. "It's just ... I don't know how else to say it. Halitosis means bad breath. No offense."

Harold stared at Joseph, trying hard to put the pieces together. "How come some of the boys don't seem to have the hell-it-toze-is then?" he asked. "They never quit drinkin."

Joseph looked over at the table and noticed the six women cozying up to six of the men, picking crumbs of pancake out of their beards, eating them, and laughing like donkeys with chest colds. Then it hit him. The men were all chewing. And their plates were empty. These men were chewing gum. Had to be. Nobody else was chewing. And nobody else sat with a woman.

He turned back to Harold, now looking sadly over at his table. His heart remembered all too well the feeling that

Harold was experiencing, as his own mind formed an image of Cherry in better days. True or not, it was an image he treasured. *Will I ever get to see her again?* He wondered. *Be with her again?* He shook his head and focused again on Harold. *Now I know the secret, I can't tell him,* he thought. *Don't try to solve their problems, Rufus said. Look how Harold got mad before, and that wasn't anything.*

Old hangdog Harold turned back, eyes pleading for an answer. *But this is just gum,* Joseph thought. *Damn it. It's not like I'm advising him to quit drinking. It's just gum. And I have some to give. What could happen?*

"Harold," Joseph said. "I think I can help you." He reached into his pocket and pulled out a pack of spearmint gum. "You can have this if you share it with your friends. It should help with your halitosis."

Harold's eyes brightened. "You got it, boss," he said, taking the pack from Joseph. "You really think so?"

"Well, don't expect miracles Harold. It's just gum. But it will help."

"Will it get my little polecat back?" Harold asked, leering over at Scarface as he unwrapped a piece and stuck it in his mouth. He didn't wait for an answer, instead leaving his plate and cup on the service counter and walking over to the table.

Joseph felt it first in the pit of his stomach, an involuntary tensing, like his body was bracing for a collision with a bus even before his mind could register what was happening. Then he heard himself, over and over repeating the words, "It's just gum. It's just gum. It's just gum."

He watched Harold go around the table to half a dozen men, whispering in their ears and slipping them a piece of gum. In his mind he saw the bus, now finished picking up its passengers, begin accelerating again. After a few minutes of furious chewing, each of the men rose and approached a woman. Harold approached his little polecat, leaning in to speak with her on the side opposite Scarface.

Joseph felt it and saw it now, clearly and in slow motion, the packed bus careening out of control, the innocent bystanders enjoying their breakfasts, or finished and chatting amiably with their neighbors, the hidden minefield that apparently only he could see. The polecat, smiling at Harold now, giving him her full attention as she turned her back on Scarface. The same scene happening at six other spots around the table. Then the wheels came off the bus at the same moment it plowed into the minefield.

Scarface and five other men erupted, Scarface diving across the polecat to land on Harold. All three crashed to the floor, then bounced back up as if from a trampoline, and went sprawling across the table, sending dishes, cups, and utensils flying. Shouts of encouragement rang out from the bystanders, most of whom quickly chose sides in the fray nearest them and piled on. In no time at all the huge table was swept clear of everything except knots of wrestlers, the floor littered with broken cups and dishes.

"STOP!" came the shout from the kitchen doorway. Rufus barged past Joseph, yelling "STOP! WHAT ARE YOU DOING?"

The writhing piles of wrestlers on the table stopped and looked up. In the sudden moment of silence everyone heard a loud CRACK. And then the table collapsed. The men and women scrambled to their feet and stood there among the detritus of the breakfast table looking suddenly sheepish. Not a sound could be heard except for perhaps a dozen people chewing gum.

"WHAT THE HELL IS GOING ON HERE!" Rufus yelled. "EVERYBODY GET BACK TO THEIR COTS! NOW!" He stood staring at the people walking heads down to their cots, then turned to look at Joseph. "What gives?" he said. "Any idea? I wasn't gone more than a few minutes."

Joseph saw Harold and the polecat approaching tentatively, he figured to apologize, so he let Harold speak first.

"I'm sorry, Mr. Rufus, sir," he said. "I just gotta clear my mind. It's this boy's fault. He give me some gum, he said to help cure my hell-it-toze-is, and instead it started a war. But I did get my little polecat back." Harold and the polecat stood there smiling sweetly at each other.

"OK, Harold. Thank you. You two go on back to your cots now." He watched them go, then turned on Joseph. "Really. You gave him gum? You had to try to help him, even though I said the only rule was to not try to solve their problems."

"It was just gum. I'm very sorry, Rufus. I didn't think ..." He let the words fade away.

"That's right, you didn't think. We're not in the savior business here, Joseph. I can't help them beyond providing beds and nourishment. Look at this place. It's trashed. What am I gonna do now? I don't have money for a new table and new dishes.

"I'm sorry, Joseph, but I'm going to have to ask you to go. And I'd suggest finding some professional help for your parents. It's not doing them any good to be here. I'll give you directions to a place I know. And Joseph," he said. "Find your boat. Or better yet, build it. It'll last longer. Until then, keep swimming."

23

A Good Universe is Hard to Swallow

Joseph took the directions from Rufous and led his parents out to their car, which he had parked on a nearby side street. The car was not there. Or rather everything that had been the car was not there except for some broken glass and the license plate. He looked at his parents but couldn't tell if they were processing this new problem. Before they did, however, he figured he better get them away from there quickly and deal with the car issue later.

The Shady Glen Refuge for Unsettled Spirits was only several blocks away, so he set out walking, his parents trudging slowly behind. He had to take their arms at one point to hurry them past a burning vehicle in a vacant lot, the fire causing them to make little high-pitched whimpering sounds. He turned to look closer at the burning car and instantly realized why. It was their car.

"This is insane," Joseph moaned. "Now their car is toast and we've been kicked out of a homeless shelter. And I'm supposed to build my own boat? With what? I mean, how low can I go? I can't even PICTURE Cherry anymore. Is this even real? How would I even know? Maybe I'm just hallucinating. This can't be my destiny, can it?"

———————————

If Destiny herself had any thoughts about the path Joseph was on, she wasn't talking. She never did anymore. When Gods talk, people listen, and Destiny had long been a God worth listening to. Or so people believed, back when she went by other names, and spoke through trusted oracles. Back when she believed that humans were not just another Johnny-come-lately species with a bigger brain and a world of possibilities. Back when she cared. Back when the other Gods just laughed at humans and threw darts at the Dartboard of Calamities whenever they wanted to have some fun.

Though Destiny was a God of the highest order, it didn't do much good, perhaps because there never was any order among the Gods. Perhaps she never really understood that they are, after all, merely a reflection of humans, a species known for their disorders. She definitely did not understand that humans could never stay on any paths that were chosen for them, no matter how golden-hued or heaven-scented they were. So it was entirely predictable when humans eventually began to stray so far from their paths that they chose to put their fates in the hands of such dubious oracles as palm readers, tea leave gazers, astrological sign interpreters, street corner prophets, baby-kissing politicians, and mind-altering drug purveyors. This treachery made her own path clear, and from that point on, no one could beat Destiny at the Dartboard of Calamities.

It is likely, though, that Joseph never truly believed in Destiny, despite the never-ending calamities that plagued his life. She just would not have seemed real to him. Not even as real as a hallucination.

———————————

The address led Joseph and his parents to a two-story yellow brick house that stood inside an eight-foot chain link fence, the fence extending down the sides of the walkway leading to the front door. A sign outside promised 'Quality Psychic Care. We Mind Your Mind.' The thought occurred to Joseph that that could be taken a couple of different ways.

And where were the trees? Shouldn't a place called Shady Glen at least have trees and shade? There was no shade at all that he could see. This place was shady alright, just not in the comforting way he had pictured. It hardly seemed to matter, though, to the dozen people staring at them through a fence as they slowly made the walk to the door.

Joseph helped his parents through the door, then turned around, startled to find a large woman in his face.

"You must be Joseph," the woman said, thrusting her hand out and causing Joseph to step back quickly to avoid getting jabbed in the stomach. "And Mr. and Mrs. Doubt. Welcome to Shady Glen. Rufus called and told me that you were on your way here, and a bit about your circumstances. Tragic. Just tragic. Well, my name is Calliope Pennyworth, and I'm certain we can help you, Joseph. Why don't you make your parents comfortable here in our lounge, and then come with me into our office."

Joseph was stunned. He couldn't process this woman's words at first, being completely astounded by her appearance. She had the largest head he had ever seen on a person, man or woman. But even aside from that, her facial features gave her an uncanny resemblance to a horse. He blinked hard and heard her say her name. *At least she didn't whinny*, he thought.

"Calliope," he said, silently scolding himself to stop staring. "I came here to get help for my parents, not for me."

"Yes, yes, of course, Joseph. But theirs is a classic case of PTSD, not much anyone can do about it except to keep them calm and away from the sort of stimulus that triggered the problem. Fire, I understand. I'm confident that they'll recover on their own time, but with your permission, I'd like to send them to a place where I know they'll get the love and support they need. If anybody can help them, it's Dr. P. No, it's you that interests me, Joseph. Come on into my office. Let's talk. Candy," she called out to a nurse that had just entered the room. "Would you come in with us please."

Joseph sat his parents down in well-worn institutional chairs and looked the place over. Everyone seemed to be staring at him. He started to follow Calliope when a bald-headed man in a bathrobe came up to him and blocked his path.

"There is no God, you know," the man said, matter-of-factly.

"No, I'm sorry. I don't know," Joseph replied.

"You're sorry that there's no God, or you're sorry that you don't know?" pressed the man.

"What? Neither. I don't know if there's a God or not. I haven't decided yet."

"It's not your decision to make. There is no God. Know how I know?"

"No, how do you know," Joseph said, trying to figure out how to politely get away.

"Cause the Buddha told me. God is all in our minds, he said, as clear as that sweet music somebody's playing. They won't let me talk to him again though. They won't let me have any more ..."

"That's very interesting," Joseph interrupted, not hearing any music, but catching sight of Nurse Candy waiting for him with a dimpled smile, a smile he took to be clearly flirtatious. "But right now I'm thinking there must be a God. How else would you explain THAT?" He brushed past the man and followed the pretty nurse to Calliope's office, unable to take his eyes off her rhythmically swaying derriere, wrapped so tightly in a short nurse's uniform, or the legs that just kept going and ...

"Most of the time their minds are perfectly fine," Calliope said as Joseph entered, misreading his thoughts. "Have a seat please. Nothing that a little professional head shrinking can't fix. The mind can be a confusing place to navigate sometimes, lots of blind alleys or dark cul-de-sacs to get stuck in, low overpasses to bang against, cliffs to fall off. We here at Shady Glen believe that getting lost in the byways of one's mind is a dangerous thing. So our aim is to nudge the patient back onto the main thoroughfare, where they can feel comfortable again in the normal flow of their thoughts."

"Ms. Pennyworth," Candy said sheepishly. "I thought it was the flow of normal thoughts we were hoping for."

Calliope Pennyworth smiled weakly. "Excuse me, Joseph. Candy, we never say normal in relation to a patient's mental state. Can you tell me what a normal thought is? No, you can't. And neither can anyone else.

"As I was saying, Joseph, from time to time we can all sense that our thoughts have lost some traction, and perhaps skidded a bit on a slick surface, or hit a bumpy patch at the edge of an abyss, or even drifted over the center divide if we've taken our minds off the road too long."

"Excuse me, Ms. Pennyworth," interrupted Candy. "Why is the center divide a problem again?"

"I'm sorry, Joseph. Candy, we've been over this a hundred times. The center divide is a metaphorical psychiatric construct that divides the direction of a patient's primary thoughts from those lesser ones travelling in the opposite direction. We want to make sure those thoughts pass by harmlessly and we avoid a head on collision. Those can be very difficult to untangle, depending on how many thoughts were involved."

"Calliope, now I'm confused," Joseph said. "Because contradictory mashups are pretty normal for my head."

"Joseph," scolded Calliope gently. "It's a question of flow.

Contradictory thoughts cause disturbance, inhibit progress. How would a person ever come to believe anything? It's our beliefs that make us who we are, that show us the way. The stronger the contradictory thoughts, the weaker the person's identity. That's the very thing that has me so interested in your case. I don't believe I've ever seen a weaker aura. Have you, Candy?"

"What about Mr. Moreau?" Candy offered. "He just sits there drooling all day."

"Mr. Moreau understands his limitations, Candy. That's something we should all strive to be better at."

"Yes, but he wasn't like that before you gave him the ..."

"Candy! That's enough. Apparently you and I need to have that talk again about understanding one's own limitations."

"I'm not a case, Ms. Pennyworth," Joseph said. "Are you saying that in order for me to figure out who I am, I have to believe something? Because every time I feel like I might be close to believing something, a contradictory idea comes up and squashes it. So does that mean I'm doomed to never know who I am?"

"No, Joseph. Remember what I said about the center divide. You just need to be vigilant about keeping those contrary ideas out of the lane you're travelling in. That's where I can help. Of course it's not easy, and it does take some time. Or, if you're game, we can take a shortcut."

Joseph saw Candy shoot her boss a look that he took to be one of horror, but as he was curious, he scaled it back to one of surprise. "A shortcut, Calliope? What kind of shortcut are you talking about?"

"Ayahuasca," Calliope said. "Nature's key to unlocking the truth."

"Is that some sort of New Age psychiatric mumbo jumbo?" Joseph asked.

"Not even close, Joseph. Ayahuasca is a powerful psychoactive drug from Nature's own medicine chest that natives in the Amazon jungle take to illuminate the essential truth of their beings, to bring forth a Holistic Remembering of Who They Really Are, and their Divine Purpose on Earth. But you have to be willing to look under the hood, so to speak."

"Wow, that sounds pretty intense, even if I don't understand what you're talking about. And all that from this ayahuasca stuff? I'm not gonna freak out or anything if I take it, am I? What can I really expect?"

"The discovery of nothing less than the universe, Joseph, and nothing more than your true self. And don't worry. I've trained to be a Shaman with a bunch of cool Indian cats from the Zaparo tribe in Peru, and have taken many excursions to the otherworldly realms of the mind myself. It's quite trippy. I myself have discovered that I was once an Inca Goddess with many thousands worshipping at my feet, and that it is my divine purpose to regain my throne. So, are you game?"

"Well, what have I got to lose, except my mind. Right, Candy?" Joseph said, looking over at the pretty nurse. She was staring at him with a deep look of worry etched on her face, but which on second thought, he decided was really probably one of admiration.

"Great. Let's go on upstairs to the Trip Room, as I call it, and we'll begin. You come too, Candy."

The Trip Room was thickly carpeted in jungle green plushness, with brown sofas and easy chairs butted up against neutral beige walls along the perimeter, a bucket beside each. The light blue ceiling, however, was like a gateway to the heavens, with planets and stars and galaxies depicted in amazing depth and detail. In the center of the room was a short table.

"Candy, you know the drill," Calliope said. "Joseph, I'd like you to sit with me on the floor by the table while I prepare the brew. After you partake, please feel free to sit or lie anywhere you like." She gathered some pieces of leaves and vine from several canisters in a cubby of the table, put them into a cup, and began macerating them. Candy brought over a kettle of boiling water, poured it into the cup, and mouthed a silent "No" at Joseph while ever so slightly shaking her head.

She really likes me, Joseph thought, deciding that she was really telling him how brave she thought he was for what he was about to do.

"Alright, Joseph, if you're ready, we can start," Calliope said. "Drink this down and make yourself comfortable. Your Voyage of Discovery is about to begin."

Joseph sipped the thick pungent brew, not tasting nearly as bad as it looked, then downed the whole cup. "What happens now?" he asked.

"Now you wait. At some point, you might feel a bit of stomach discomfort. That's what the buckets are for. Other than that, relax and enjoy your trip. Many people find that lying down and looking at the ceiling is a good way to start."

Joseph lay down, closed his eyes, and wondered what he had gotten himself into. Minutes ticked by, one as boring as the next. Then he remembered the ceiling, and all the interesting ceilings he had known. He opened his eyes on the universe, or at least a little corner of it. *Maybe if I count the stars,* he thought.

Somewhere around the one hundred and twenty-fourth star, they began to move, swirling slowly, drawing him in deeper. Soon he was passing too many stars to count, pulsing and winking at him from all sides, urging him onward. The center of the galaxy sped by, then countless more stars, and then out the other side, into a cold, empty void, sweet melancholy music surrounding him, entering him. He looked out upon countless new galaxies, each one both near and far at the same time, impossible to comprehend. Scale meant nothing. There was no scale, just space, emptiness to which each star clung to its galaxy, emptiness through which each galaxy spun its lonely trajectory through the universe, enough emptiness to fill his soul. If he had a soul. He thought of Cherry and began to cry.

"Buddha's Universal Lost & Found Department," a serene and knowing voice declared from somewhere. "How can I help you?"

Joseph searched the void for the source, sensing that something was approaching. In the vastness he could just make out a hazy form, coming nearer out of the blackness. It was the Buddha, floating before him now, orange robe billowing, though he felt no breeze, eyes like mirrors reflecting his own confused visage.

"I've lost my way," Joseph said, wiping his eyes.

"Have you tried looking into your soul?" questioned the Buddha.

"No sir. I don't even know the way to my soul."

"There's your first problem. Name please."

"Joseph Doubt."

"Let me check my inventory. OK, Lost Minds, Lost Souls, plenty of Lost Baggage – you'd be amazed how often baggage is left behind, only to be reclaimed at a later time. Ah, here it is. Lost Ways. And yes, Joseph Doubt, right there in the log. So it's gotta be in here somewhere. You may enter, Joseph, and continue your search. Believe in me and you will find your way. The universe will always be open to you."

Joseph looked at the Buddha, then into the emptiness of the universe. "That's a little on the vague side, isn't it?"

"Alright. Believe in me and the Doors of Enlightenment will open to you. How's that?"

"Well, I mean, I like the sound of these Doors of Enlightenment and all, but sorry, I still don't get it."

"Joseph, look at me and tell me what you see."

Joseph looked into the Buddha's mirrored eyes. "I see myself."

"Do you? And who are you?"

"I – I don't know," stuttered Joseph.

"You need to look deeper then, Joseph. Find your soul."

"But I just told you, I don't know where my soul is."

"Whoa, Buddha, Baby!" boomed another voice. "Give the boy some space, will you? Get it, Joseph? Give him some space."

Joseph looked around wildly for the source of the directionless voice and saw a large figure in a Lucha Libre mask suddenly appear, piecemeal like the Cheshire Cat, a red cape with a large green letter G in the center billowing out from his back. "Are you G-G-G?" he stuttered. "G-G-G."

"No, I'm his brother, Garth," the voice replied, before breaking into a wide grin. "Of course I'm God, Joseph. Now listen closely, we don't have much time. Your soul ..."

"But don't you command time?" Joseph interrupted. "Are you saying we're almost out of it?"

"No, that's not what I'm saying. Time is a difficult concept to understand. I don't think we should get into that right now. First you need to believe in me. Your soul ..."

"Are you saying that you can't explain time?" Joseph persisted. "You're the one that brought it up. I think you owe me an explanation at least. I'd really hate to run out of time. I've left a lot of my life unfinished back there. Cherry, for instance. She ..."

"Oh for God's sake, Joseph," God snapped, storm clouds raging in his eye holes. "Alright, so I can't explain time. What of it?" The storm clouds abated. "Now let's please turn our attention to where I can help. Your soul, Joseph. Believe me, it's in jeopardy. What you need to do ..."

"Is my soul almost out of time then?" Joseph interrupted again.

God shouted, "WILL YOU FORGET ABOUT FREAKIN' TIME? This isn't how it's supposed to go. I command, you obey, got it? Now ..."

A loud chuckling sound turned God's attention to the Buddha. "What are YOU laughing at?"

The Buddha began to sing, "Ti -i – i – ime, is on my side, yes it is."

God poked a long crooked finger into the Buddha's ample belly. "Get back to Earth, Saffron Breath. You don't belong here. The universe is not yours to give."

"But it is his to take," the Buddha replied coolly, with a hint of a smile. "Who's going to stop him? You? You're not even real."

"Why you ungrateful little poser," seethed God. "Worst mistake I ever made was creating you. Well, second worst actually, but I don't want to talk about that other one in front of the boy."

"Still can't admit that we each create ourselves, can you? The universe is in all of us, if we but open our minds to it."

"Open your mind to this, you pretentious creep," fumed God, delivering a powerful right to the Buddha's temple that sent him sprawling towards the Andromeda galaxy.

The Buddha shook his head and floated smoothly back. "Violence is never the answer," he said calmly. "You must look inside and seek peace."

"I AM Peace, you nitwit!" God bellowed. "I am Love! I am the Beginning and the End! I am All Things! I am Omnipotent!"

"Is it you that makes stars explode then, and asteroids and

meteors crash into planets and wipe out life? Or make civiliza-
tions annihilate themselves? Maybe a little less of your peace
and love would be appreciated."

"Are you challenging me? You're just an overgrown pimple
that's waiting to be popped. I've a good mind to drop a meteor
on you – see how you like it. But I'm here for Joseph. Joseph's
only chance to be saved is to believe in ME. I AM THE WAY!"

"That's it. Take it back," shouted the Buddha suddenly as
he leapt on God, showing surprising agility for his size.

"Never," God shouted, flipping the Buddha onto his back
and diving across his midsection.

The Buddha was pinned, but saw the hand of God reaching up towards his face. He lifted his head and bit into it hard.

"Ow!" yelled God. "No fair biting!" He turned the Buddha onto his stomach, sat on him and pulled one of his arms
behind his back, twisting hard and jerking it upwards. "How's
this for Nirvana, you Dharma Bum?" he taunted. "Say uncle."

"Ignore those wackos, Joseph," said an oily voice behind
him.

Joseph turned and saw another unusual figure approaching, this one red, with horns, a tail, a pitchfork, and ... Oh My
God! It was Pono! Eyes of fire stared at him.

"Have I got a deal for you, Joseph," Pono said, grinning.
"Give me your soul and I'll give you Cherry. Whadaya say?
All you have to do is put your faith in me. Your path is clear.
Cherry is waiting."

"Where, Pono? I don't see her. If I didn't believe you before,
why should I believe you now?"

"Because, Joseph, I have Cherry. You'll see her as soon as
you sign this little, uh, waiver," Pono said, producing a long
scroll and shoving the bottom towards Joseph. "It's completely
legitimate. Reviewed by COD, the Council of Deities. See,
that's their seal right there."

"I don't know, Pono. Sounds a little fishy to me. Why do you need such a long document if it's just a simple transaction?"

"Oh, you know lawyers. If you think they're bad on Earth, you should see them up here."

"Up here? Wait a minute," Joseph demurred, working it out. "There wouldn't be any lawyers up here. I'm pretty sure they'd all be down there. For sure not on any Council of Deities. You made a mistake, Pono. The Devil's always in the details. I'll take my chances without you."

"YOU'LL BE SORRY, JOSEPH!" Pono thundered, flames shooting from his eyes. "I'M NOT THROUGH WITH YOU!" Maniacal laughter poured from his mouth.

A strange sensation washed over Joseph at that moment, and God, the Buddha, and Pono began to swirl. Then so too did the galaxies, until they were all spinning faster, faster, like an enormous carousel with a maniac at the throttle, pushing it ever faster and laughing at the riders struggling to hang on. He felt sick, opened his mouth for air, and before he could stop it, the whole universe spiraled inside. The taste was horrible, unpalatable even, but he had no choice. He swallowed. His stomach had never felt so uncomfortable, God and the Buddha still wrestling, Pono laughing, the universe spinning. Suddenly he felt that it was all more than he could handle. He grabbed a bucket and vomited it all back up, God, the Buddha, Pono, the universe, everything. It all spewed out in a partially digested, foul-smelling stream of unrecognizable dross that seemed like it would never end.

He lay back, exhausted, feeling someone wiping his brow and his chin, and opened his eyes. Through the haze he saw a large horse face watching over him. "Is it over?" he heard himself say.

"If you have to ask, Joseph, then no," said Calliope. "You haven't found your way yet. You need to let go and believe."

24

The Carousel of Beliefs

Joseph closed his eyes again. A swirling circle of fantastic, fragmented colors greeted him and slowly coalesced into Cherry's kaleidoscopic image, transforming her face into a psychedelic Picasso masterpiece. Over and over her image changed, as if the kaleidoscope was being turned by a child with a new toy. Abruptly, Cherry's fragmented face stopped turning. The circle faded and vanished.

A road appeared. A lonely dirt road that cut through an endless meadow lying wide open to the sky. Joseph felt like a child as he stood there, lost in wonderment. A great gathering of worlds rustled in the tall grass; tiny, teeming worlds, so tiny they were like the sighing of the breeze that carried their dreams away. He strained to listen, amazed at the miracles he knew to be there, hidden, each one needing a lifetime to understand.

The road looked the same in both directions. He wondered which way he should go, or even IF he should go. A horse that he hadn't noticed before stopped grazing and picked up its head to look at him.

The horse walked over to him and nudged him hard in the side. "Hop on, Joseph. We need to ride," it said, urgency in its voice.

"What's the hurry," Joseph replied, stepping back before the horse could nudge him again. "I kind of like it right here. Why can't I stay?"

"You DO want to find out who you are and what your purpose is, don't you?"

"Yes, of course, but I have a feeling I can find that out right here. There's life and mystery all around me."

"Nonsense, Joseph. You won't find any answers just standing there. You need to kick up a little dust. Feel the wind in your face. Let's go." The horse stamped its foot impatiently.

"Hold your horses," Joseph countered, before noticing the horse's apparent distaste for that expression. "I mean, wait a minute. You're not saying that all we are is dust in the wind, are you? That's a bit trite, don't you think?"

"No, Joseph, get serious please. I'm saying that the answer, my friend, is blowing in the wind."

"OK then. That sounds much better. Which way do we go?"

"It doesn't matter," the horse replied. "Pick a direction if you like. It's your life. In my humble opinion, one road's the same as the next. It's what you do on that road that matters."

Joseph chose east and climbed on. Without a word, the horse galloped off. The dirt road soon turned treacherous in places, narrow and potholed as it wound past swamps and cliffs, giant boulders threatening to fall in their path. He hung on for dear life, feeling like he could be thrown to his demise at any moment. Then the road straightened out and improved, and he settled in to watch the countryside pass by. Sunset came and still they rode. Then sunrise, and sunset again. It began to rain. Many sunrises later, it snowed. He lost track of the seasons and the years. "Are we close yet?" he asked for the thousandth time.

"Almost, Joseph," came the reply each time. "Be patient."

"But we've ridden for years," Joseph complained, finally getting frustrated. "This road's going nowhere. And I haven't learned anything new."

"Let go of the reins, Joseph," the horse ordered. "Grab my neck tight. Trust me. You've got to feel the road or you won't get anywhere."

Joseph dropped the reins and threw himself on the horse's neck. Instantly he could feel its powerful muscles, straining and slacking, straining and slacking, as the horse's neck pumped like a piston. Its steaming breath was in his ears and threw foamy spittle into his face. Every hoof fall rippled through his body.

Another hill was approaching. Upward they rode, Joseph beginning to feel all tingly with the excitement and anticipation of a momentous discovery. He shouted for the horse to go faster. It responded with a powerful surge, legs churning and kicking up great clumps of earth, little creatures scurrying out of their way. At last they reached the summit. And came to a jarring stop that nearly sent him flying over the horse's neck.

"Well I can't say I was expecting THAT," the horse said, looking down into the valley. "But each person's ride is unique, they tell me. What do I know? I'm just a horse. Eat grass and die. And you humans think you got stuff to complain about."

Joseph looked down on a strange sight indeed. An enormous merry-go-round filled the plain below. Gaily painted wooden horses slowly bobbed up and down and circled around and around. Sprightly carnival music blared out from beneath the red, yellow, and blue striped canopy. His heart ached with memories he had never been allowed to experience, which were promptly shoved aside by a growing anger. The ride stopped and the passengers exited.

From the hilltop, Joseph watched the operator collecting tickets for the next ride. "A merry-go-round?" he asked, incredulous. "This is my destination? A merry-go-round? Is this some kind of a joke?"

"This explains a lot," the horse mused. "I've heard it's a long and difficult road for your sort. You must be an agnostic. They say you can lead an agnostic to the answer, but you can't make him believe. Is that right? At least horses have to drink water eventually."

Joseph shrugged, feeling helpless again. "I don't know," was all he had to offer.

"There you go. Man, you've got it bad. You see, that's not just any merry-go-round, Joseph. That's the 'Carousel of Beliefs.' I've never actually seen it before. Each ride is supposed to be a horse of a different color or stripe."

"What does it do?" Joseph asked, curiosity now beginning to take the reins.

"It's a training facility of sorts. Lets people hop on a belief of their own choosing and give it a ride, see if they like it. Or lets them freshen up their stale beliefs, put a fresh coat of paint on it. That's the only downside I've heard. The ride's usually crawling with politicians. Helps them figure out what they actually stand for. Now off you go. Good luck, Joseph. May the Horse be with you."

"Thank you, I guess," Joseph said, jumping to the ground. He walked down the hill. Several new passengers had boarded by the time he reached the carousel. He stood waiting for the operator to finish with her instructions. She turned around, and he was surprised to see Calliope Pennyworth standing before him.

"Welcome, Joseph," she said. "I was beginning to wonder if you'd come. I trust your trip is going well?"

"I really don't know, Calliope," he said. "I was hoping to find Cherry, but instead I get God, the Buddha, and the Devil wrestling over my soul. Does that mean anything to you?"

"Holy Smokes! God, the Buddha, and the Devil! Wrestling! Over your soul! I don't like the sound of that one bit! I believe it means you got here just in time, Joseph. But please don't panic. Hopefully that was just a bit of cosmic horseplay."

"I'm not panicking. Actually, I thought it was kind of funny. Buddha bit the hand of God and then God was twisting the Buddha's arm, and ..."

"Focus please, Joseph. And forget about this Cherry person. You need to find yourself first. The 'Carousel of Beliefs' will help you. We are what we believe, you know."

"But I don't seem to believe in ANYTHING, Calliope."

"Yes, I know, Joseph. That's how you found us. At the moment you're nothing but a bit of imagination, a chimera in the cosmos of the mind. A lost chord on the soundtrack of life, if you prefer."

"A metaphor for the ultimate search perhaps?"

"A warning for others, more like it. But don't worry, even an imagination needs sustenance. Something it can feel. Something it can believe. I'm quite certain there are rides here that can help you. Now, let me give you your instructions. Every horse here is saddled with a different belief, ranging from the ridiculously trivial to the truly grandiose. Understand so far?"

"They don't look so different to me, Calliope. They're all horses. They all go up and down and round and round. They're just different colors. But they're all stuck on a platform."

"No, no, Joseph, you don't understand. Believe me, they are all different. Plus I can vary the speed of the ride, or turn the strobe lights on for a spectacular effect. I can change the music, perhaps to something you find more appealing, say something inspirational like Brahms's Requiem, or the Hallelujah Chorus, by Handel. Personally, I prefer something with a sweet groove to it that carries you along for the whole ride. I'm talking soul music here, Joseph. You with me?"

"Calliope, the horses still don't go anywhere except around in circles, don't you see that? If that's what beliefs do, how's that supposed to help me?'

"You prefer squares, maybe? Look, Joseph, circles are the beginning and the end. They represent wholeness, the infinite, eternity, timelessness, the very Self. Ride the Carousel and you can't help but find yourself. There are no contrary horses here to confuse you. Each one is steadfast in the belief it carries. But see, the unusual thing about this ride is that not only do you have to believe in the horse, the horse has to believe in you, too."

A gleeful grunting sound from behind caused Joseph to turn around, just as a large hairy creature brushed past him and leapt onto the carousel. It made a beeline for an enormous, brown, shaggy horse which whinnied happily at its approach. Still grunting, the creature hugged the horse's neck before climbing into its saddle, grinning and thumping its chest.

"Bigfoot," Calliope said in response to Joseph's raised eyebrows. "He often comes here to ride the horse that believes in him. To reassure himself that he's real." She shrugged. "Makes him happy."

"So, what's up with that green and brown striped horse then?" Joseph asked. "It looks so sad. Why does everybody seem to be avoiding it?"

Calliope shook her head. "That horse, Joseph, carries the belief that money is the root of all evil. Needless to say, Francis doesn't get many riders."

"What about that pretty gold one next to it? The one that seems to be mocking it. It's so radiant I can barely look at it."

Calliope chuckled. "Very perceptive of you. I think you ARE beginning to understand. That horse doesn't believe in evil. It believes in greed. The mega-rich and the wannabees can't get enough of Ole Midas. They like nothing more than to ride him and laugh at all the other horses. Particularly poor Francis.

"Anyway, Joseph, quit stalling. YOUR ride awaits. It's time to find out who Joseph Doubt really is. So please, Joseph, pick a horse. It won't hurt you to give it a try. May I suggest starting in the middle somewhere, say that red one there with the blinders on. That spunky one carries the belief that this country is going to hell, that things aren't what they used to be, and that the poor and the immigrants are to blame. You might recognize them as Republicans where you come from.

"Or opposite that is this blue one here with the rose-colored glasses. That one's harnessed to the belief that this country has unlimited potential, that things are better than before and that any problem can be fixed rationally. Even things like war, inequality, and racism. Those you might know as Democrats."

"Well, I guess if I'm nothing," Joseph replied, "I've got nothing to lose." He jumped up on the red horse and felt the anger building in him almost immediately. Nothing definitive, just an anger he couldn't quite put his finger on. Strangely, though, he had a sudden yearning for Budweiser beer and country music, things he had never enjoyed before, as he tried desperately to remember the words to the Pledge of Allegiance. Looking around for an American flag, his eyes fell on the blue horse, and all the vague anger he felt before welled up and coalesced into a raging inferno of unbridled hate. He pleaded with himself to calm down, which may have been a mistake, because the horse responded by bucking so furiously that before one revolution had been completed, it threw him clear off the ride. He landed, bruised and dirty, on the ground next to Calliope.

He stood up and brushed himself off. "I thought you said the horses couldn't hurt me, Calliope."

Calliope scratched her head. "Wow. I've never seen such an extreme reaction. Did you do or say something to anger the horse?"

"I was just trying to understand it, that's all."

"Alright, I believe you. Perhaps we just started too strong. I think we'll skip the blue horse then. I'm sensing a similar reaction. So what say we start near the bottom and work our way up? Now that little purple horse there believes it can accurately know someone's character in ten seconds or less. A very helpful belief to acquire. Oh, you'll likely miss out on any nuanced interest people have to offer, but since 98% of people in this world are duller than a tractor pull at a country fair, you'll be thankful for the quick judgement. Go ahead, hop right on up there."

In three seconds flat, Joseph again found himself in the dirt.

"Double Wow!" Calliope exclaimed. "Tried, judged and sentenced in three seconds. I believe that's a new record. OK then," she said, still hopeful, "forget what I said about tractor pulls. Now, at the very beginning we have that brown pony there, who carries the belief that a roll of toilet paper should always be installed so that you pull the end down from the top, not up from the bottom. So how about ..."

"Wait, Calliope," Joseph interrupted, catching sight of a horse deep on the inside, a horse that was constantly changing its color and giving its rider all she could handle. But it was the rider that interested him. Though he could only get a partial glimpse of her when she went by, she looked familiar. Finally she turned his way, smiled the smile that he remembered, the one that he thought could melt the polar ice caps, and waved enthusiastically. He couldn't believe it. It was Cherry Givens.

"Joseph! Look at me!" Cherry called out, before turning serious and grabbing the saddle horn with both hands. The horse appeared to be bucking for all it was worth, but still she stayed on.

"I see somebody likes you, Joseph," Calliope said. "Who's the girl?"

"That's Cherry Givens," Joseph answered breathlessly. "Can I get on that horse with her?"

"Definitely not. One rider to a horse. It's a process, Joseph, and you can see that horse is really challenging her, and she it. You can't rush it and you can't interfere."

"What's the horse, Calliope? What belief does it carry? Tell me please, I've gotta know."

"Easy there. That's our most difficult horse. It's not easy to stay on her, but everyone wants to try. That's Loco, and she believes in love, Joseph. But if I were you, I wouldn't wait up. Cherry looks like she's in for one hell of a ride."

Joseph watched Cherry, the avowed denier of love, go round and round, one-handed and woo-hooing like a rodeo professional one second, and hanging on for dear life the next. He was dumbfounded. What did this mean? Was she changing right in front of him?

"Please, Calliope, I beg you. I need to talk with Cherry, and I need to ride that horse. I think I can do it. I don't have much time."

"Sorry, Joseph. There's nothing I can do. If you could be patient and wait ..."

Already her voice was getting faint. He tried to focus on Cherry, but her image was fading. She was becoming more of a phantom with each passing circuit, blurring into the background of circling horses. Strobe lights flicked on suddenly and pulsed madly over the horses as 'Bye, Bye, Love' blared from an echo chamber. For a second, Cherry's voice broke through. "Bye, Joseph. Believe in me," it may have said. He couldn't lose her. Not again. But it was too late, he was drifting, crossing over the center divide, hitting the bumpy patch at the edge of the road before flying out into the abyss. He was crashing.

He awoke, sweating and disoriented, mumbling "I believe in you," over and over, trying hard to open his eyes. Someone was holding his head in her lap. *Could it be*, he thought.

"I believe in you, too, Joseph, my brave boy," Nurse Candy answered. "I believe in you too." She raised his head and let him sip a little water, then brushed the damp hair off his forehead and gently kissed him.

Joseph opened his eyes with a start. His mouth felt like the Mojave Desert. A fat lizard was crawling around inside, pretending to be his tongue. "I have to go," he croaked, pushing himself up to a standing position. He swayed unsteadily in place for a moment, located the door, and staggered towards it. "Have to find her," he said.

Candy sighed. "I'm right here, Joseph. I believe in you."

25

How Can You Lie if You Don't Know the Truth?

Joseph was relieved to find Pono's business card still in his wallet, listing an address in Centerport. *If Pono is a businessman*, he wondered, *who's he giving the business to now? Ah, who cares?* he finally concluded. He was in a hurry, and Pono was his best lead to finding Cherry. At least that's what his hallucination had told him, though it had also told him that Pono was the Devil. To believe or not to believe, that is the question.

Joseph hurried downstairs and saw Calliope with her back to him, arms outstretched to a crowd of devotees who were on their knees before her, begging for ayahuasca with shouts of "More!" Maybe she HAD become the Goddess she believed she was.

He briefly wondered what she had done with his parents, then remembered something about them being sent to a doctor, a Dr. P., she had said. He tucked the thought away and hustled out the front door and down the steps, surprised to see that it was late afternoon or early evening. He had been lost in his head for much longer than he had realized. His whole life really, when he thought about it. *But maybe that means there's a lot in my head*, he thought, *and I just need to be a better navigator.*

BOOM! You hit the nail on the head, Joseph. Or the bulls-eye on the dart board of the brain. If there's anything the author of this little tale is certain of, it's that EVERYBODY needs to be a better navigator of their brains. But even with a neuroscientist, a mindfulness teacher, or a psychedelic drug trip sitter on board to guide the way, it's not easy. The odds of any of us ending up exhausted and scared in the brain's equivalent of Hoboken after dark is always high.

The neuroscientists like to say that there are 100 billion neurons in the human brain – more neurons, in fact, if not outright scientific conjecture, than stars in the milky way. And that these 100 billion neurons form 100 trillion synaptic connections, a number, ironically, that is too big for the brain to grasp, or all the neuroscientists in the milky way to map. It's no wonder that so many people put their brains on auto-pilot.

The mindfulness teachers like to say that our minds are filled with mindless chatter, and that this easily disorients us, and leads us down pathways that negatively affect our mental health, happiness, and even our physical well-being. But just where in the mind this mindless chatter originates has never been determined, a fact that can make it rather hard to avoid. Even to the mindfulness teachers, apparently, any map of the brain still has large parts marked, "Danger! There be dragons here!"

The psychedelic drug trip sitters just like to say, "Groovy, Man!" Perhaps to them, one path makes as much, or as little, sense as the next one.

Who's to say, then, whether Joseph was on the right path?

For better or worse, Joseph decided that he'd steer his hopes and dreams towards a horse named Loco, and the phantom it carried. So what if he had only seen them in a hallucination. Seeing is believing, if that's what you choose to believe.

Well, there was no choice now but to navigate his way back to the shelter and tell Rufus about his fantastic vision. Surely Rufus would see the boat that was floating now within his reach, and help him out.

He broke into a run. *Maybe things do happen for a reason,* he thought, before passing the smoldering remains of his parent's car. *Or maybe reasons are like burning cars and houses, just more fodder for some cosmic scorched earth campaign. Depends on one's perspective.* "Come on, Joseph, keep it real," he said to himself as he barged into the shelter. "You have a dream to chase now." He found Rufus in the kitchen and poured out his story.

Rufus listened patiently, grinned, and punched Joseph's shoulder. "That's some vision, yo," he said. "I was you I'd get all over that. But it's late. So you need to stay here tonight, OK? Eat, sleep, shower. You smell like the floors in here. Then I'll drive you to your car in the morning after breakfast. And Joseph? If you've got any more gum, hand it over now."

The next morning dawned clear for the first time in Joseph's recent memory. He tried to read the paper while waiting for Rufus to finish with breakfast, but he knew only so much bad news could mix with pancakes and coffee. The catastrophic earthquakes, tornadoes, cyclones, volcanic eruptions, wildfires, floods, and droughts he knew he could stomach because they were a big part of everyone's diet now, and the discovery and potential devastating impacts of new solar flares, asteroids, and black holes he could put off worrying about for another time. But to now see whales and dolphins inexplicably beaching themselves in mass suicides around the world was too much. They were the brains of the oceans. What did they know? Where was it all heading? How many more pancakes would it take to absorb this news?

A short while later, Joseph sat in Rufus's car and stared at the remains of his home. He hadn't expected the sight to hit him as hard as it did. He felt empty, numb, like a big piece of his life had gone up in smoke too. It hadn't been much of a life, he thought, certainly not enough to support a complete burn. So maybe there was enough left to start over.

He thought about his parents, and wondered where they might be and how they were doing. This had been everything to them. Their whole lives had been in there. All they had now was each other, and that flame had burned out long ago.

"You're a Phoenix, Joseph," said Rufus, putting a calming hand on his shoulder. "Rise from the ashes. Make a new life. Don't look back."

"If I don't look back, Rufus, how can I tell how far I'm getting?"

"It's not the miles, Joseph. It's the smiles. Go find Cherry."

Joseph got into his car and took a last look at the remains of his old life. Then he waved goodbye to Rufus and began the two-hour drive to Centerport, all the while trying to channel his inner Phoenix. All it got him was some concerned looks.

Once off the highway, he couldn't help noticing the decrepitude of the ravaged city. Everywhere he looked he saw ominous warnings. 'The Apocalypse Is Coming' was written in dripping blood red script on signs nailed to telephone poles, or painted in swirling graffiti on abandoned buildings and bridge abutments. Even the few people he saw looked more like zombies than the actors on a set of 'The Walking Dead.'

When he arrived at the address he was seeking and saw the sign on the small office building, it all made sense. 'Pono & Sons. Apocalypse Insurance for a Better Tomorrow.' As if on cue, he watched Pono's five chubby nephews, the ones he now apparently called his sons, exit the office and get into a van with stacks of signs and armfuls of spray paint cans. Just as he had before, Pono was laying the groundwork for a new endeavor. Only this time he was putting his faith in fear, not forgiveness. Joseph parked, took a deep breath, and went to meet his old roommate and tormentor.

"Well, well, well, if it isn't the Duke of Doubt," Pono announced, grinning mischievously from behind a large, polished desk. He recrossed his stubby legs that barely reached the desktop and blew out the smoke from a fat cigar. "Come on in, Joseph. Have a seat. I was beginning to have some doubts myself that you would ever get here."

"You were expecting me?" Joseph asked.

"Of course I was expecting you," Pono said. "I know people better than they know themselves. Haven't you figured that out yet?"

"You got my resume from Reaperson Arms, right? I'm not looking for a job, Pono. You do understand I could never work for you."

"You still don't know who I am, do you? Or who you are? Or the meaning of life and all that silly stuff. Well, God knows how desperate you must be to come to me for help. The question is, what's in it for me? You made it clear that you couldn't work for me. But I say Honest Joe is a liar. Because not only CAN you work for me, but you WILL work for me."

"I'm not a liar, Pono. And I won't work for you. I just came here for a little information. A little truthful information. Surely that's not too much to ask?"

"If you find any around here, let me know. I'll have it taken care of immediately."

"What?"

"Never mind. I'll help you, trust me, it'll be fun. I'm gonna help you by making you a liar. 'Cause if you really want something bad enough, you'll do what everybody else does. You'll lie. You're no different, you'll see when I prove it to you. There's nothing that you can't get with a good lie or two. How do you think your new President got to be where he is? He makes the rest of you liars look like a bunch of Dudley Do-Rights. I'm already thinking that when he comes my way, I'm going to make him Regional Director of our Southern District. With all those people who follow him, no questions asked, just think of the business he'll bring in."

"That's not me, Pono. I wouldn't be able to look myself in the mirror."

"Wake up and smell the outhouse, Joseph. Those are carnival mirrors you're looking at. Now I'm a pretty good liar, wouldn't you say? A great liar, to hear others tell it. Maybe even The Great Liar, if you know what I mean. You don't, do you? Of course not. Look, I'm gonna let you in on a little secret. Lies beat truth any day of the week, and it's not even close in the dark of night. This has been the way since the beginning of life. How do I know, you ask? Let me just say there's no one alive who's made more of a study of the subject than I. From the earliest life forms on up, mimicry, camouflage, sexual lures, and deception of all kinds have been the basis for survival. Anything for an advantage. Those that couldn't lie, or lied poorly, were given an E, for Extinction. Didn't pass the test. But all that was nothing, a simple warm up, minor league stuff. Just practice for the Big Leagues.

"The arrival of humans, and in particular that wonderful piece of manipulative matter called the human mind, allowed lying to expand into fertile new territories, like conquistadores in a new world. It took no prisoners. Hell, man, humans even lie to themselves! And more convincingly, I might add, than they lie to others. It's as much a part of their make-up as the carnival mirrors they see themselves in, or the language they speak. Language, now there was a game changer! The truth of it is, language was INVENTED to make it easier to lie.

"Unless I'm lying about that.

"Anyway, of course you remember the time I told that one about being the King of some small island somewhere, and being the Second Son of the Universe, the Prince of Penance, no less. Talk about a 180! But it sure got me what I wanted at the time. I think I nailed every girl on that campus."

"Seriously? That's all you were after?"

"No, but it was a great little demonstration, wouldn't you say? Like I said, anything for an advantage. If there's anything you need to understand, it's this. If humans didn't lie, they'd go extinct too. A lot quicker than they would otherwise, I mean. There it is Joseph, Lying, the Real Secret to Life."

"So according to you then, everything is just a big old con game?"

"Not at all. There's no con. There's only the lies people want to hear. You see, people everywhere desperately want to believe in a good fiction, 'cause reality sucks. That's why the first job of anybody who wants to get anywhere in life is to make up a good story and sell it. Look no further than the three P's - parents, priests, and politicians. They know better than most the kinds of stories that make people feel better after they buy them. You see, life is actually a business proposition. You got your buyers and you got your sellers, and then you got your losers standing in the aisles who can't decide what story to buy 'cause they're afraid they might choose wrong. I'm talking about you, Joseph. People like you are like dodo birds. Not only couldn't the dodos sell a story to convince predators that they were more valuable alive than dead, but they didn't even buy the story that the end was near for them. So they did nothing. No wonder they went extinct."

A second after he stopped talking a white projectile exploded through a window, sending glass shards flying and making Pono and Joseph jump. They watched a seagull flop around on the floor for a few seconds, bleeding profusely, and die.

Joseph stared at the seagull. "I don't think that bird bought your story, Pono. And I don't either. Dodos went extinct because they couldn't fly and escape the predators that were introduced to their island. Well, God knows who introduced YOU, but I think you're just a predator, preying on people's weaknesses and killing the good in them. I remember when you said that the secret to life was to use the tools that you were given, like your volcano birthmark. Now you say it's telling a good story. I don't know why anyone would believe you."

"Dodo," coughed Pono into his hand. "My stories may change but not the fact that I'm right. That first story was all for sex. Now it's all about business. Money and power. It doesn't matter. They're all interconnected anyway. There's only one story with a happy ending, and it's not the story of the dodo. But enough of this nonsense. What brings you here anyway? Wait. Don't tell me. You want to find Cherry, don't you?"

"You know where she is?" Joseph asked, his eyes widening. "I had a dream about her. She was calling to me."

Joseph was stunned to see Pono's haughty look suddenly disappear, to be replaced by a look he had never seen on the man before. Pono looked like a big kid, staring open-mouthed through a toy store window at the other kids buying things he knew he could never have. Joseph recognized that look. From when he was a young boy. He'd seen it a hundred times on himself in the window's reflection. And felt the hurt, envy, and anger. But he'd long since adjusted.

Pono recovered quickly, turning the open mouth into a nasty leer. "A dream, huh?" he spit. "Dreams are like turds, Joseph. Everybody has 'em but nobody wants to hear about em. And the more you try to pull them apart, to see what they're made of, the more you understand their origins in the stinking crap factory they come from. I've got some free advice for you. Don't look too close at dreams. Flush 'em and forget 'em. Cherry doesn't want to be with a dodo like you. Her soul's on my side. She doesn't believe in luh, in luh, in lu-uh-uuve."

An unexpected rumble of thunder caused Joseph to look out the broken window at a rapidly darkening sky. Another seagull crashed into the building and fell past his view to the sidewalk.

"You said you would help me, Pono," Joseph persisted. "That's not help."

"I know where she is, Joseph. Or I have a pretty good idea anyway. Like I said, I know people better than they know themselves. But why should I tell you?"

"Please, Pono. I'll do anything. I need to find her."

"Anything?" Pono stared at Joseph, his wheels turning. Finally he blew out a great cloud of cigar smoke, crushed the stub in an ashtray, put his feet on the floor, and spoke. "Alright then. You asked for it. Oh, this is gonna be fun. Tomorrow morning, ConspiraCon is coming to town. They've booked the Exhibition Hall in the Convention Center. There'll be a lot of people there, and I want you to sell them our insurance policies."

Joseph looked as confused as a heavy metal head banger at a poetry reading. "I don't know anything about selling insurance," he said. "And what's a ConspiraCon?"

"It's the annual circle jerk of conspiracy believers, whack jobs who believe there's a sinister organized force distorting the truth of everything."

Joseph burst out laughing. "You're a sinister organized force. Are they gonna have a Pono conspiracy booth there? I'd be glad to man that one."

"Not funny, Joseph. This is a business opportunity for

the right salesperson. A bit sketchy maybe, and one that I first ruled out for me or my sons, but now you're here. In any case, the managers of this year's event are trying to be more inclusive, so their theme this year is 'A Conspiracy For Everyone.' I'll call them and get an 'Apocalypse Is Coming' booth in there. The problem is that once they see you're looking to profit from it by selling insurance, they'll be extremely suspicious. Possibly even dangerous." Pono grinned. "Maybe that would be a good time to tell them about your dream."

"Are you're crazy? You want me to sell apocalypse insurance to dangerous skeptics? Why would they believe me? I don't think I could sell a raincoat to Noah."

"How badly do you want to find Cherry?" Pono slid a ConspiraCon convention brochure across the desk. "Who knows? Maybe you'll get lucky. Maybe these nuts that believe in conspiracies about vaccines, jet contrails, and the Reptilian Elite are crazy enough to buy apocalypse insurance from a dodo. And let's make this even more interesting. Let's say you need to sell at least ten policies."

"That's impossible, Pono," despaired Joseph. "Why are you doing this? Just to torture me? You might as well make it twenty!"

"Good idea. Twenty it is."

"What? Oh, I get it now. You don't know where she is, do you? That's why you're making this impossible."

"I'll tell you what. I'll sweeten the deal. Sell twenty or more policies and I'll take you to her personally, no matter where she is or how long it takes. But if you don't sell them, you're gonna have to come work for me. Either up here, like my, uh, sons, or else in my basement pad, which is actually a pretty hot place. I'll even give you a choice. Do we have a deal?"

"That's not a deal, Pono. I'd have to sell my soul to the devil to even have a chance of selling one policy."

"Just call me Mephistopheles, Joseph. Look, all you need to do is figure out a good enough lie. That's what makes this so fun. Admittedly it'll have to be a pretty big lie if you don't want to get strung up by these freaks."

Joseph looked up at the black, hard to read ceiling. It wasn't giving him anything to work with. "Alright, already," Joseph groaned. "What choice do I have? But explain to me how this apocalypse insurance is supposed to work. Correct me if I'm wrong, but if there is an apocalypse, doesn't that mean that everybody will die? So what's the point of insurance?"

"See, this is exactly why you're a dodo. You can't see the big picture. Who knows if there'll be an apocalypse, that's for God and Satan to battle out, but it's now your job to sell that story. If people believe the apocalypse is coming, it's human nature to believe that some people will be left alive, and of course they'll believe that includes them. Those are the ones you're gonna have to target."

"That's a big 'if,' Pono. Again, why would people believe me, especially since I don't know what the truth is myself? So how can I lie if I don't know the truth?"

"The truth is a dream for dodos, when are you going to understand that? It didn't save them, did it? The important thing is to get these people to believe that an apocalypse is coming, any way you can. Then it's a simple fact that they'll believe they'll live through it, because everyone believes they have a purpose."

"Do you believe that people have a purpose?" Joseph asked.

"I believe I have a purpose, Joseph. To get rich selling apocalypse insurance. Then I'll have even more influence over the weak souls of the world. You should believe that as well."

"That I'll be rich too?"

"You? Don't be an idiot. You're a dodo, not a phoenix. You should believe that I'll be rich."

"You're wrong, Pono. I'm a phoenix. I'm still rising up. I know because I know that I haven't found myself yet. And I still have dreams to chase. At least I still have hope that I'll like what I find. Unlike you."

"Joseph? You couldn't find yourself in a Hall of Mirrors."

"Maybe, maybe not. But I'm not looking to find myself in some crazy carnival attraction. I'm hoping to find myself on the Carousel of Beliefs with a horse named Loco. I believe that's where Cherry is."

26

A Conspiracy for Everyone

After a restless night at the Centerport shelter Rufus had told him about, Joseph headed out into the new morning. He couldn't believe he had agreed to do Pono's bidding, thereby lying just as Pono had said he would. And now if he was to ever see Cherry again, he'd have to lie his tail off to even have a chance of selling some stupid insurance designed to make crazy people feel better about the end of the world. Well, dammit, the end of the world for them would be a new beginning for him! But how the hell was he ever going to pull this off?

He parked in the Convention Center's garage and grabbed Pono's bulging briefcase filled with insurance policies, plus propaganda flyers, disaster photos, and terrible news headlines with which to decorate his booth, and headed for the entrance. The bumper stickers on the cars he walked past gave him a small sampling of the people he would need to lie to. 'Genetically Modified Foods Create Government Modified People,' 'When They Come For Your Guns, Show Them Your Rocket Launcher,' 'Beware the Vast Right Wing Conspiracy' parked alongside 'Stand Up to the Vast Left Wing Conspiracy,' and 'I Brake For Bigfoot.' It promised to be an interesting convention at least, if he survived.

Wait a minute, he thought. *Talk about a Carousel of Beliefs. This couldn't be where Cherry is, could it?*

No, he decided. *This place is for one trick ponies, conspiracy believers only, not horses like Loco and searchers of the truth like Cherry and me. And Pono wouldn't make it that easy. But I'll certainly keep my eyes and ears open. 'You can't find if you don't seek,' my mother always said, even if her own search field was limited to herself, and those views that fit neatly into her belief system. But isn't that true for most people? For some reason, it's apparently not easy to look outside one's established beliefs. Why is that? Could our minds be controlled by some outside forces? The government? Aliens? What don't our minds want us to see?* He watched a couple walking towards the door with a large poster of a cat shooting mind waves out of its eyes, then laughed. *Now who's the conspiracy nut?*

'A Conspiracy For Everyone' read the large banner outside the entrance, above a smaller one reading, 'There's Something Going On.' Joseph walked in. Small groups of people were milling about, talking excitedly and punctuating the air with expressive hand motions. He approached a woman with an ID badge that identified her as Laureen, Floor Manager, and waited until she was alone before introducing himself.

"Welcome, Joseph," Laureen said warmly. She checked through the pages on her clipboard and found what she was looking for. "Here you are. A first timer, I see, with a brand-new conspiracy, 'The Apocalypse Is Coming.' Great to have you. Let's all hope the apocalypse doesn't come before the convention's over at least," she said, winking conspiratorially.

"I've placed you in the rookie section," Laureen continued. "I hope you don't mind. I've put you next to Lenny and Liz, the couple that came in right before you. They have this very interesting cat conspiracy that says that cats transmit parasites that hijack their owner's minds, so that they can then control all humans and take over the world. They say to just look at how cats take, take, take, take and never give, and how they don't do anything but eat and sleep, and yet they still make people want them. And you gotta admit, that unblinking staring thing they do is downright creepy.

"And they've got an old crazy neighbor lady with a couple dozen cats who still keeps taking in new ones. The lady used to be normal, Lenny said, but now the cats have complete control of her. He said it's places like this that are the cat's control centers, and they're springing up everywhere. He said they only managed to figure this all out one day and break their cat's hold on them when the little cutie got so blissed out on catnip that it slipped and told them about their plan. On the spot they swore off drinking and drugs and made it their life's mission to warn the world.

"So, this 'Apocalypse Is Coming' conspiracy of yours sounds interesting too. Have you got evidence like that?"

"No, sorry," Joseph answered.

"None at all?" Laureen asked, eyes narrowing.

Joseph could almost feel his perspiration ducts snap open. He gulped. "Well, uh, no." He shifted his feet and stared at the floor, just making out Laureen raising her hand in a signal of some kind. *This can't be good*, he thought. *Is my dream over already? What would Pono do? Think, Joseph, think! Of course! He'd lie.*

He straightened up and looked Laureen dead in the eye. "It's the cats," he said. "The cats are planning the apocalypse. Yeah, that's it. They do have nine lives you know. So what's an apocalypse to them?" Laureen waved her hand again and he saw two large men stop and back up.

"I see," Laureen said, eyes widening slightly. She put an

asterisk by his name though. "I'll let you in, but I'm sure Bannon and his crew are gonna want to talk to you before long. We really don't want to have any more FLEAS in here. They were grandfathered in, but we're kind of sticklers for evidence now. We have standards. Don't want to be seen as a bunch of nuts, you know."

"Sure, I understand," Joseph said. "No worries," he lied. That one slipped out as easy a fart at a bean supper. *Stop with the lying*, he scolded himself. *You're playing right into Pono's hands. Just be yourself.* "Who are the fleas, if you don't mind my asking?"

"Sorry, I have to take care of this line behind you, Joseph. Why don't you go on in and mingle, and talk to some of the wisest people you'll ever meet. Except for the FLEAS, but you'll see them inside too. Doors open to the public at ten o'clock."

Joseph walked over to a refreshment table he spied in the corner and picked out a three-sided pastry labelled a 'Bermuda Triangle.' He wolfed that down and grabbed a cup of coffee guaranteed to be made with fluoride free water. *So far, so good*, he thought. *Now let's go see who I'm dealing with.*

Heading for the main hall entrance, he took note of the prominent sign stating that all cell phones and other electronic devices be left outside, then let the two large men check him over to make sure he complied. The first thing he noticed upon entering the hall were the strange cone shaped devices in the upper corners, with some kind of flexible wands projecting out of them that were dancing spasmodically. One of the guards had told him that these were new to the market Acme X-13 thought wave disrupters, designed to prevent any outside attempts to mentally infiltrate the convention, and to prevent any inside spies from telepathically radiating information to outside agents. Whatever. He did notice, though, that he was feeling a bit light-headed. He closed his eyes for a minute to regain his composure.

In fact, at that very moment, everyone in the hall was suddenly feeling very light-headed, and mentally accusing everyone else of being a spy and employing secret government thought-mining tactics on them. Each of them, however, had been well versed in close-quarter mind infiltration measures for just this possibility, and knew exactly what to do. It was well known by most convention goers that the silent repetition of the children's nursery rhyme that began 'Hey Diddle Diddle' for one minute while sticking one's fingers in one's ears, would scramble any such attempt.

Joseph opened his eyes to the strange spectacle of people with plugged ears and moving lips. He chuckled to himself as they resumed their activities as if nothing unusual had happened.

Right next to where he had stopped, a man and woman talked quietly to each other. Their darting eyes and hushed, nervous voices added to their general appearance of teachers who suddenly realized that their students knew more than them. Joseph watched as others gave the couple a wide berth, all the while grinning mischievously and scratching themselves in an exaggerated fashion. He stepped up and introduced himself.

"Excuse me," he began, "I'm Joseph. Sorry for the interruption, but what's bugging these people, if you don't mind my asking?"

The couple turned to look at him. "Is that your idea of a joke?" the man humpfed.

"Pardon?" Joseph replied. "I don't know what you mean. This is my first time here."

"Oh. In that case, sorry," the woman said. "Please excuse my partner, we're just a little sensitive. I'm Carol, and this is

Maurice. You see, SOME people around here think our distinguished organization is a bit old-fashioned. It's quite sad, since it's been around for such a long time, shining light into the darkness and conceit. We're ..."

"Hey, FLEAS," a well-dressed man shouted from a passing group. "I just got a call from King Ferdinand and Queen Isabella. You're wanted back in the fifteenth century." The group laughed hysterically and patted the man on the back.

"Why are they making fun of you?" Joseph asked. "What's this organization that you're talking about?"

"We're representing the Flat Earth Society," Maurice said. "The ignorant Globalists gave us the acronym FLEAS. Actually, we call ourselves Flatists."

Joseph couldn't help himself. "Flat Earth Society?" he snorted. "As in you believe the earth is flat?"

Carol stared at him hard. "You're not going to mock us too, are you?"

"I don't mean to, but surely you can't refute hundreds of years of science and exploration."

"All faked," Maurice stated, arms crossed.

"Forget about science then. What about simple observation? You've seen pictures of the earth from space right, showing the earth is a globe?"

"Fakes," said Maurice. "If people lived on the other side of a globe, they'd be upside down and fall off."

"You never heard of gravity?"

"Gravity is a lie," Carol said. "If gravity was a force pushing us in a downward direction, then it would have to keep pushing in that direction, which means it would push anyone on the bottom of a globe right off. And if you say the force somehow pushes in the opposite direction down there, then that means the two forces would be pushing towards each other, squishing any globe and making it flat. Therefore, gravity is a lie. Case closed. So, what about you? Why are YOU here?"

"I'll be manning 'The Apocalypse Is Coming' booth, when I get there."

Maurice threw his arms up. "The Apocalypse Is Coming! Talk about hoaxes! How'd they ever let you in here? People have been predicting the end of the world since, like, forever. And where are those people now?"

"I don't know," Joseph said, walking away. "Maybe they fell off the edge of the world." *This isn't good*, he thought. *Even these idiots are suspicious of me.* He moved deeper into the hall. *Don't quit, Joseph. Keep trying. Remember the dream.* He picked out two somewhat normal looking people from the packed crowd and settled in next to them, waiting for an opportunity to introduce himself.

The tall, scruffy, bearded guy with the small eyes and the lumberjack shirt gave him a quick appraisal, and continued talking. "Look at his tiny hands. His orange skin. The strange hand motions. The weird hair. That's a dead giveaway, Pete. The President's a Reptile. Probably head of the Reptilian Elite."

"Hey, I agree with you, Boyd," said the pink, fleshy man with the large owly glasses and a bow tie. "These lizard people can shape shift all they want, but there's some things they'll never get right."

"Yeah, we should all be worried. Remember the last great Reptilian leader that tried to go it alone? 1930's Germany? The feet, the hair, the skin, the weird hand motions. He almost succeeded. But he ended up having to kill himself. Or did he? His body was never found you know. Makes you think."

"Well, either way, Boyd, the damn reptiles are getting more and more control of us. How do we hope to fight that?"

"Yeah, I don't know," Boyd said, shaking his head.

"Well, I've been giving this a lot of thought. What bothers a reptile most? Cold. They're cold blooded. They need heat. That's why they've been warming the earth lately. They want it hotter. We need to figure out how to make it colder. That'll drive them out."

"That might work for earth reptiles, Pete. But these are alien reptiles. We don't know what they want. Except for power, of course. And control. Global warming is a hoax. A conspiracy by scientists."

"It's a conspiracy alright," Pete said. "A conspiracy by the government. The Reptilian Elite. I'm sure even these alien reptiles hate the cold. Why else would they keep blocking environmental progress, and making environmentalists the bad guys? They're the real heroes. We need more environmentalists to win this battle."

"You're crazy. Those greenies are putting us out of work. Making us weak and ready for the alien takeover."

"Yeah, sure. Next you'll be saying that crop circles are a hoax too. A conspiracy by farmers."

"Don't get me started on crop circles, Pete. In the first place, they're not only circles you know. That's the elite reptile media conspiracy dumbing it down to make us sound stupid. Crop circles are part of a highly complicated geometric alien messaging system using pictographic coding beyond the possibility of earthly understanding. Except for the farmers, they know, but they've all been corrupted. Why do you think they're so eager to genetically modify their crops? What better way to infect us and make us more pliable. That's why I eat only yogurt now."

"So now scientists are too dumb to understand some pictures in a field? Oh, I forgot. According to you, scientists, environmentalists, and farmers are the enemies. Oh, and the media." Pete turned to Joseph. "Can you believe this guy?"

"Sorry, guys," Joseph said. "You lost me when you started talking about shape-shifting alien reptiles controlling the world. I was trying to imagine what they look like. Do they actually have scales? And forked tongues?"

"Well, nobody's ever actually seen them in their reptile form," Boyd said. "Except for L. Ron Hubbard of course. Wait a minute. Are you mocking us? Who are you? I've never seen you before. What are you doing here?"

"No, no. Really, I'm not. It's all very fascinating. My name's Joseph Doubt. It's my first time here. I'm on my way to set up my 'Apocalypse Is Coming' booth."

"Doubt, huh? You hear this guy, Boyd? If that doesn't sound suspicious. You must be the one putting up all those 'The Apocalypse Is Coming!' signs I've seen. Since when does a conspiracy need to advertise? That's a sure sign of a lie. What are you really up to?"

"Nothing. Guys, really. I swear." Their rising voices made him swivel his head nervously. Sure enough, people were tuning in to the commotion.

Boyd pointed at Joseph. "Hey, Pete. Look at the size of his hands. And his skin color's a little off, don't you think?"

"OK then," Joseph said, more annoyed than angry. "I'm just gonna go over there and set up now. Nice talking with you. Don't let the reptiles bite."

27

Charity Without Love is Like Hope Without Insurance

Joseph kept his eyes straight ahead, trying hard not to notice all the other eyes he sensed following him as he made his way to the rookie section in a nook at the far end of the hall. He couldn't help noticing that conversations stopped when he passed, however. It was beginning to seem like his task was just the pipedream it had probably always been. It had been born in a hallucination and now it would die in a place that made hallucinations seem like the stuff of Kindergarten paste eaters. How could he fight what he couldn't understand? How could he sell something as ludicrous as apocalypse insurance to people who were already suspicious of him? How could he find his way back to Cherry when he'd never make it out of the land of the Abominable Snowman, and all the other abominables? God, he hated it when Pono was right.

He found his booth easily enough by the 'Apocalypse Is Coming' placard on his front table. Nodding to Lenny and Liz, the crazy cat couple to his left, he mechanically began pulling out the contents of his briefcase and setting up. The woodsy looking man with the Sasquatch booth to his right, however, was giving him the stink eye, and it was getting harder to ignore it. His own mood wasn't getting any better, so he decided he would just tell him to stuff it if the guy gave him any crap. He was almost to the point of not caring anymore.

"I can't believe they demoted me to the loser's section," the woodsy man said, loudly, eyes daring Joseph to challenge him. "Ya touch up one little teensy piece of evidence and they kick ya back to the freaks. Do they really think those old photos of Champ and Nessie are real? That's all they got! I've got footprints! Besides the photo. You can't argue with that!"

"Hey, Buddy," Joseph snapped, in no mood for this tangential attack. "Keep your big mouth to yourself!"

"It's Big Foot, loser," the man snapped back. "Don't ya know anything? Big Mouth. No wonder you're here with the other freaks."

"I know this much. Bigfoot's nothing but a Big Joke. He apparently can't even cut it with the other nuts in this place."

"What'd you say? You calling everyone in here nuts? Wait till Bannon hears this! One thing we don't put up with is mockers or spies!"

"That's two things, Champ," said Joseph. "But look. I'm sorry. I went too far. Can we at least agree that Bigfoot's not one of the Reptilian Elite then? 'Cause of the size of his hands and feet, I mean," he added, after seeing the man's horrified look.

"Course he's not one of the freakin' Reptiles! He may be a lot of things, but he'd never be a traitor to his planet. Why would you even say that? What proof do YOU have of this apocalypse that you're advertising?"

"Well, for one thing," Joseph said, thinking of something he figured everyone would get upset about, "whales and dolphins around the world are killing themselves. Swimming right up onto the shore and dying."

The woodsy man smirked. "Shows how much YOU know. The government's been testing mind control methods on mammals for years. The fact that they can now make whales and dolphins kill themselves should make any sane person worry that they're close to trying it on humans."

"You guys are both wrong," interjected Lenny. "It's the cats. They're controlling the oceans now. They're getting stronger and more cunning than we thought. I hear that kids are even self-identifying as cats now, and demanding that schools put out litter boxes for them! The cats are coming for us, man!"

"Well, I'm just saying it ain't no stinkin' apocalypse," the woodsy man said. "The world's not coming to an end. Not before I see a Sasquatch. I mean, another one. Another Sasquatch. Hey, Cat Man? Does that brochure I see say that this guy's selling apocalypse insurance?"

"Yes," Lenny said, squinting at Joseph's table. "Yes, I believe it does."

"That's it," the woodsy man barked. "This imposter's gotta be exposed. I'm gonna go get Bannon."

Joseph hung his head and stared at the piles of lies on his table. *What's the use? Could I have failed any more spectacularly? Pono knew I'd never sell any insurance policies in this place. I wonder what this guy Bannon's gonna do to me? Ah, screw him. From now on I'm gonna just say what I think. I don't care anymore.*

He watched a short man approaching, dark eyes fixed on him. The man's hard eyes, goatee, thinning black hair pulled back in a short ponytail, and impassive face gave him a look that seemed to be saying, 'I know what you're thinking.' His black polyester suit with an orange tie and yellow sneakers, however, told Joseph that a career government drone from the Office of Duplication and Redundancy could easily out-think this bozo. He was flanked by the two large bouncers he had encountered before, and trailed by an ever growing contingent of grumbling angry-faced people who clearly smelled blood. Joseph swallowed hard and waited.

The short man stopped directly in front of Joseph's table, picked up a pamphlet and an insurance policy, and said nothing. He leafed through them casually, then put them down and looked at Joseph. "Are you Joseph Doubt?" he asked.

"Yes," Joseph replied.

"My name is Bartholomew Bannon," the man announced, "and I'm in charge of 'FACT', the Fearless Association of Conspiracy Theorists. Already this first morning I've had a number of complaints about you, and I can see why. It looks like you're brazenly stoking the fears of an imminent apocalypse in order to sell insurance. That's like if the cat folks over here were to market some fake medical marvel that claimed to resist a cat's mental incursions. Joseph turned to see Lenny and Liz look at each other, then slyly slide a stack of flyers off their table.

"Or if Jasper over here ...."

"Jethro."

"Or if Jethro here were to advertise Bigfoot tours for a price." Joseph watched Jethro pick up a clipboard and place it atop a pile of papers. "You see what I'm saying? We cannot allow the integrity of our experts to be compromised. A conspiracy is only as strong as its evidence. I'll not have it said on MY watch that conspiracy believers jump to conclusions BEFORE considering the evidence. You say an apocalypse is coming soon. Why should we believe you?"

Joseph scanned the angry crowd pressing closer, then looked back at Bannon. "You shouldn't," was all he said.

"Now don't even try to play me ..." Bannon began, then

stopped. His impassive face took on a puzzled look. "What? Did you say we shouldn't believe you?"

"No. Why should you?"

"Be-cause your sign and your pamphlets say the apocalypse is coming?" Bannon answered, a bit defensively now. "And because you're selling insurance to profit from it? Is the apocalypse near or not?"

"How do I know? Do I look like Nostradumbass?"

A loud murmur spread through the crowd at the intentional bastardizing of the revered name.

Bannon motioned for the people to settle down. "Then we shouldn't buy your insurance either? Is that what you're saying?"

"I wouldn't."

"OK," Bannon said, more to himself. "What the hell's wrong with this picture? Are you trying to con us?"

"No, no, Mr. Bannon. Certainly not." Joseph paused, then dropped his payload. "You're doing that to yourselves."

Bannon clenched his fists and turned beet red. "Why you impudent little ..." Then he remembered something and looked at his watch. "Bam. Snake. It's a half hour before the doors open. Please escort this twerp to the back room. We need to ask him a few more questions."

"Wait a minute," Joseph said. "Maybe your congregation would like to hear what I have to say. Or are you afraid of me?"

"Well. Don't you have some nerve. But if we're not afraid of the Shadow Government, aliens, or the secret Pokemon police, why would we be afraid of what a little nobody has to say? Speak your piece."

"In the first place, Mr. Bannon, everybody," Joseph began, "it's true I don't belong here. I don't believe these things you all believe. That's not a crime, is it? And as for the apocalypse? I really don't know if it's coming soon, but it certainly appears that way to me. What I DO think, however ..., oh, you're really not gonna like this, is that there's a conspiracy behind your conspiracy theories. Why do you think your conspiracies never get very far with the general public? Why are they laughing at you behind your backs?"

"Because the government suppresses the evidence we need to show people the whole truth, of course. Any fool knows that."

"What if there is evidence that is far worse than you think? What if the government secretly leaks fake evidence from time to time so that people like you pounce on it and create a conspiracy theory? What if the truth is that the government needs people like you to make them look sane and believable? What if you all are the VICTIMS of a conspiracy instead of the exposers? And now that they know who you are, they can marginalize you, track you, and control you for their purposes. Maybe you people need to wake up and break up, then shine a stronger light back on them. Show them that you're smarter than you look."

Joseph knew he had either hit gold or he was in deep doo doo. There's nothing conspiracy people loved to do more than talk, and this crowd had just fallen as silent as Bigfoot with laryngitis.

"Oh, my, God!" blurted out Bannon then. "He's right! Look at us! What are we doing? We're having a convention! How conventional can we get? We need to go underground, build a shadow network of resistance warriors, penetrate the government propaganda machine for the truth, and get our messages out without fear of mockery by the corrupt media. THE TRUTH MUST BE HEARD!" he thundered, as the cheering rose to a crescendo.

Bannon looked at his watch again. He quickly ordered that Joseph's booth be switched with the FLEAS, who had long held a prominent position in the main hall, and further told the FLEAS that he would scratch them from the convention completely if they said one word about it. On the sly he whispered to Joseph that he was sure to be a shoo-in for that year's Most Valuable Conspiracy award, and would get to take home the coveted Golden Loon. Then he proudly bought the first insurance policy from Joseph, which triggered such a rush among the convention exhibitors that Joseph sold out even before the doors opened to the public.

Sixty-two policies! Joseph was back in business. The fates had conspired to make a mockery of the truth yet again. The story with the happy ending was still alive! At the first break he would blow this convention and wave the signed policies in Pono's face. He felt a bit like Dorothy about to bring the witch's broom stick back to the Wizard. Now Pono HAD to bring him to find Cherry. He just needed the Wizard to be a Wizard, and not the con man he had always been.

At the first break, Joseph raced out of the Convention Center with his prize secured, and sped back to Pono's office. He waded past the dead seagulls littering the sidewalk and burst in. A scantily clad young woman jumped off Pono's lap and hastily threw her clothes back on, then grabbed the dollar bills scattered across the desk.

"What the hell are you doing here?" Pono barked. "You're supposed to be selling my insurance. Or trying to."

Joseph walked over to the desk, nodded to the woman, and dropped the stack of signed policies in front of him. "Take me to Cherry like you promised," he said.

"I'm a little busy with Charity at the moment, Joseph. Why don't you go on home. You weren't supposed to sell any of these things. I lied. I really don't know where Cherry is."

Everything seemed to freeze up inside Joseph. He wanted to scream at Pono and dive across his desk and strangle him, but he couldn't speak, couldn't move.

"Aww, isn't that sweet. This man's in love," Charity said. "You've got to help him, Pono."

"Don't give me luh, luh ... Don't give me ... that, Charity," Pono said, grimacing. "Gag me with a pitchfork."

"Seriously, Pono?" Charity said. "You don't believe in love? What am I even doing here?"

"We're having fun, baby. What else?"

"Have fun with yourself, baby," Charity snapped. "Don't call me no more, got it? You're really not fun." She slammed the door on her way out.

"Man, what a buzz kill you are, Joseph," griped Pono. "Charity may begin at home, but man, can she finish at the office. I really don't know where she is you know."

Joseph came alive again. "Sixty-two policies, Pono. You promised."

"And you believed me. You really are a dodo. But before you wet yourself, I've got nothing better to do now. So, let me think, if I were Cherry, where would I be? Ahh, I know. Based on her last trajectory, she's either in a convent, or she's searching for herself at Dr. Platonic's Love Spa & Celibacy Clinic. But I gotta warn you, Joseph. Your dream's dead. She doesn't want you. So if I'm gonna go to all this trouble to take you to her, once she tells you to get lost, you're mine. I've got a little job for you, working in my basement pad. Making cold calls on hot deals. OK?"

"Sure, Pono. Whatever," Joseph answered. "Let's go."

"Alright. So it's your choice. Where do you want to try first?"

"Let's try Dr. Platonic's. I like the sound of that."

Pono grinned. "Good choice, Joseph. I like the sound of that too. Sounds like the kind of place I can bring a little chaos to. Should be fun."

28

An Apocalypse of Love

Joseph and Pono stepped outside amongst the dead and dying seagulls. To their right a posse of cats meowed menacingly at a man walking a terrified dog. Back the other way, two women were screaming and swinging their purses wildly, but were having little luck keeping another pack of cats off them. A fire truck roared up, sirens wailing, and began hosing the cats away. Three more fire trucks screamed past. Joseph and Pono scrambled inside Joseph's car, set the GPS, and sped away.

"What the heck's happening to this world, Pono?" Joseph asked. "It almost seems like ever since you started selling apocalypse insurance things have been getting even crazier than before."

"Yeah, funny thing, that," Pono said, smiling to himself. "But it's not any crazier than chasing this dream of yours."

"It's not just a dream, Pono. I can feel it. Cherry loves me. I hope."

"That's something else you're feeling, Joseph. It's called loneliness. Just like all those other lonely losers at Dr. Platonic's.

Looking to fill their hearts with loo, with luh, with luh-uve,"
he mocked. "Cherry's an atheist. And she doesn't believe in ...
that. You're searching in vain. Her soul's already locked away,
and I've got the key."

There was a long pause. Suddenly Pono slammed the
dash with his fist. "Man, you people have the best fun factories imaginable sitting right there in your heads, and hardly
anyone ever goes there because of your phony morals. You
oughta shut the damn things down if you're not gonna use
them properly. Stamp a 'Brain Out of Order' sign on your
foreheads. I think there should be mandatory lobotomies for
anyone caught saying 'I'm In L-L-L-L-Luuve'. What a waste
of millions of years of evolution. You people deserve what's
coming."

Joseph listened for the thunder that he noticed always
seemed to come when Pono mentioned love. A weird coincidence certainly, how else to explain it, but this time it didn't
come. Instead he saw Pono staring out the window with a puzzled look on his face. "What do you mean by that?" he asked.
"You talk like you know something the rest of us don't."

Pono smirked. "You're getting warmer."

"What gives, Pono? You've been acting awfully devilish
lately."

"And we have a winner. Sorry, Joseph. Can't help myself.
I guess you could say it's in my nature. But hey, the GPS says
we're getting close now. You notice how disgustingly beautiful
the countryside's been getting? Looks like this place could
use a few shuttered factories. Or burned-over forests at least."

They drove on, one marveling at the lushness of the landscape, the other bemoaning it. No signs of crazed animals,
threatening skies, or war planes streaking overhead. Only
babbling brook-laced meadows in a peaceable kingdom, with

bunnies, deer, fox, and bears posing together under a clear blue sky.

They turned left at a heart-shaped sign proclaiming 'Dr. Platonic's Love Spa & Celibacy Clinic, For Pure Hearts Only,' and followed the narrow winding lane until they were confronted by a gatehouse with a bar across the road. Two armed guards outside and one inside stiffened as the car rolled to a stop, their rifle stocks nicely matching their blush-red uniforms.

"Registration ticket, please," the unsmiling gatehouse guard intoned.

"I-I don't have a ticket," panicked Joseph. "But please, sir, I need to get in there."

"Sorry, sir. Rules are rules. No one gets to see the Doctor without a pass. That's how she knows that your heart is pure. Now please turn around and go back the way you came."

Joseph was crestfallen. His hands slipped off the wheel and his head dropped to his chest, like the weight of it had suddenly become too much.

Pono stepped out of the car and nodded to the outside guards. They immediately raised their rifles and levelled them, at the ready.

"Get back in the car, sir," one guard sneered. "We have orders to shoot anyone who gives us any trouble."

Pono smiled. He walked around the car and stopped, facing them. "Your obedience is commendable, gentlemen," he said. "Feel free to shoot me." He stood there and examined his fingernails.

The guards looked at each other, eyebrows raised, and turned back. "Look, will you please get back in the car?" the second guard begged. "Without a pass we have no way of telling if your heart is pure."

Pono's smile broadened. "My good man," he said, "show

me someone you say has a pure heart, and I'll show you someone with a heart yearning for a little romp with the devil. No
one's heart is THAT pure."

"You haven't met Dr. Platonic," the first guard sighed.
"She's heavenly." The second guard nodded dreamily.

The smile faded from Pono's face for a moment, then came
back. "So, this Dr. Platonic is a woman," he said. "Of course.
Who's also heavenly and has a pure heart. Actually, I believe
I have met her, though it's been a while. But we keep in touch
in other ways." Thunder rumbled in the distance, causing the
guards to look up into a clear blue sky.

"Anyway," Pono continued, "it's not the heart that con-
cerns me. It's the soul. More specifically, your souls. I know
you don't really want to shoot anybody. Your souls are in tur-
moil now, so just think what they'd be like if you shot me.
Believe me, I know about souls. That's something I can help
you with. Here, take my card," he said, passing out cards he
pulled from his shirt pocket. They say, 'Pono's Soul Repair.'
That's me, Pono Nui. Souls trump hearts any day of the week.
And I offer discounts on Sundays. So stop by sometime for a
free soul evaluation." The next words he whispered. "And I've
got some pretty hot women there to show you and your souls
the devil of a time." He winked, then resumed in his smooth
baritone. "Now lower your guns please. I'm just going to chat
with your friend over here."

Pono approached the gatehouse and stepped in front of
Joseph, facing the guard. Noting his heart-shaped name tag,
he said, "Curtis, my man, "What seems to be the problem?
Can't you see we have an emergency here? The answer to this
poor man's dream may be inside. Surely you're not gonna let
a little piece of paper get in the way of that, are you?"

"Please step back, sir," said the guard, unmoved. "He can
look for love in a bar like everyone else."

"Look," Pono said, leaning in and whispering. "I didn't want to have to tell you this, but I happen to know that they're dropping the celibacy rule, today only, so there's going to be a lot of horny women in there. Ordinarily I hate to share, but why don't you come with us and let the other guards take over here? Kind of our little secret. Those women will go nuts for a good-looking guy in uniform like you."

A short while later, Joseph and Pono let Curtis off in front of the women's dormitory, and continued on to the outdoor amphitheater, where Curtis had said Dr. Platonic would be speaking. They parked and followed the signs down the primrose-lined gravel path and through the dappled shade of birch trees, until arriving at the back of the Edenic glen where Dr. Platonic was talking.

Joseph looked impatiently for Cherry across the sea of white-robed people seated in front of him, perhaps two hundred strong, all facing forward. Gradually, though, the hypnotically smooth voice of Dr. Platonic took hold of him and forced his eyes upward. An unmistakable aura of love and serenity radiated from her white-robed figure, wavy brown hair spilling across her shoulders and framing a face that glowed with an unearthly light, a face he knew would have to be the most beautiful he had ever seen. He wished more than anything on earth that he was closer so that he could see her face better, or maybe even touch it.

"Most people ask themselves the question," Dr. Platonic continued, "Why are we here? Now, certainly that's an interesting question, one that implies a search for meaning in our lives. But I ask you all to take a step back. Before we can answer that question, we should all be asking ourselves, 'HOW do we know we're here?' We know we're here because we feel things, right? And what's the strongest feeling you've ever felt? The answer is ..."

"Constipation!" shouted Pono.

An awkward silence fell over the amphitheater before Dr. Platonic resumed. "The answer, people, is love. The problem is that the feeling of love is elusive, but it doesn't have to be. And before you leave here, I promise you that you will be feeling so much love, so much good, clean, pure love, that my Celibacy Clinic will make you feel like you're in a Disney movie. Impure thoughts will simply cease to exist. So that brings us back to the first question, 'Why are we here?' and our search for meaning.

"Now let me tell the story of our good friend, Jerry. Are you here today, Jerry? Stand up please. Ah, there you are. Everybody say, 'I love you,' to Jerry."

Two hundred voices responded with a sincere, "I love you, Jerry."

"You may be seated, Jerry," Dr. Platonic said. "Now some years ago, Jerry was involved in a terrible bus crash that claimed the lives of his family and everyone on board except for him. A heartbreaking, inconsolable loss that spun him into the depths of depression, alcohol abuse, and drug dependency. For him, life lost all meaning. Until the day, that is, he came to realize that God must certainly have spared him for a reason, and he was forced to face the fact that his family and the others were sadly lacking sufficient reason to live. So his search for that reason has driven him over many roads, until they finally led him here, to the home of love. Love is a reason to live unto itself. It heals all souls, people, just like it has Jerry's."

"Watch out, Jerry. It's a trap!" Pono called out. "Your soul has been hijacked!"

This time angry murmurs rippled through the audience at the disturbance.

"Settle down, everybody," soothed Dr. Platonic. "Alright. To continue then, I would like to talk next about our friend

Emily. Would you stand up please, Emily. Thank you. Everyone say, 'I love you,' to Emily."

Again the audience declared their love.

"Now, Emily's problem is that she has crippling anxiety," she continued. "She can't shake the feeling that terrible things are going to happen, no matter what she does, and as a result she can't make herself do anything."

"Terrible things ARE happening Emily," Pono yelled. "The apocalypse is coming!"

Dr. Platonic again ignored the outburst, and again motioned to the crowd to quell their rising anger. "Emily's problem is a very common one. She is paralyzed by fear. A fear of being inadequate, a fear of not having any control of the things in her life, a fear that people are out to get her, a fear of being afraid. It's a fear of things that haven't happened. A fear of the future, to put it plainly. What Emily needs is more love. Love conquers fear. With more love, her fears will roll off her like water from a gull's back."

"The gulls are dying, Emily. I've seen the fear in their eyes!" shouted Pono.

Again the audience erupted, murmurs escalating to loud chatter this time, though everyone was still unsure of the proper response to such disrespect for the Master. Dr. Platonic knew she was on the verge of losing the peace, love, and understanding she was known for, and also knew she couldn't ever let them see THAT happen. There would be no turning back from THAT wrath, no explanations that would suffice. Who knew what the consequences of such drastic action would be? Well, she did of course, but ... The first dark thundercloud rolled in nevertheless.

"Please, my friends," she said with a voice that could have calmed an angry sea. "Do not show the unbelievers among us the dark side to your souls. Show them love instead. Speaking of which, we have another friend with us this morning with yet a different problem. She's an atheist who can't see her way to believe in the love that never dies, the eternal love, Love Almighty. She's been talking to me about trying to find the truth of love, and trying to find someone she's been dreaming about. Well, I can tell you with the utmost certainty that our friend has been looking in all the wrong places. Fortunately, she's found her way here. Now let me introduce ..."

"Truth is a dream for dodos," Pono shouted. "And dreams are like turds ..."

"Shut up, Pono!" screamed Joseph suddenly. "Shut up! Shut up! Shut up! Shut up! Let her talk!"

"Let her talk!" echoed the audience.

"Quiet! Everybody calm down! NOW!" thundered Dr. Platonic. More threatening clouds moved in overhead, echoing her displeasure, and adding some disquieting rumbling of their own. "As I was trying to say, I'd like you all to show a little love to our atheist friend in the audience, Ms. Cherry Givens. She ..."

"Cherry!" boomed Joseph, racing up an aisle.

A white-robed figure shot to her feet and turned to the back. "Joseph!" Cherry cried, pushing her way through the row. Grinning from ear to ear, they threw themselves into each other's arms as the audience cheered wildly.

Two other figures in the audience, however, were decidedly not cheering. For a moment they sat there and looked at each other, shocked almost beyond comprehension at this unexpected turn of events in their slow rehabilitation. Then Alvin and Naomi Doubt began shrieking as if their house was on fire, and raced towards their son.

"Oh, for the love of God," Dr. Platonic groaned. "Is anybody listening to me? This is not the kind of love I've been talking about. Damn atheists. Don't they realize who I am?"

"I hear you," Pono shouted above the crowd. "And just so's ya know, her friend there's an agnostic. Whaddaya think of them apples? Ya gonna send a serpent after them?"

Dr. Platonic stared at Pono now, seeing him clearly for the first time. "I think you better come up here right now," she warned. "Are you who I think you are?"

"I'm coming, DOCTOR," Pono answered, smirking. "Are you who I think YOU are?" He approached Joseph and Cherry on his way to the stage, still entwined and talking rapidly over each other. The middle-aged couple that had been shrieking was now trying hard to pull them apart, babbling futilely. Amused, he stopped to listen.

"Joseph, Joseph, you can't do this to us," the woman pleaded. "She's an atheist for God's sake. Let her go now and come with us. We'll forget this ever happened. You know we raised you right. I tried to anyway."

"Tried!" the man bellowed, livid, eyes on fire. "Ye couldnae hae guided him any worse if ye'd a'had him gift wrapped and delivered to Satan. The lad's soul hae drifted a long wie from the Highlands, and ye say ye tried! Oh, how I wish we cuid go back and start over."

"Yeah, like starting over would help, you stubborn Scotsman," shot back the woman. "Pull your fat head out of the bog. You'd still be the same intractable, righteous fool you've always been. If his soul is lost, it's because you never bothered to understand his soul. You can't treat it like it's made out of stone. You have to be gentle with it, carefully bending it and molding it into the shape you want."

"Oh, this is just dreich," moaned the man. "We're getting nowhere. We shuid go talk to Dr. Platonic. Maybe she can help."

"Dodos!" sneered Pono, moving on. He climbed the steps to the stage and stood in front of Dr. Platonic.

"Well, well, well," Dr. Platonic said softly, extending her hand. "I thought I detected an evil presence. Play nice now." She smiled and nodded towards the audience.

"Believe me," Pono whispered back. "I wasn't expecting to find YOU here. And evil's so subjective, isn't it?"

"That's easy for you to say," Dr. Platonic replied. "You invented it. But it's not so subjective if you're the victim of evil, not that you'd know anything about that. Do you even understand the difference between pleasure and pain?"

"Hey, what do you take me for, some kind of insensitive monster? I have feelings. Pleasure just happens to be my specialty, and one of my many pleasures is to cause pain. I'm not some one-dimensional freak who thinks that l-l-l-luuuve for you is the answer to everything. I mean, as hot as you are, that's pretty shallow, wouldn't you say?"

"One-dimensional! Shallow! What nerve to come here and ... So you think I'm hot, eh? How hot do ..."

"Dr. Platonic! Dr. Platonic!"

Dr. Platonic and Pono turned to see a man and a woman rushing towards the stage, the middle-aged couple that had been trying hard to get Joseph's attention. They watched as the couple dropped to their knees in front of Dr. Platonic, clasped their hands together as if in prayer, and wailed.

"Please, Dr. Platonic," beseeched the man. "Help us! Our only son hae fallen in love with an atheist! His soul is in jeopardy! That's him over there, Joseph Doubt, with that fallen woman!"

Pono turned back to Dr. Platonic and held up his hand. "Excuse me, Doctor, I've got this," he said, smugly. He turned back to the Doubts. "Sir, Ma'am, I know your son quite well. And you're quite right, his soul IS hanging by a thread, and that woman is not helping any. I'm sure I can fix that. What we need to do ..."

"Stand down, Mister," thundered Dr. Platonic. "This is MY house." She turned to face Alvin and Naomi Doubt. "Of course I'll help you. Saving souls is MY specialty." Dr. Platonic looked up at the audience. "Please, everyone, excuse this interruption. I'll just be a few moments. My friend here was just about to leave. As a bonus for being so patient, would you good folks like to witness a soul being saved?"

Raucous applause and shouts of "Go! Go! Go! Go!" erupted from the crowd.

"OK, it's unanimous," Dr. Platonic said triumphantly. "Mr. and Mrs. Doubt, please take a seat. Your son's soul is in good hands here. Love is all around. But first I need to introduce my, uh, associate here, to the audience, and then he'll be leaving. Right, my friend?" she said to Pono.

Pono scowled at Dr. Platonic, his jaw tight and his clenched hands straining.

Alvin and Naomi thanked Dr. Platonic profusely, both of them bowing over and over as they made their way back to their seats. At last they were able to pull their eyes from Dr. Platonic's ethereal beauty. They felt a peace and tranquility they hadn't felt in years. They turned to look at their son, still wrapped in a tight embrace, but felt calm now, certain that the evil spell he was under was about to be broken.

Steam was rising from Pono's bald head. "Look, Doctor," he blared, razor blades in his voice. "That boy's agnostic soul is MINE! I've been waiting for a long time, and finally had him leaning solidly my way till that damn atheist had to go and discover l-l-luuuve. I blame you for that. So back off. I'm taking em both down!" The anger was back. A sharp bolt of lightning flashed from the clouds, followed by a low rumble of thunder.

The audience applauded uneasily, shifting in their seats.

"OK, I got your point," Dr. Platonic said, smiling through

her teeth while nodding reassuringly towards the audience. "But two can play THAT game!" The clouds thickened and grew darker, twin lightning bolts shot earthward with a crackling ferocity, and groaning peals of thunder added a tense exclamation point.

A sharp gasp escaped from the crowd, followed by indistinct murmuring.

Pono grinned. "Still have the touch, I see."

Dr. Platonic grinned back. "Anything you can do, I can do better. But let's control ourselves for the moment, shall we? I still have to introduce you. And then, my friend, you'll be leaving. Just don't forget, this is MY home field. Tell me, what name do you go by now?"

"Pono Nui."

"Attention please," Dr. Platonic announced to the audience. "Attention. Everybody, this is an old, uh, acquaintance, Pono Nui. Everyone say, 'I love you, Pono Nui.'"

"I love you, Pono Nui," raptured the crowd.

Pono shifted uneasily under the barrage of love.

Dr. Platonic, grinning wider now, whispered "Go on. You have to say it back."

"I don't want to," grunted Pono.

"This is MY house," Dr. Platonic whispered, grinning more forcibly now. Three successive lightning bolts rent the sky, followed by a loud crash of thunder that trailed off slowly. "Say it!"

This time the audience fell trembling into their neighbor's arms and prayed for salvation.

"OK, OK, I get the message," Pono said. He faced the crowd but looked down and shifted his feet. "I l-l-luuu-uve you everybody," he mumbled.

"Louder. And with feeling."

Pono raised his head and looked the crowd over. "I

L-L-LUUVE YOU EVERYBODY!" he boomed, with such a ferocious intensity that he turned deep red for an instant. Birds fell from trees and small animals ran for cover as multiple successive flashes of lightning lit up the sky, one breaking loose and forking down to split a nearby tree, toppling one half and leaving the standing half on fire. The entire audience leapt to their feet and began running and screaming over the cannonading waves of thunder. In seconds the amphitheater was empty, except for Dr. Platonic, Pono, and Joseph and Cherry, who were still locked in a tight embrace. Pono smiled. "What do you think, Doctor? Too much l-l-luuuve?"

Dr. Platonic looked over Her empty amphitheater and sighed. "Crazy weather we've been having lately," she said, before turning back to Pono. "Right in your wheelhouse though I'd say. You never were content when things were going smoothly. Always looking for trouble. I can't believe I fell for it. I'm so embarrassed."

"Please don't be, Doctor. I just got carried away as usual. Probably out of frustration. I think we both must be losing our touch. More and more these humans act like they don't need us, you know? Can I confess something to you, Doctor? Sometimes I wonder if we're even real. Look at those kids. Totally oblivious to us. But you, I must say, Doctor, are looking lovelier than ever."

"Oh, you. You always were the charmer. But I know your tricks, don't I?"

"Like I know yours, Doctor."

"Please, call me God," She said, winking. "Might as well drop the façade. There's no one here that believes in either one of us now."

Pono suddenly looked sheepish. "I will if you call me Beelzebub," he said. Of all the crazy names people have given me, no one ever calls me Beelzebub anymore. It's my favorite." He paused, wondering if God was going to laugh at him. When it was safe, he continued. "Don't laugh, but do you know how I came to be here today? It's because I got outsmarted by that agnostic dodo over there into searching for Cherry! Me! Encouraging love! Hey, will you look at me. I can say the word now. Love, love, love, love. Can you believe it? Hey, you didn't have anything to do with that, did you?"

"Now, now, Beelzebub," said God. "You know love doesn't need any help. It works in mysterious ways."

"Yeah, just like you, my dear. Tell me, what brings YOU here?"

"Well, my team says I've been showing all the signs of being under a lot of stress lately, snapping at Gabriel, barking at St. Peter for his tough border policy. Uh, you didn't have anything to do with THAT, did you? You're not bribing him somehow for those borderline souls, are you?"

"Me? Come now, God. Does that sound like something I would do?"

"Well, anyway," said God, "it's all true. I guess my little angels thought this would be good therapy for me. Get back to basics, you know? They had good intentions, but ..." She let her voice trail off.

"You know, Beelzey?" God continued, angry this time. "These humans have really been pushing my buttons lately, especially with the way they've been treating the planet I gave them. Best one of the litter too. They don't love their planet, they don't love each other. They only love themselves, and where does that get them on date night? No wonder I haven't been getting the number of souls I used to get. My numbers are way down. I suppose that means yours are way up. Go on, you know you want to gloat."

Beelzebub stared at God, his mind trying to process a feeling he had never experienced before – confusion. His face looked like it was struggling with it too. "W-what are you saying? You're not getting the souls? I'm not getting them either! Where are they going then?"

Now it was God's turn to be surprised. God doesn't like surprises. She threw up her hands and looked heavenward, shouting, "For Heaven's sake - What the Hell's going on around here? What do you angels DO all day? We've got millions of lost souls, and you don't tell me? Don't you understand that love is the only thing that can save people? YOU'RE ALL FIRED!"

"Now, now, God, take it easy," Beelzebub implored. "Forget about those lost souls. They're probably lost because they don't have their cell phones with them. That probably puts them in some new kind of Hell, one that not even I could create. We don't want THOSE souls, do we? You can't do anything with souls like that."

God lowered Her arms, looked at Beelzebub, and managed a smile. "I guess you're right."

"That's good," Beelzebub said. "Relax. Now, God, you trust me, right?"

"Like Hell I do," laughed God. "But I'll pretend to trust you if you pretend to trust me."

"Very funny. But see, I can really help you here. This is my area of expertise, you might say. I can take that stress away in a jiffy." Beelzebub moved behind God and began massaging Her shoulders. "See, doesn't that feel good? You've got to relax though. You really do feel tense."

29

A Roller Coaster of Feelings

Joseph and Cherry at last broke apart, and stood grinning at each other. A second later Cherry blurted, "Oh my God. Look at Pono and Dr. P. Let's get the hell out of here before we see something we'll regret. Hey, where did everybody go?" she wondered, looking around.

"I don't know," Joseph replied. "It's like there was a fire or something. Hey, there is a fire. In that tree! Cherry, do you ever get the weird feeling that God and Satan are actually real and fighting all around us? But that's just crazy, isn't it?"

"I sure hope so," said Cherry. "Can you imagine good and evil superpowers fighting for control of Earth? And we're the prize? Sounds like a silly video game to me, but what do I know? Come on, let's go back to my room and continue getting reacquainted. I've got to tell you about my strange dreams. About you, Joseph. We were riding a crazy horse together."

"I know," Joseph said, unable to stop grinning. "I think the horse is still with us, Cherry. I can feel it."

As they reached the women's dormitory, Joseph saw Curtis

standing forlornly outside, and nodded to him. Curtis gave Joseph the thumbs up as they went in.

"I don't know what made me think of it, Cherry," said Joseph, "maybe what you said before. But I just remembered a story Pono told me about how life is like an arcade game. You know, the kind where you maneuver the crane with the claw on the end to try and pick your prize? He said that you have to learn to manipulate the tools at your disposal to get what you want in life."

"Correct me if I'm wrong, Joseph," Cherry said, "but the only prizes in those games are cheap, inconsequential trinkets."

"That's what I said. So he says, 'Welcome to reality, Joseph. It doesn't seem to keep people from playing, though, does it? They try and try, spending their precious time, money and effort to win some meaningless prize, and win or lose, they're never satisfied. So they keep coming back.'"

They stood outside Cherry's room. "So what are you saying, Joseph?" Cherry asked, suddenly grim faced. "That I'm a meaningless prize? Is that how you feel?"

"No, no," Joseph said. "On the contrary. I feel like I just won the lottery."

Again they embraced. "Me too," Cherry sighed.

"If I've learned anything so far," Joseph said, "it's that nothing in life is certain. But that's OK. Certainty just gets in the way of appreciating all the uncertainty."

"I know one thing that's certain," Cherry said, pulling Joseph into her room. "You talk too much." She backed him up and pushed him onto the bed. "This chapter is so over. Time to get back on the horse."

"Let's ride," Joseph said, stripping off his clothes as fast as he could.

Three times the horse took them around the track, the wild, frenzied rush of the first lap giving way to a slow canter by the third as they each learned to feel and guide the powerful beast's spirited rhythms to suit their needs. Three times they passed the finish line, each time more satisfying than the last. Exhausted, Joseph and Cherry finally lay back and stared at the ceiling.

"You know, Cherry," Joseph said, "I just realized something. I've been communing with ceilings my whole life. It's like they've been watching out for me."

"Oh," said Cherry, eyebrows raised. "And is this one saying anything to you I should know about?"

"No. It's completely silent. What do you make of that?"

"I can think of three things, Joseph. Either you're nuts, the ceiling's defective, or you don't need a ceiling anymore. I guess most people usually seek guidance from an authority figure that's a little higher up than a ceiling, but hey, whatever floats your soul if you know what I mean."

"Or it could be a little of each. But I think you're right, Cherry. I don't think I need a ceiling anymore. I feel like the whole universe is open to me now. So, my love, where do we go from here? Still trying to figure out who you are?"

"Nah. I realized something too. I don't think I can ever know who I am, just like I can never truly know who you are. We keep changing, like we're on a freakin' carousel of beliefs or something."

Joseph stared at her, a vision of Cherry taming Loco the Love Horse overwhelming his mind.

"What? What is it? Joseph, why are you staring at me like that?"

"Cherry," Joseph said, eyes like saucers of champagne. "What are you feeling right now?"

"I don't know," Cherry answered. "Love, maybe. Yeah, I think I'm feeling love. And peace. And happiness. Why? You're spooking me. What are you feeling?"

"Same things. Pretty weird, huh, seeing as how you never

believed in love before. I was ON the Carousel of Beliefs, Cherry. The real thing. At least it seemed real. And it led me to you. What do you think of that?"

"I think ... I think that's some carousel you were on, Joseph. I guess it ended up taking us both for a helluva ride. But I think the real reason we feel the way we do right now is because we just got laid. No one ever feels angry or hateful after they get laid. It's impossible. It's really too bad people can't stay laid, you know?"

"Well, Babe," said Joseph, grinning like a horse in a patch of locoweed. "What do you say? I'm feeling the need for some more peace, love, and happiness."

"Easy there, Cowboy, give the horses a rest, will ya? We don't want to get saddle sore. Besides, I was just talking about feelings, not beliefs. If there is such a thing as a Carousel of Beliefs like you say, then there must be a Roller Coaster of Feelings too. Hey, I like the sound of that. It's like we're living in an amusement park. But you know, none of these rides are really gonna help us figure out who we are, they keep spinning and swooping, rising and plummeting ... Still, as long as we're on these rides together, I figure that we'll at least have fun trying to figure out who we are, don't you?"

"Couldn't have said it any better myself."

"What about you, Joseph? Your ceilings ever give you any answers?"

"Not really," he replied, running his index finger over the question mark on his right temple. "But thanks to them I realized that I don't believe in answers anyway. The Carousel of Beliefs is just a search engine, or the opening chapter of a great mystery. It's not the end of the story."

And so it was thanks to the Carousel of Beliefs that Joseph and Cherry lived happily in uncertainty ever after. Even if it really was the end of the story.

Epilogue

—

THE END?

God sighed as Beelzebub dug deeper with his thumbs, his fingers gently probing her neck and shoulders. "This is only a taste of what I can do for you, my dear."

"Ohhh, that feels good," God moaned.

Beelzebub leaned in closer and whispered something in her ear.

"No, no, Beelzy, I can't," she sighed. "I must remain celibate. I must love everyone equally and abstain from physical love."

"My lamb, we're two sides of the same coin, you and I," wooed Beelzebub, increasing the pressure on Her shoulders and Her mind, and nuzzling Her neck. "Love and ... hmm, I don't remember. Whatever's the opposite of love. But what I mean is, we belong together. I don't know why we always fought. This feels so much better, doesn't it? Don't fight it, I'm all yours."

"And I'm all yours," sighed God finally, sinking with him to the floor. "Be gentle with me, it's my first time."

"First time?" questioned Beelzebub between kisses. "Whose idea of heaven is THAT you live in? What do you and the angels DO all day?"

"Shut up and take me, you little devil."

Thunder crashed and lightning flashed, winds moaned and animals groaned, and humans everywhere quaked in fear. One hour passed, then two, and then a third, with no sign of a let up in the untamed tumult. "It's the apocalypse!" the humans cried. "We're doomed!"

And then, suddenly it was over, as quickly as it had begun. The sky cleared, the sun came out, the wind died, the animals quieted, and the humans went back to doing what they were best at, blaming the weatherman. "Take THAT apocalypse! You don't scare ME!" they boasted.

Beelzebub and God lay on their backs and stared at the sun.

"WOW! Wowie, wow, wow, WOW!" said Beelzebub. "Oh, My Beautiful Omnipotence, that was Heavenly! THE BEST EVER! Your first time, you say? Wherever did you learn those moves?"

"Are you kidding me, my sexy, insatiable satyr? I've been watching over humans for eons. That's all they ever think about."

"I know. You can thank me for that. So, my Heavenly Hostess with the Mostest, how was your first time?"

"Let's just say I answered my own prayers, you incorrigible incubus you," smiled God. "Do you still respect me?"

"Respect you? My Sweet Salvation, I feel – I feel like there's a warm blanky inside me. You ARE love, aren't you? Why did I always have to fight you? But I have one question. Since it's my first time in love, I'm not really sure what it's supposed to be like. Are you supposed to hear angels singing?"

"That's my choir," cooed God, still smiling serenely. "I hear them too, but to me it sounds like they're smashing their harps and cursing you. Oh well, they've had it pretty soft for a long time."

"You know, God," Beelzebub said, "this love thing is all right. I had the sex, but something was missing."

"Yeah, copy that, Beelzy," said God. "I had the love, but something was missing for me too."

"Hey, God, I had an idea. Whadaya say we blow this popsicle stand and trip the light fantastic. I think we've got a lot of making up to do. I can make you feel things that'll make your angels blush, and you can teach me more about love."

"I'd love to, Beelzy. But what about all the people that need me? I can't just leave them high and dry."

"I'll tell you what then, my little Redeemer," Beelzebub said. "Let's throw them a bone. The selfish little whiners don't deserve more than that anyway. How about we call a truce on this crazy apocalyptic battle we've been waging forever? Just let the people deal with things without us for a change. Let them take their natural course."

"You'd do that for me? How could people ever call you the Prince of Darkness? They just never saw your good side."

"Well, God, in all fairness, you never really let them, did you?"

"Yeah, you're right. I'm really sorry for that now. It just goes to show you it's never too late to find true love. So, do you think the people will be all right without us?"

For three seconds, Beelzebub and God stared at each other, contemplating the fate of the souls they had battled over all their existence. Then they both erupted in a laughter so free and uncontrolled that after five minutes they were still gasping for breath, only to have it start all over again when they looked at each other. At last they could wipe the tears away and speak.

"That's a good one, My Eternal Muse," Beelzebub said. "These are humans we're talking about. They'll destroy the earth in no time. There's not a chance in Hell they'll make it."

God sighed. "Heaven either, I'm afraid."

**Bob Lorentson** is a retired environmental scientist and an active daydreamer. When not writing or dreaming, he hikes, bikes, kayaks, plays guitar, travels, reads, gardens, drinks beer, and searches for his soul, which in all likelihood is avoiding him due to philosophical differences. Currently his body lives in East Haddam, Connecticut, with his wife and two rescue animals, none of whom can ever say for sure where his mind is located. He is also the author of *You Only Go Extinct Once (Stuck in the Anthropocene with the Pleistocene Blues Again*, and *Hold the Apocalypse–Pass Me a Scientist Please.*

A Note to the Reader

This book was locally sourced, organically written, and is guaranteed to be free of chatbots and other artificial ingredients. If you find that your beliefs have become healthier as a result of reading The Carousel of Beliefs, you can thank me by leaving a brief review on the platform of your choice. If, on the other hand, your beliefs have taken a sudden turn for the worse, I must advise you that burning the book may feel good, but will only bring you temporary relief. It's always best to pick yourself up and get back on the Carousel.

Seriously, I sincerely hope you had as much fun reading *The Carousel of Beliefs* as I had writing it. Thank you for your support.

Bob Lorentson

www.ingramcontent.com/pod-product-compliance
Lightning Source LLC
Chambersburg PA
CBHW051940220626
47052CB00004B/739